THE DEEPEST GRAVE

THE DEEPEST GRAVE

A Crispin Guest Medieval Noir Mystery

Jeri Westerson

Severn House Large Print
London & New York

This first large print edition published 2019
in Great Britain and the USA by
SEVERN HOUSE PUBLISHERS LTD of
Eardley House, 4 Uxbridge Street, London W8 7SY.
First world regular print edition published 2018 by
Severn House Publishers Ltd.

British Library Cataloguing in Publication Data
A CIP catalogue record for this title is available from the British Library.

ISBN-13: 9780727829634

Severn House Publishers support the Forest Stewardship Council™
[FSC™], the leading international forest certification organisation. All
our titles that are printed on FSC certified paper carry the FSC logo.

Typeset by Palimpsest Book Production Ltd.,
Falkirk, Stirlingshire, Scotland.
Printed and bound in Great Britain by
T J International, Padstow, Cornwall.

To Craig, the least grave person I know.

Glossary

Ambry	Cupboard for storing linens or clothing.
Cabinet with a stool	Implying that the 'stool' is a chamber pot.
Caltrop	An antipersonnel spiky weapon left on a road to impede the progress of horses or foot soldiers.
Chequy	A checkered pattern.
Ciborium	A container to hold the communion bread after consecration, similar to a chalice only with a lid.
Degraded	In terms of one's knighthood, to be demoted, downgraded. To lose the right to be called a knight.
Disseized	To be dispossessed of one's estates, title, and other possessions by force or edict.
Furnager	A baker of other people's meals.
Galette	Like a pie but without a pan, the pastry simply folded inward over the filling, not quite covering it.

Hobby horse	A child's toy of a carved horse's head attached to a stick, on which the child could ride astride.
Jetty	Second floor of a house or shop that juts out over the lower floor.
Liripipe	A long tail of cloth attached to a hat, long enough to swag over the chest.
Lychgate	A covered gate leading to a churchyard. *Lych* from an Old English word meaning corpse; a place a corpse would be left – sometimes for days – to await burial.
Paten	A flat saucer usually made of precious metals, used to hold the bread during consecration at mass.
Prie-dieu	A kneeling stool for praying.
Rectory	Housing for a priest.
Sacramental	A ceremony, action, or sacred object (a blessing, the sign of the cross, or rosary, for instance), used to help an individual receive sanctifying grace (the state of one's soul being infused by God).

Sanctuary lamp	The candle that burns in a church sanctuary near the altar 'to indicate and honor the presence of Christ'. Usually held in a red container.
Scopperel	A child's plaything, similar to a pinwheel.
Sexton	A man responsible for a church, its property, and certain church tasks.
Shrive	To give confession in the sacrament.

One

A hand tapped Crispin's shoulder from behind as he was finishing his business against an alley wall. 'Can't a man take a piss without being harassed?' he growled.

'You're Crispin Guest,' said the male voice.

Crispin finished, set his cote-hardie to rights, and turned. 'What the hell do you want?' But then he shut his mouth when he recognized that the young man was a priest in a dark gown.

'I had no wish to disturb you, but I could not find you. I looked on the Shambles—'

'I am situated in the same place where I have been for these last four years, my lord. On the Shambles, in an old poulterer's shop. I used to be above a tinker's, but it burned down . . .'

'So I have been told.'

Crispin set off in that direction, hoping to make it before the streets got too dark. But of course, the sun lingered longer in these warmer months at the beginning of summer. It wasn't likely to grow dark until near compline.

The priest scuttled behind him, catching up to walk beside him. A client. He needed them. But clerics gave him the shivers. There had once been a day when he could trust most of them

1

. . . but that day seemed to have disappeared, along with his knighthood.

He glanced at the man sidelong. 'And why do you seek me, Father?'

'I scarcely know how to begin.'

'At the beginning is generally the best.'

'But I do not know when it began. Only that it has. And I fear the answer when it comes.'

Crispin stopped and slowly turned to the man. 'You speak in riddles.'

'Do I? It was not my intention, Master Guest. Only that . . . I can barely explain it myself.'

Crispin rubbed his clean-shaven chin. 'I think a drink is in order. Come.' He led the way just up to the Shambles, but turned sharply and headed up Gutter Lane to the Boar's Tusk.

He caught Gilbert's eye as he entered, and the tavern keeper quickly deposited drink for them. He did not stay to talk with Crispin as he usually did, but curiously noted his clerical companion.

The priest settled in and took up the cup, drinking thirstily. Crispin sipped his. As usual, he sat with his back to the wall and a view of the smoky room, with its sagging rafters and dingy walls. 'Now then. What is it that concerns you and needs my help, my lord?'

The priest poured more and drank another dose before he finally set the cup down. Close and in the light, Crispin could study his dark gown, threadbare in some spots, patched in others. The priest had a square jaw, darkened by beard stubble. His eyes were small but glowed with an intensity of fear. His hair could only be described as luxurious, black, in thick waves, unlike

2

Crispin's own dark hair that hung lankly nearly to his shoulders. The priest's facial features were pleasant and slightly patrician. Crispin wondered vaguely which noble family he might have come from. He thought the man would be just as at home in mail as in his clerical garb.

'It is horrific, Master Guest,' he said, shaking his head. 'I can scarce speak of it.' He leaned into the table and spoke confidentially, his heavy brows clutched together over his eyes like fists. 'They walk. At night.'

Crispin leaned in. 'Who does?'

'Them. The . . . c-corpses.'

Crispin slowly sat back and measured the man. 'You jest.'

'I assure you, I do not. Come. See for yourself. After the sun sets.' He took another hasty gulp. 'You'll see them.'

Crispin eyed the man's unsteady hand on his cup and wondered if strong drink were not more to the point. He leaned in again. 'Has anyone else seen these . . . these apparitions?'

'You think I'm mad. I thought so, too. Until the gravedigger saw them as well. I was telling him about it, exhorting him to get inside, to stop tending to the grass so late after dark. He was as skeptical as you are. I warned him to go inside. And it wasn't more than a quarter hour later that he was pounding on my door, begging to be let in. White as bone, his face was. Eyes as wide as mazers. "Yes," he said, he'd seen them. Dragging their coffins over their shoulders, treading through the churchyard into the mist. He called out at first, and then one of them turned

3

to face him. Oh, he gave such a description that would curdle your blood, Master Guest. The same I knew in my own heart when I looked upon those poor devils. And not only them, Master Guest, but my own brother Noll not long from All Hallows Barking, remarked that he had seen similar strange doings. He will not come to my church. I have scarce seen him since. My own brother!'

Crispin raised an admonishing finger. 'Now hold. You all saw these supposed walking corpses?'

'There is nothing "supposed" about it. We saw them.'

'And . . . did they cause . . . er, mischief?'

'As soon as I spied them, I fled into the rectory. The next morning, I went about the churchyard, sprinkling holy water. I found . . .' He licked his lips. 'Disturbed graves. Some were opened, clods of earth cast aside, and those that had coffins, I found the lids ajar. When I inspected further – with fervent prayers and the large crucifix from the altar, mind you – what I saw . . . Oh, Master Guest! I do not know what mischief they might have got up to, but when I moved the lids, I saw blood upon the linens covering their faces. Blood . . . on their mouths. They had become bloodsuckers!'

The man seemed genuinely alarmed, and Crispin had no doubt that something had awakened such dread in him, but he could not reconcile it to this fantastic tale. 'Something has disturbed you greatly, Father . . . Father—?'

'Bulthius Braydon. Of St Modwen's Church.'

4

'Father Bulthius. Something is amiss. I shall
. . . I shall investigate it for you tonight, if you
wish. My fee is sixpence a day.'

'I will pay it. Anything is better than going on
with this demon's march night after night.' He
struggled at his belt, and dug deep into his pouch,
pulling out more than sixpence. 'Here, Master
Guest. Sixpence, and more. For I cannot imagine
it shall all be resolved in one night.'

'You might be surprised, my lord. Depending
on what I find.'

'You will find demons. And when you do,
then I will gird myself and help you dispatch
them.' He rose. 'Meet me at my churchyard. The
vicarage is near All Hallows Barking.'

'In the shadow of the tower. I am aware of it.'

'Tonight, Master Guest. And then you will see.
God save us.'

Two

When Crispin entered the old poulterer's, the heavenly aroma of cooking food greeted him instead of the smell of chickens. Isabel Tucker tended to the fire and the meat pie baking in its pan beside it. Her apron could barely encompass her swollen belly and, as she straightened, one hand went to the small of her back, fingers digging in and kneading the muscle.

She had been barely seventeen when she'd married Jack last year and, though a slight thing, she had proved her worth carrying in the water and fuel, and never shirking hard labor. She possessed a wit that more than once offered Crispin and Jack a practical direction to follow on their rounds of investigating. Yes, she was an asset, right enough, though with a forthcoming babe she'd be too busy to intercede in their work again. *More's the pity*, he thought. For those bright hazel eyes of hers would spark and light with a fact neither of them had spotted, though he was loath to give her too much credit.

'Master Crispin,' she said with a smile. She had freckles on her nose, but not as many as his ginger apprentice. 'I'm glad you're home for supper.'

'As am I. It smells delightful.'

'It's just a bit of pork pie and pottage. Not as

6

grand as it could be, but not as bland as it might have been.'

He hung his cloak by the door, and doffed his shoulder hood, hanging it beside the heavy mantle. 'You are a miracle-maker with what little you have to work with.'

'With two proud men to feed, I must do my best.'

'And so you do. Is Master Tucker here?'

There was a clatter at the door as it was kicked open, and Jack, arms full, slipped through.

'Speak of the devil,' muttered Crispin.

Jack smiled. 'Master! I have news. Look. Come see what I've brought.'

Crispin winked at Isabel and gave his apprentice his attention. Jack set the cradle down upon the floor.

'Oh Jack, you got it!' Isabel set her spoon hurriedly aside and rushed to the cradle, kneeling beside it. 'Just look at that.'

'Where did you come by it?' asked Crispin.

'I did a service for the furnager and he paid me in kind. He had this cradle, and since his wife and son had passed over a year ago – God rest them – he had no further need of it.'

'That was enterprising of you.'

'I try, master. It's hard to spend good coin on such when we haven't any to spare.'

'It won't always be so,' Isabel said to him, and kissed his cheek. He reddened, and took her by the widened waist, though he had little to grab hold of these days.

'But it is so for now, my love. How's our boy? Is he still making a merry jig in there?'

She rubbed her belly and sighed. 'Aye, he likes to rest while I work, and dance while I rest. You tell him to calm himself.'

Jack leaned over and spoke gently but firmly to her round belly. 'Here now. Did you hear that, my lad? Your mother is weary and needs her rest. You take your ease when she sits, do you hear me?'

He smiled up at her and she grabbed his curly head in an embrace.

Crispin turned away from the domestic scene. Something in his heart ached with the sight of it. He was not a part of that intimate moment, though there were times when he was treated more as the patriarch of their little triad, rather than merely the master of the house.

When Crispin turned back, Jack had taken a spoon and dipped it into the pottage from the iron pot and lifted it to his pursed lips, blowing on it as he noisily slurped. 'Is it ready, woman?'

'It is. Bring the ewer for Master Crispin so he can wash his hands.'

Jack grabbed the basin and ladled some warm water from the other pot on the hob into the ewer, and with a towel draped over his arm, presented the basin to him. Crispin pushed up his sleeves and held his hands over the basin, while Jack poured the warmed water over his fingers.

Isabel had brought these niceties. In the intervening years between Crispin's banishment from court and when he had met the boy, Crispin had set aside his courtly manners, even his prayers

8

before eating. But Isabel insisted on it. At first, he had balked, but eventually he was pleased at her persistence. It was good to get back to the routine of a civilized life.

Jack followed suit, and set the ewer and basin by the fire. He sat opposite Crispin and waited as Isabel served. Upon her moving in after they had wed, both of them served Crispin and waited for him to eat before they partook. And, as proper as this was, it wasn't expeditious, particularly if Crispin needed Jack in some pursuit of justice. It left the boy hungry and unfocused. Crispin had to put his foot down. The men were to eat. And if the men ate, then it sufficed that she would serve and then sit with them to eat as well. His insistence had made of them a strange family: servants and master, all together, as it had been with Jack alone. Sometimes the arrangement caused a twinge of discomfort, but sometimes – as it did now – he welcomed the feeling that seemed to fill that empty place in his soul that had stood by itself for so long.

Crispin sliced the fat but squat pork pie, laying a modest wedge on his bread slice, distributing wedges and pottage until they got their fill.

Chewing the last of his bread and wiping his hands on the tablecloth, Crispin glanced at the twilight sky visible through the shutter sitting ajar. 'An excellent repast, Isabel, my dear. But Jack. I didn't tell you about our own adventure tonight.'

'Tonight, sir? What have we to do tonight? Did you get another client?'

'Indeed, I did. A priest, Father Bulthius of St Modwen's Church, near All Hallows by the tower. And you'll never guess what he would have us do.'

'Tell me.'

'We are to watch and wait in the churchyard for walking corpses.'

Jack spit his beer across the table.

When Crispin looked up with distaste, Jack wiped his bearded chin with the tablecloth. 'I'm sorry for that, master, but what did you say? Surely I didn't hear you aright.'

'You did. We are to watch for walking corpses, for he claims that in his churchyard, the dead walk again, like Lazarus; but then, like boys under curfew, return to their graves after their nightly ritual.'

Jack's mouth hung open. Crispin hid his smile of amusement in his cup.

'He thinks they're bloodsuckers, for he found one with blood upon his face cloth.'

Jack snapped to his feet and looked desperately at a suddenly stilled Isabel. 'Master, we can't go on such an unholy vigil.'

'And why not? The man paid me, after all.'

'But Master Crispin, it isn't anything a Christian should be doing after hours. It isn't right, sir.'

'Don't be a fool, Jack. I don't believe any of it for one moment.'

'Oh.' He sank down to his chair again.

'But there is clearly something going on that vexes this priest, and so we must investigate. It's near sunset now. We'll be leaving presently.

10

That will allow us to enjoy a bit more wine and digest our meal.'

Jack rubbed his belly. 'I feel all queer inside now.'

'It isn't *you* with child, after all,' he said with a chuckle.

Isabel rose and stacked the wooden bowls on the serving tray. She seemed to have shaken off her initial misgivings, and elbowed Jack. 'You do as Master Crispin says. He'll not let you fall into harm's way.'

'Certainly not,' said Crispin cheerfully, tilting his chair on its back legs and sipping more wine. 'I find the whole thing amusing and invigorating. What could it possibly be that has vexed this man so? I tell you, I cannot get it out of my head.'

'Me neither,' said Jack sullenly.

Crispin finished his wine slowly, watching Jack fidget and Isabel clean the bowls and plate. She dried it all with a towel and all was swiftly back in order. She threw more peat on the fire and sat in her chair before it, picking up her sewing again. He noticed she was repairing one of his stockings. Her needlework wasn't as fine as some he had seen, but it was serviceable, and that was all he could expect these days.

'Are you ready, Jack?' he asked after a time.

Startled, Jack looked up. Eyes wide, he nodded. Crispin went to the door and donned his shoulder cape and hood. As he buttoned the mantle, he turned. 'Well?'

The boy dragged himself to his feet and shuffled toward the door and his own cloak and hood.

'If we don't return, Isabel,' he said solemnly, 'go on to your uncle.'

Rolling his eyes, Crispin spun him toward the door. He looked back at Isabel in the firelight. Her face was drawn and seemed thin in the shadows cast over her features. He smiled to reassure. 'He's being overdramatic. We'll return well after midnight. Don't wait up.'

He saw the cast of relief in her eyes before he closed the door and slapped Jack's ear. 'Are you a fool? Why would you worry her so?'

'Master, we're off to see *corpses* walking abroad.'

'I told you that it was foolishness. Now come along.'

The Tower of London was at the other end of the city and it would take a while to get there, particularly since they had to skirt the Watch. Only thieves were abroad at night, and Crispin never needed an excuse to get himself involved with the sheriffs.

He jabbed Jack with his elbow. 'Stay alert for the Watch,' he admonished.

Jack straightened and pulled his hood up over his head. The boy was tall, as tall if not a bit taller than Crispin, and huskier than he'd ever been. In fact, with Jack at his side these days, Crispin felt more at ease than he had in many years. Jack Tucker was a skilled fighter and strong enough where it mattered. The two of them were a formidable pair and, what's more, all of London knew it. Crispin smiled. He didn't truly fear the Watch, for it was more than likely that the Watch was skirting *them*.

12

He was able to enjoy the night, the stars peeking in and out of the cloud cover, wisping across the night sky between the tall buildings. The glittering stars marched ahead of them on a cloudy trail. The shops and houses were blue in the falling light. Only the wealthier houses had gleaming candles shining through glass windows. The rest were barred with shutters, with only a stripe or two of light. London was inside, sharing the hearth with family and servant. As he should have been doing. But, alas. A man had to make a living.

They made it up to Aldgate and cut over to a narrow lane. St Modwen's was a stubby church with a single tower and arched entry. She was an old church of mossy stone, nearly by itself. Worn paths through the surrounding fields shone like white veins when the moonlight showed itself between the clouds. These were old, meandering paths from the dwindling houses at the outskirts of London that led directly to the parish church. And, all around it, sparse woodland. Though a lonely parish, as with all of God's houses, there was comfort there within the stone. It shone with a single lantern within – the sanctuary lamp – through its tall, dark windows.

They walked up the few steps to the door and Crispin pushed them ope\n. They yawned wide, their hinges expressing a laconic whine. The church was no warmer in its nave than it was outside in the night, but they followed the lantern light up the tiled path to the rood screen, its carvings creating a welcoming gate. They passed under the arch and nearly up to the altar, where a figure knelt before it, praying. He must have heard their steps and finally turned. The fear in his eyes was even greater now than before. Crispin rested his hand on his sword hilt.

'You came.' Father Bulthius seemed surprised at such a boon and rose, wringing his hands.

'Of course I came. And I brought my apprentice, Jack Tucker.'

Jack bowed. 'Father.'

'You are most welcome, young man.' He glanced back toward the crucifix and crossed himself. 'Shall we go to this dread deed?' He handed Jack a glass vessel. 'Here is holy water.' He clutched a silver crucifix which he showed to Crispin. 'Now we are prepared.'

Jack clasped the holy water as if his life depended on it.

The priest led the way to a side door which opened out to the churchyard.

The moonlight painted the trees and gravestones with silver-blue. But the shadows it cast churned even Crispin's imagination. The gnarled shapes of trees that stretched to horrific heights wove a tapestry of disquiet all around them. A rustling in the underbrush didn't help. He knew it was mice or other night creatures, but the circumstances suddenly made much of nothing. Something winged overhead, and Jack ducked, releasing a squeaked curse. He apologized to the priest for it, but Bulthius didn't seem to notice. He held his lantern aloft. It shook and rattled from the trembling of his hand.

Crispin cast about, narrowing his eyes into the

14

darkness around them. A mist was rising, making distances foggy and shadows all that much more filled with omens. He found himself clutching his dagger hilt and, feeling foolish, released it, opening and closing his tensed hand.

The air smelled damp and earthy. Ears sharp, eyes searching, Crispin moved purposefully behind the priest, waiting. Perhaps that was the worst of it. The waiting. Was anything truly going to happen?

Abruptly, the priest stopped. He raised his arm and pointed. 'Look!' he rasped.

Crispin turned toward the direction of his pointing hand but saw nothing. Until there was movement in the distant mist. A sluggish figure with a heavy burden.

Jack gasped and took a step back, crossing himself vigorously, holy water pressed tight to his breast.

Crispin slowly drew his sword. 'What manner of sorcery is this?'

A man was walking toward the field, dragging each step; on his back, a large object. Was it a coffin? Crispin wasn't certain at that distance, but he wasn't about to stand around wondering.

He stepped around the priest but Father Bulthius grabbed him and held him back. 'What are you doing?'

'I'm going to see what it is.'

'I know what it is, Master Guest. It is the walking dead.'

Crispin gripped the sword tighter. 'And so we shall see.'

15

'Master, don't go.'

You too, Jack? He gave his apprentice a disgusted sneer. 'If you're afraid, stay back.'

That prodded him. Jack visibly swallowed, screwed up his courage, and drew his knife. He pulled off the cork from the vessel with his teeth, and brandished the holy water with his other hand. They set off together, and perhaps not willing to be left behind, Bulthius trotted after them. Suddenly, the lantern winked out as the priest tripped and clattered to the ground.

The moonlight hid behind a crest of clouds, and the apparition vanished into the darkness. 'God's blood!' Crispin swore. 'Did you see in which direction it went?'

'No, master. It just disappeared into the night.'

'Forgive me, Master Guest.' Bulthius brushed himself off and grabbed the lantern. The metal was battered and the candle within bent. 'We'll need a new flame.' He trudged back toward the church, skirting around a crooked headstone when he suddenly stopped. 'Bless me. Almighty Father, save us.'

Crispin came around the stone and saw the empty grave. It looked as if it was dug that day, the piles of dirt on either side of it. And, on closer examination, something heavy had been dragged out of it, collapsing the side of the perfectly rectangular hole. Something heavy . . . like a coffin.

'This proves nothing.' He sputtered when he was hit in the face with something wet. Scowling, he glared at Tucker.

16

'Sorry, master. I was just sprinkling the grave.' He held up the vessel of holy water.

'This was a funeral today?' he asked the priest.

Bulthius slowly shook his head. 'No, good master. At least a sennight ago.'

Crispin glared at the empty grave, almost blaming it for its empty state. He pressed a fist to his hip. 'Was it a wealthy man?'

'Yes. He left a large sum to our chantry.'

'Then that is your answer. A grave robbery.'

'But . . . the whole grave? Why would anyone wish to steal everything, coffin and all?'

That *was* unusual, and Crispin bit his lip, pondering. Usually the grave was opened and the body only disturbed enough to steal jewelry and weaponry. Certainly no one desired the body. Unless there *was* some sort of evil witchery involved.

He glanced back at the last place he saw the trudging figure. 'Jack, stay here.'

'Not on your life, sir.'

Crispin hurried toward the mist. He felt better with a blade in his hand and Jack beside him. He kept his ears open and eyes sharp, scanning the churning fog. His head turned this way and that, listening, fooling himself with suddenly looming shadows of trees and rocks. He gestured to Jack to stop and they both listened.

Was that the slow progress of a tread?

Listening hard offered nothing more.

The moon slid out from the clouds long enough for Crispin to look around, finally seeing the outline of trees, a stone wall, a headstone . . .

but no figure. He crouched down to examine the mud. 'Jack,' he whispered. 'Look here.'

Jack got in close beside him, and with the moon shining over their shoulders, Crispin pointed out the footsteps in the mud . . . and something heavy being dragged behind it.

'God have mercy,' Jack gasped.

Three

The priest offered Crispin warmed wine as the three of them sat before the small hearth in his rectory.

'You are convinced now, are you not, Master Guest?'

Crispin mumbled to himself and sipped the hot wine. He stared into the flames, trying to reckon just what it was he saw. 'I believe there is something, good Father. And we must continue to investigate. What happens in the morning when you go out to the churchyard?'

'The graves are returned to the way they were. With dirt cast back over the hole.'

'Then how do you know of the instance of the blood on the face cloth?'

'I had my gravediggers uncover it, Master Guest. I had to know if they had returned . . . and that was when I saw it.'

'It's ghastly,' murmured Jack.

'Perhaps we should sit outside the grave. See when this apparition returns.'

'Oh no, Master Crispin!' shrieked Jack. 'We mustn't, sir!'

'There are only so many ways to solve this mystery, Jack.'

Jack downed his wine and clutched the empty cup in whitening fingers. 'Maybe there are some mysteries Man was not meant to know.'

Crispin rose. 'Not this man.' He crossed to the door and paused. 'You coming?'

He could almost feel Jack's trepidation sweep over him, but the boy rose, dusted himself off carefully as if girding himself, and followed Crispin through the door.

The cold was a slap in the face as he ventured once again into the night. 'Where was that grave?' he muttered.

Jack pointed. His hand trembled but he stood by his master, hand on his dagger hilt. And when Crispin strode forth through the mist to where the open grave had been, he made sure to keep Jack on his left so he could pull his sword if need be.

They rounded the corner of the church and stopped. The grave was covered. The dark earth sheltered it loosely, hastily, as if the corpse could not wait to be home again.

Crispin knelt and ran his fingers over the scuff marks of something large and heavy, saw footprints . . . and snatched his hand away.

Slowly he rose. The priest stood behind him, holding a rosary to his lips. 'Father Bulthius. I will solve this puzzle. But it looks like that will not be tonight.'

He and Jack strode through a darkened London, saying nothing. Crispin stole glances at the boy and finally asked, 'What did you think of that, Jack?'

'I could barely stop m'self from pissing me braies.'

'Besides that.'

Jack screwed up his mouth, beard twitching. 'You're trying to say it isn't what we thought it was. But master, what the hell else could it be?'

Crispin passed a hand over the cold skin of his face. 'I don't know . . . but it was damned queer.'

'Aye, that it was.'

'There is no choice. We shall have to return tomorrow night.'

The boy shook his head. 'Ah, it's a sore thing indeed when a man must do so unholy a task to earn food for his wife and child.'

'It is indeed. May I remind you that you chose this life? I tried to discourage you.'

'I remember it, master. It is at times like these that I remember it very well.'

They reached their lodgings before midnight. Isabel had fallen asleep before the hearth in the hall, and Jack, with gentle cooing sounds, urged her to her feet and helped her up the stairs. Crispin followed, and Jack turned to him as he opened his own chamber door. 'I'll be in anon to help you undress, sir.'

'Don't be a fool. I don't need your help. See to your wife, man.'

Jack gave him a grateful smile and disappeared behind his door. The soft sounds of Jack helping her to bed gave Crispin that pang again; the pang of a thousand regrets fluttering against his heart like a butterfly's wings. He turned away, entered his solitary room and closed the door.

The hearth had not gone completely cold. There were still embers glowing beneath the ash,

21

and he grabbed his iron and stirred it up, tossing bits of peat and sticks upon it. But even as the room warmed, and he drew off his cote-hardie and laid it carefully over his coffer, he knew he was too tired to sleep. He fell into his chair and settled before the fire, a mangy fur – that Jack had managed to bargain God-knows-what for – thrown over his legs.

Staring into the flames, he ruminated on the couple in the room across from his. He imagined Jack pulling her close, covering her with a warm blanket, petting her unbound hair; she would snuggle against his chest, her nose perhaps dug into the underside of his blazing ginger beard. They were content with one another. Jack had been smitten at the first. And soon they'd have a child.

And who was Crispin but the lonely middle-aged man who lived with them, who sometimes grumbled and groused and even raved when he had too much drink in him. What would this child see when they beheld him? Who would they think he was?

He couldn't help himself. He leaned back and stretched to retrieve the strange miniature portrait that he kept under the mattress. It was clearly torn from a breviary. An indulgent husband had hired some monk to pen the prayer book and paint the likeness of his wife within, perhaps as a saint or even the Holy Virgin. It was just her face and shoulders, much less than the size of half his palm width. And then torn from the prayers, it was hastily pasted into a small gold-leafed frame for the secret enjoyment of her long-dead husband.

Philippa Walcote. She had been married to the rich mercer . . . or so she thought. No one knew who he was, for he masqueraded as Nicholas Walcote, the famed but reclusive trader in cloth. And it wasn't until the imposter had been murdered and Nicholas's brothers came to claim the body that he was discovered. Many declared it had been she that had done the deed and, truly, there had been many secrets. Crispin had uncovered each one, peeling them back like the skin of an onion. He'd saved her from the gallows but, in the end, just like an onion, it had produced its share of tears.

He stared at the portrait of Philippa. Hair of brassy gold, a dimpled smile, and that heavy-lidded gaze that had always intrigued. Why had he kept the damned thing? It only caused him misery. But every time he tried to throw it into the fire, the thought of its loss ached his heart that much more.

He clutched it in his fingers till they hurt. He could have had her. He could have had a child and more with her, but his stubborn pride had not allowed it. What was it about him that foiled every chance at happiness over and over again? Was it his curse, his penance for dashing his greatest honor against the rocks, forswearing his oaths to the old king? Had his treason been the cause of his damnation?

Almost, *almost* he tossed the portrait to the flames, but once again he couldn't. And again, he leaned over and stuffed it beneath the mattress once more.

* * *

23

He awoke stiff and cold. Naturally. What can one expect when one sleeps all night in a straight-backed chair?

He didn't so much as rise from the chair as climb out of it, cracking and stretching his back, his muscles, and rolling his stiff shoulders.

He pried a flame out of the hearth, fed it and wondered, as his own stomach growled, if there was something about with which he could feed himself.

A knock on the door told him that at least others were up with the day.

'Master Crispin,' came the voice of Isabel through the door. 'I brought you your mixtum.'

'Come in.'

She shoved the door open with a hip and waddled in with a tray. She looked him over. 'You don't look so good. I've warmed some wine for you. You should drink it up while it's still hot.'

'Thank you, Isabel. You take good care of me.'

'I'm grateful that you take such good care of Jack, for he sorely needs someone looking after him.'

'I rather think that he's the one who looks after me.'

Jack tromped up the stairs and passed through the doorway. He used a cloth to carry the hot handle of the kettle with Crispin's hot water for his wash.

'It's nice and hot for you, master. Oh. You don't look good this morning, sir. A bit gray around the edges. Well, a good shave will content you, I'll wager.'

24

'Perhaps all I need is a good bleed. You don't happen to have a leech about, do you?'

'I'd get a barber if we had the funds, sir.'

'Never mind. I'm sure your steady hand will remedy that.'

Jack gave him the eye as he prepared the soap and razor. 'Now Master Crispin, I haven't nicked you but once or twice, and that was when I was first learning.'

'Which is why *you* wear a beard, I see.'

Jack cracked a smile. 'See how much we save on leeches?'

Crispin allowed Jack to shave him as he sipped the wine. It did invigorate and he was able to relax into the feel of hot water on his face, the soap lathering his chin and cheeks, and the smooth glide of the razor making all right again.

He passed his hand over his newly shaved chin and smiled. 'Well done, Jack. As good as any barber.'

'Thank you, sir. And now to your mixtum. Don't let it get cold.'

Pottage from the night before and a piece of bread was kept warm under a cloth, and Crispin pulled it off and dug into his bowl. The pottage was even better the next day, and he slurped it down, running his bread around the bowl to sop up the rest.

He'd been a fool last night, feeling sorry for himself. It was the late hour, surely, that had flung him into such a morose state. No more of that! He had a problem of roving corpses to solve.

Jack seemed to know when he was ready to dress, for he appeared just as Crispin was buttoning up his cote-hardie. He stood still, enduring Jack's vigorous brushing of the woolen cloth, taking care to rid it of churchyard mud.

Crispin affixed his belt and his dagger's scabbard. 'Jack, have you given any thought to last night's happenings?'

'Nothing but thought, sir. I tried to think logically, as you taught me, laying it out like skittles. But I could not for the life of me explain it.'

'Nor could I. Puzzling. I intend to examine the churchyard and then talk of walking corpses with Abbot William.'

'Shall I go with you, sir?'

'If you've a mind to it.'

The morning work bells had rung, starting the business day for all. Thank goodness the day had dawned with a glorious spray of sunshine instead of gloom, thought Crispin, for he had had enough of gloom.

They walked through London toward the tower, shining white in the distance on its hill. 'What are your thoughts on the matter?' asked Jack suddenly, after a long portion of silence.

'I haven't a clue.'

'What – or *who* – would cause a corpse to rise, sir?'

'Sorcery. Forcing a corpse to rise to do their evil bidding. I have heard tell of such but have never seen it. I'm not certain I've seen it now.'

26

'Ever the skeptic.'

'It is best not to assume, Jack. *The ultimate value of life depends upon awareness, and the power of contemplation rather than upon mere survival.*'

'And *it is the mark of an educated mind to be able to entertain a thought without accepting it.*' Jack turned a self-satisfied smile on Crispin.

Crispin returned the smile. 'So it is. I'm glad to see you're still reading your Aristotle.'

'For self-defense as much as anything else, sir.'

Crispin carried his smile with him all the way to the church, and promptly lost it when he surveyed the churchyard over its stone wall.

'Will we go into the church, sir, and seek out Father Bulthius?'

'Not at the moment. I want to view the graves first.' He passed through the lychgate, with its wooden arches and slate-covered roof, and held the gate open for Jack, who grumbled behind him. 'Better in the light of day, eh, Jack?'

'Much, sir. But it still crawls me skin with shivers.'

And mine too, but he didn't wish to say that aloud. He made his way between the mossy headstones and found the disturbed grave of last night. The dirt covered the hole and all seemed as if the funeral had only just come to pass.

They stood silently, both staring at it warily, as if the corpse would suddenly burst from the ground.

Crispin shook his head as he folded his arms,

casting his cloak back off his shoulders. 'I confess, I don't know what to look for.'

Jack knelt tentatively by the grave and took the dirt in his hand, crumbling it between his fingers. 'Lately tilled.'

A twig cracked and they both jerked, heads snapping in the direction of the sound. A man with a wheelbarrow and a spade worked in the distance. A younger man was with him, using a rake. Crispin headed there with Jack at his heels.

'Good sirs,' said Crispin, hailing them.

They looked up. The older man wore a wide-brimmed hat over his thin leather hood and a dirt-laden apron over his tunic. He bowed to Crispin and gave a nod to Jack. The younger man – about fifteen or so – wore a simple leather cap with its straps untied and hanging loose, with a tunic streaked with dirt.

'Are you the gardeners?'

'Among other things, master,' said the older man. 'We are gardeners, ostlers, gravediggers, and anything else that Father Bulthius requires.'

'Can you tell me about these graves, then? Those that Father Bulthius claims were . . . disturbed.'

The man's eyes widened and he exchanged a look with the young man. 'I can't talk about that.'

'Why not?'

'Beggin' your mercy, but who are you?'

Jack got in his face. 'That there's Crispin Guest, the Tracker of London. If he asks you a question, it's best you answer sharp, and no smarting back.'

'Now Jack.' Crispin edged him back and with a mild expression faced the man. 'If you could answer me.' Sometimes Crispin found it more advantageous when Jack served as an angry underling, while Crispin played the pacifying lord.

'You're the Tracker? Aye, I heard o' you. Well then. We did see something strange hereabouts, didn't we, Hal?' He got in closer, voice down to a gravelly whisper. 'Graves all dug up, coffins opened. I thought it was robbers. But then what I seen at twilight . . .' He shook himself. 'Made all me hairs stand straight up.'

'Mine, too,' echoed Hal, the younger one.

'And what exactly did you see?'

'The grave was open and Father and me and Hal seen it. We seen him walking with his coffin on his back. My heart was pumping so loud I thought it would burst.'

'And when was that?'

'Less than a sennight ago.'

'And what did you do about it?'

'Do? We ran – that's what we did. Like any sane Christian man would!'

Jack nodded soberly.

Crispin folded his arms over his chest. 'And what did you do the following day?'

'I thought mighty long and hard about leaving my position . . . but where else was I to go? And Hal here and leaving poor Father Bulthius alone and all, well. So I came back and we all scoured the churchyard, but the grave was all put to rights. But the next night, the same thing happened again.'

29

Hal crossed himself and closed his eyes in prayer.

'To the same grave?'

'Aye. And then another new grave the next night.'

'Did you or Father Bulthius tell this to the grieving families?'

'I don't know, sir. I didn't tell them. How do you tell them families that their loved ones is going about sucking blood in the countryside?'

'And how do you know there is, er, blood-sucking going on?'

Hal snapped his eyes open and jerked forward. 'Why, their faces. I seen the blood on their face cloths. Oh, it's horrific is what it is. We saw it for ourselves, didn't we, Tom?'

'Aye, that we did.'

'I see. Thank you.'

Crispin gave each man a farthing and both gravediggers bowed, Tom leaning on his wooden spade and Hal holding tight to his rake. They watched as Crispin and Jack walked away.

'Just as the priest said,' Jack insisted.

'Yes. Strange.'

They made it to the lychgate, but Crispin wanted to check again where he had seen the 'walking corpse'. He pivoted on his heel and set off for the meadow.

'Master Crispin!' hissed Jack. He heard the boy swear and then the tramp of his feet as he ran to catch up. 'I thought we were done here.'

'You're so hasty, Jack. Frightened away. Has it ever occurred to you that this is precisely why we've both been told this story . . . with a performance to back it up?'

'Or maybe we saw what we saw because it's true. Master, I don't understand you. You saw it plain as me. Why are you so skeptical all the time? Why must there be more than we see with our own eyes?'

'Because the alternative is . . . is impossible. I would rather be at the mercy of some treacherous plot than at the supernatural urgings of some great evil.'

Jack grumbled for a time, until his rumblings formed words Crispin could discern. 'And relics?' asked Jack. 'That's God's grace, not evil. We come across them all the time and you don't believe in their power. You never do, and yet they do affect us.'

Crispin automatically put his hand to his scrip, where at the very bottom lay a thorn from a certain venerated object. Jack told the truth. Crispin seldom believed in the relics that came their way. But some had affected him more than others. The thorn had seemed to give him an unexplained confidence when it pricked his finger, but he had never dared toy with the notion again.

Yet this was no religious relic. This was the rising of corpses, that which was spoken of in the end times of Revelations. There had been a terrible plague before he was born. It had devastated London and all of England and Europe. Surely it meant the end times were coming. How could he accept *that*?

He tamped down his fears and put on his

logical mask, a shield to protect himself. His intellect could ferret it out. But if it truly was the intercession of the Devil, then he would fight that, too, with his very soul if need be.

Saying nothing more, he reached the spot where he thought he saw the apparition. The mud showed footprints – his and perhaps the other. Something heavy was dragged as well. And then the footsteps simply stopped. Vanished.

'Do you see that, sir?' said Jack anxiously.

'Yes.'

Jack shook his head. 'Right before your eyes and you do not believe it. Let us go to Abbot William. Maybe he can convince you.'

Perhaps Jack was right. Perhaps his skepticism was preventing him from seeing the truth of it. He strode quickly back through the churchyard and through the lychgate from where they had come.

They'd have to travel across all of London and then on to Westminster, to the Abbot of Westminster Abbey. In the last few years, Abbot William de Colchester had become a friend and confidant. He had been cold at first to Crispin, unlike his predecessor Abbot Nicholas de Litlyngton. But as Crispin proved his worth, the stoic abbot warmed to him. They played chess often. As often as Crispin could get away from his duties as Tracker. And in the intervening year, while Crispin was accustoming himself to a woman in the household, that had been his escape.

He wondered if Jack knew it, or knew how uncomfortable Crispin had been in their new circumstances. Surely he did, for the boy was nothing if not astute. And tactful, for he never broached the subject. There was nothing to be done, in any case. It was up to Crispin to gird himself and live with it. Especially if he didn't want to lose his apprentice.

The road to Westminster was busy as always, with more wagons than usual with the doings of summer, what with hay carts and drovers bringing lambs to market, with produce beginning to come in from the fields.

Once they passed Charing Cross's tall stone structure of arches and pediment, Westminster Abbey's two towers, one on the north side and one at the west entrance, were finally visible.

They took the familiar worn path to the cloister and rang the bell.

As many times as Crispin had been there since, pulling on that same bell rope, he still expected to see Brother Eric . . . and the ache of betrayal in his heart that this was not to be jabbed at him once more. He could not help himself as he sent up a silent prayer for the man.

One of the abbot's own chaplains, Brother John, served as porter today and slowly approached, giving a courteous nod upon recognizing Crispin. 'Here again, Master Guest?' he said, unlocking the gate. 'Your winning the last chess game put the abbot in a foul temper.'

'Sore loser, is he?' Crispin chuckled.

'I'm afraid so. Though, I would appreciate it if you didn't mention I said so.'

'Of course. Not a game of chess, unfortunately, but I do need to speak with him.'

33

They walked together, all three, through the windswept arcade to the abbot's apartments at the cloister's west end. Brother John knocked upon the door, and without waiting for a reply, pushed it open. A man playing melancholy strains on a flute sat on a stool by the fire, while the abbot sat at his table, carefully going over parchments with quill poised. He did not look up.

'Yes, Brother John?'

'Crispin Guest is here, my lord.'

Abbot William raised his head and his pale blue eyes sought out Crispin and crinkled in pleasure. He set down his quill. 'Ah, Master Guest. But you have your man in tow. This tells me this is no mere social call.'

'Astute as always, Lord Abbot.'

'Osbert,' said Abbot William to the musician. 'You may go.'

The man bowed, picked up a scrip, and followed Brother John out the door.

'Have your man Jack pour us some wine, Crispin.'

'Aye, m'lord,' said Jack with a bow. He took the familiar trek to the sideboard and poured wine into two goblets.

Abbot William skirted his table and came to the fire, seating himself in one chair while Crispin took the other. 'What is it you have come to me to discuss, Crispin?'

'I have a very strange tale, Lord Abbot. It is one I am loath to tell you.'

'I am adequately intrigued.'

Crispin glanced at the abbot's face. Intrigued

34

he might be, but his broad face never revealed what he was thinking. His many years as archdeacon and envoy to Rome had schooled his features into an unreadable mask. 'I was called to investigate . . . walking corpses.'

The abbot's brows raised as he took the wine Jack offered. 'Indeed. And where were these moveable deceased?'

'St Modwen's near the tower.'

'Now that has sparked my memory.' He rose and walked to his bookshelves. They housed an array of precious leather-bound volumes and a collection of parchment scrolls piled atop one another, their only indication as to what they might contain were dangling labels attached to cords. He reached for a leather volume and took it down, opening it on his table. Gently, he turned the pages, searching through the carefully penned texts. 'An Abbot Geoffrey of Burton upon Trent made mention of these same happenings, coincidentally, in his *Life and Miracles of St Modwenna*. He wrote about the precious saint almost three hundred years ago. Let me see if I can find the passage . . . yes. Here it is. Listen. "*That very same day on which they were interred they appeared at evening, while the sun was still up, carrying on their shoulders the wooden coffins in which they had been buried. The whole following night they walked through the paths and fields of the village, now in the shape of men carrying wooden coffins on their shoulders, now in the likeness of bears or dogs or other animals.*"'

35

'Holy Mother,' gasped Jack. 'That's it, Master Crispin!'

'Hush, Jack. The abbot has more to read.'

'Indeed,' the abbot went on. 'Apparently, this went on for days, afflicting the nearby peasants with disease and terror. Finally, they talked to the bishop. See here: ". . . *they received permission from the bishop to go to their graves and dig them up. They found them intact, but the linen cloths over their faces were stained with blood. They cut off the men's heads and placed them in the graves between their legs, tore out their hearts from their corpses, and covered their bodies with earth again.*"'

Jack looked down at the book with pale cheeks. 'What did they do with the hearts?'

'Burned them at a crossroads from morning till evening. It's the only way to rid the demon from the revenant.'

'Revenant?'

'Yes, young Jack. From the Latin *reveniens*. The "returned". Animated corpses such as you have described. I'm curious. Did you see them?'

'We did, sir,' Jack put in hastily before Crispin could reply.

'Truly?' Abbot William put his hand to his heart and walked thoughtfully around the table. Jack peered over the Latin text, reading it, his lips moving slowly and silently.

'Master Guest, do I take it that you intend to investigate this . . . this event?'

'I was hired for that very thing, my lord. If necessary, I suppose I shall be required to

36

perform this ritual of beheading and heart burning.' He sneered. 'Though I am reluctant to do so.'

'Indeed. As any Christian would be. It is such a coincidence this happening at a church bearing the name of the same saint who encountered the like before.'

'Yes.' Crispin nodded. 'Quite a coincidence.'

Abbot William rubbed his hand over his knuckles. 'I am very intrigued by this. Crispin, I know it is an unusual request, but I should very much like to accompany you on this quest.'

Taken aback, Crispin took several moments before he replied. 'You would?'

'Indeed. It isn't every day that one is faced with a *reveniens*.'

'If you tarry nigh, Master Crispin,' muttered Jack, 'you'll see plenty. It isn't all that uncommon.'

He laughed and pointed toward Jack. 'Oh ho! Young Master Tucker is not as enamored of your adventures as you are, I see.'

Crispin gave Jack a narrow-eyed glare. 'Not this adventure.'

'Then we shall all go together. If I may.'

Crispin gestured with a bow. 'You are most certainly welcome to do so.'

The abbot looked giddy. 'Bless me. I have not been this excited since . . . well. I don't know when. Perhaps my first journey to Rome, when I was a young man, and quite naive. Though this is purely as a matter of research, you understand. And in my abundant abilities to excise evil. I shall be ready. Where can we meet?'

37

Crispin kept his face neutral, but he was certain he could feel the warmth at his cheeks. 'My lodgings, I suppose. On the Shambles. An old poulterer's.'

'Oh, excellent. I should like to see your lodgings.'

'They are . . . humble, my lord.'

'Humble is nothing to be ashamed of. After all, our Lord was born in a stable and lived his life in humble surrounds.'

Crispin couldn't help but raise his eyes to the ribbed vaulted ceiling, its arched windows of reticulated colored glass, the tapestries, the carved furniture. Not quite as humble in the Church these days. 'Indeed.'

They bade their farewells to the abbot and trudged back toward London. The Thames was particularly pungent as the sun beat down on the shore. The smell of dead fish, brackish water, and wet water plants wafted up from the banks. Crispin unbuttoned the top few buttons of his cote-hardie. The sun was overwarming him with his caped hood and mantle.

'Why would the abbot want to see such a horrific sight, master?' asked Jack, his long strides curtailed to keep himself abreast of Crispin.

'As he said, he is a man interested in these doings. And perhaps – if it is something beyond our ken – it might be expeditious to have his proficiency. I judge that he might have more experience with the excising of demons than our dear priest Father Bulthius.'

'Aye. I've been thinking about what you said,

38

sir. If it isn't as our eyes tell us, what else *could* it be?'

'A deception of the human variety. Man's weakness and sin.'

'I hope you don't take this the wrong way, Master Crispin, but I hope it *is* that.'

'So do I.'

There didn't seem much else to do but return to their lodgings to ponder it all and wait until the evening. Isabel was happy to see them and, with broom in hand, urged Crispin to take his ease on the armed chair while she aired out the place, with both front-window shutters open wide and the door standing open as well. She merrily swept, only stopping now and again to put a hand to the small of her back.

Crispin's black and white cat, Gyb, made free use of the open windows and doors, taking turns wandering inside, and then out again, weaving around Isabel's skirts. 'You troublesome cat,' she sighed. 'Why don't you make yourself useful and catch us a fat hen?' She shooed him once or twice with her broom, but the cat wasn't the least disturbed by her prodding one way or the other.

Crispin watched the street, vaguely aware of the progress of people parading before him: merchants, servants, women at their shopping tasks. He pictured the, well, the *revenant* striding through the churchyard, of the Latin texts about St Modwen on that very subject. What were these corpses up to? Father Bulthius said they had become bloodsuckers. Whose blood were they sucking? Horses? Pigs? People? He hadn't

39

yet heard of anyone complaining, but he hadn't been out there among London's citizens lately. Perhaps he should go and listen. It was better than sitting here and waiting.

He rose and waved off Isabel and Jack as they offered to help. 'I just feel like a walk.' He left them. It was good for a married couple to be alone for a time. At least he imagined it would be so. He looked back and caught the soppy gaze Jack turned on his wife.

Gyb popped out of nowhere and followed him for a bit, his tail straight up like a century's spear. 'Are you to accompany me?' he asked the feline.

The cat looked up at him once, then turned his gaze toward the street, his ears flicking and twitching. Finally, the animal turned at an inter-section and went on his way to his own business. Crispin watched him go, envious of his cat's carefree nature.

He walked on, reckoning he'd hear more if he were closer to St Modwen's. He took the long trek through the heart of London, thinking wist-fully of the Boar's Tusk, and how nice it would be to spend the afternoon within the tavern, drinking the harsh wine and taking his ease, listening to Gilbert talk. But, of course, he could not afford that. He was earning his second day of coins investigating. There was no time to shirk.

He wondered what these graves looked like as they opened for these corpses. Did they dig their own way out or did it yawn for them like a parting curtain? He actually felt better knowing that Abbot William would be with them. He didn't suppose the man – the sort of man he knew the abbot to be – would run screaming in the opposite direction. Not a man who had faced the pope on a regular basis.

He spied an alehouse not too far from the little church and ventured inside, taking a seat near the middle of the establishment, surrounded by men who seemed to be familiar with the small room and wobbly tables. He ordered a goblet of wine and leaned in over his cup, pushing back his hood the better to hear.

'That priest must be mad,' said one man with a tattered cote-hardie and a walking staff leaning against the table. 'Have any of you heard of such ravings before?'

The men beside him shook their heads. One gray-haired fellow with a leather cap and a grizzled beard nodded. 'We once had a priest way back when the old king reigned, who raved and foamed when he gave a sermon. Oh, he was legendary.'

'I remember him,' said the third in a blue tunic. 'Died of apoplexy right in the middle of mass one day, didn't he?'

'He did. There was many a man who, for once, regretted missing church that day.'

They all chuckled and clinked their cups together.

'You ever seen them corpses, then, Will?' said Blue Tunic to the first man.

'I haven't, but my goat was struck dead.'

'No!' said the man with the staff. 'What happened?'

41

'Found it in the morning, throat torn out and blood all over the yard.'

'Probably a dog,' said the grizzle-bearded fellow.

'There would have been a row. Growling and such. Heard nothing at all.' He shivered. 'The wife won't leave the house alone now.'

Blue Tunic shuffled in his seat. 'I thought you said that priest was mad.'

'Aye, he is. But he might also be right.'

They drew silent, sipping their ale.

Crispin drank his wine and rose. 'My good men,' he said as he stood over their table.

They all looked up at him, some with mouths hanging open, lips wet and slick with ale.

'I couldn't help overhearing—'

'Nasty habit, eavesdropping,' said Grizzle Beard.

Crispin smiled. 'Ordinarily I'd agree. But since I came to this very alehouse to discover the exact nature of your conversation, I feel I must ask my questions.'

'And who are you anyway?' Blue Tunic arose and squared with him. The others got up from their seats and joined him; an impenetrable wall of grease-stained tunics, and hairy arms.

'I am Crispin Guest. They call me the Tracker. Have you heard of me?'

Blue Tunic exchanged chastened glances with his fellows and slowly sat. The others followed suit. 'What if we have?'

'I'd like to talk to you about this . . . this dead goat of yours.'

'Buy us another round of ale and we'll loosen our tongues.'

Crispin pulled up a stool and sat with them.

He let them talk while he listened. The tavern keeper came around and filled their cups from a round-bellied jug. It seemed everyone in the parish appeared to be talking of these walking corpses. The news had spread fast. But there was little to add to the tale. One of the men had heard of another instance of a dead animal and related the address to Crispin. He thanked the men, they waved at him, and he left them there with their jug of ale.

The house was at the other side of the lane from St Modwen's, a lone house at the bottom of Tower Hill, bordered by tall grass and a stand of plump trees.

Geese wandered and honked at him from the courtyard. Their gray bodies gathered close, but one lone gander propelled forward, neck outstretched and serrated beak ready to do battle. Crispin stood his ground and waved his arms, yelling at the creature. It pulled up short, turned its head to eye him warily, then gave a flourish of honks before it waddled haughtily away.

'Here now,' said a man coming out of the cottage. 'You must be blessed indeed for Old Lucifer to give you a wide berth.'

Crispin watched the gander as it retreated, its tufted tail flicking at him. *Old Lucifer, eh?* 'I have no special powers or blessings, good man. Only a fierce determination to avoid being nipped.'

'That you have. Well then. Are you in the market for goose, sir?'

'I might be. But, more importantly, I've come to ask you a question about dead geese found on your property.'

The man's friendly smile faded. 'Why ask about those?'

'Forgive me.' He bowed. 'I am Crispin Guest, the Tracker of London. And I am enquiring about strange occurrences that have been reported in this part of the city.'

'Strange occurrences indeed. My geese were killed. What am I to do about that?'

'Was it animals? Foxes, for instance?'

'If it were foxes they would have taken them away, eaten them, left entrails or somethin' behind. But these were just dead. Bloodied.'

'Have you ever seen the like before?'

'No. And bless me, but I never want to see it again. There is something queer out there in the meadow.'

'Like what?'

'I seen it, just at twilight. Strange lights a-floating about, strange sounds like moaning. I stayed inside, I can tell you.'

'And what of the animals?'

'I keep them in the shed back there.' He pointed to a structure leaning more than the cottage. 'And it's locked up good, with a sturdy door and a latch. Something got in there and dragged out me geese.'

'But didn't take them away or consume them.'

'No. That's the queer thing.'

'Yes, it is. Do you have a feud with someone, someone who may wish to cause you grief?'

'I've got no more enemies than any other man.

44

But what fool would kill a goose and not take the meat home?'

'Who indeed. Have you heard of any other similar animal killings, where the animal was simply left to die?'

The man scratched his behind, hitching up his tunic in the process. There was a large hole in the thigh of his stocking. 'I can't say that I have.'

'Well, I thank you for your time, good man.'

'Erm . . . are you certain I can't interest you in a fine goose for the table, sir? They're plump and tasty.'

Crispin looked back at the flock of squat bodies and long necks. It had been a while since he had goose, but he shook his head. He knew they weren't cheap. 'I'm afraid not.'

'Well . . . see that you track this foul fiend then. We've no use for such a miscreant going about scaring folk with bloody animals and strange sounds.'

'I will do my best.' He bowed, and turned away.

He followed the track again toward the main road, but stopped at the edge of the tall grasses and dips in the land of the meadow. It was daytime now, and none of it looked mysterious or strange. But he well knew how night can change a landscape . . . and one's imagination. Every shadow creates a question, every rustling of the grass a stray thought. Had he truly seen what he saw last night, or was it simply the suggestion that put it in his head, painted with shadow and moonlight?

45

Still, it was strange that animals had been bled and left to die. A fox or a stray dog would have carried a goose off. Weasels would have eaten it. Even someone plying mischief wouldn't have left such valuable meat behind.

He sighed.

Had not the revenants' mouths and faces had blood upon them?

He strode by the churchyard, marking where the graves were again and finally made his way home.

He was suddenly faced by the solemn features of both his servants. Isabel busied herself, perhaps hoping Crispin had not noted the worried expression on her face, but Jack stood in the center of the room, biting his lip, and rubbing the elbow of his coat.

Crispin eyed them both. 'What is it?'

Jack caught Isabel's eye before she turned hastily away once more, stirring the pot over the fire with more attention and vigor than was likely necessary.

'Jack, what's amiss?'

'We . . . we got a messenger. From a possible client.'

'A *possible* client? Who, then?'

'Well . . .'

'Tucker . . .'

'You should not get angry, Master Crispin. Or ignore the missive. After all. A client is a client. You've always said.'

He frowned. Isabel was facing studiously away, and Jack was biting his lip again. 'Yes. But who could it possibly be that vexes you so?'

46

'You mustn't get angry.'

'I'll get angrier the longer you delay.'

'Well . . . bless you, Master Crispin. You can't say I didn't warn you.' He dug the parchment out of his scrip and crumpled it in his hand for a moment more. Crispin was ready to leap at him but, just as he was about to strangle the boy, Jack handed it over.

When Crispin unfolded it, he looked at the signature at the bottom.

It was from Philippa Walcote.

Four

The name rang out in his head amid the quiet room as his heartbeat ticked away, growing sharper and faster as Crispin rolled the name over in his mind. Philippa? Wanted *his* help? A younger more naive Crispin would have jumped at the chance, but this older, jaded, present self merely took in the sharp etchings of her name, walked to the table, and traced his finger on the worn surface.

'You received this today?' He prided himself on the steadiness of his voice.

'Aye, sir.'

Crispin swallowed and this time, read from the beginning:

> *I hope you are well, Master Guest, and that this missive does not come as a great shock to you, for surely you never intended to hear from me again. Indeed, I never intended to contact you. But I am at a loss as to what to do. It is urgent that I speak with you. Will you come to my home to discuss the matter? I beg that you do.*
> *Philippa Walcote*

Stupidly, he turned the parchment over, but found it blank on its reverse. 'Did the . . . the messenger have no other tidings to convey?'

'No, sir. Only this message. It is very short on pertinent facts.'

'Yes.' He read it over again, hearing the lilt of her voice recite it in his head. But this was foolishness. Why should he accede to this? He already had a client. He need not answer this.

As if Jack could read his thoughts, he suddenly said, 'The messenger specifically asked for "the Tracker", sir.'

'I could send you, I suppose,' Crispin said, but even as the words left his lips it left a bad taste in his mouth. Did he *fear* to go? Was he so much less of a man that he was afraid of this woman who had broken his heart by marrying another so soon after his refusal?

Jack wisely remained silent.

Crispin shook his head, ashamed of himself. 'This is foolish. I will go and see what the wench wants and be done with it. Likely it is something equally as foolish as she is herself.'

'I will go with you, master.'

'There's no need—'

'I'm going.'

Jack snatched the letter out of his hands, stuffed it into his own scrip again, and opened the door. He'd wisely left his cloak hanging by the entry, for the weather had grown warm. Crispin unbuttoned his own cloak and hung it, and removed his hooded cape as well. Feeling lighter and cooler, he led the way out the door with Jack following.

He tried to blank his mind as he made the familiar trek to the mercer's house. It had been nearly nine years since he'd last seen her. He

49

had tried to avoid that street, avoid gazing upon that house of stone, with its walled garden and courtyard entry. There was little reason to be there, after all.

It took no time. Not enough time. The gatehouse lay before them and Crispin hesitated across the lane, simply looking at the place. It had little changed. Why should it have? It was still the house of a wealthy mercer, though this time it was the brother of the deceased, though that was a long tale in itself.

He took a step forward and his boots marked the route and stopped again before the porter. 'Crispin Guest. I was invited by the . . . the mistress of the household.'

The porter only nodded and opened the gate for him. It wasn't the same porter from eight years ago, of that he was certain. Crispin walked across the flagged-stone courtyard and up to the arched doorway. He pulled the bell rope and heard the jangling ringing on the other side of the heavy oaken door. Jack stood tall beside him, his bearded chin raised – ready, it seemed, to leap before Crispin to protect him should some danger streak toward them. It might have amused under other circumstances.

The door opened and a servant Crispin didn't recognize stood in the doorway.

Jack announced, 'Crispin Guest, the Tracker.'

The man's eyes widened slightly before he gestured for Crispin to follow him into the parlor. *Not the solar*, he said to himself, for that was where all the mischief had begun in this house the last time he was here. It was best, then, to

50

meet in the downstairs parlor, the proper place to receive business associates.

They waited as the servant escaped to get the mistress. He wondered if Clarence Walcote would be on hand to greet him, and scowled at the thought. He couldn't help but glance about the room. It was much the same as he remembered it, but somehow more lived-in. The tapestries were different: more colorful, more joyful. The painted mural on the walls depicted a tranquil scene of animals of various sorts gathering together in a glade. The sideboard had not one but two silver candelabras with fine beeswax tapers.

The woven rush mat on the floor seemed fresh when he walked across it, and he accidentally kicked a wooden toy he had not seen. He bent to pick it up and examined it. A wooden knight on a horse, its paint rubbed off in some places from being played with to excess. He remembered having something similar as a child and placed it upon the sideboard with care. Jack had told him some years ago that she had a babe who had obviously grown into a child who liked to play with wooden knights. A boy then.

Crispin's unease grew the longer they waited. He tapped his fingers irritably on his knife hilt, and then he couldn't help looking down at his coat and brushing it smooth. Several times.

Jack must have noticed, for he was suddenly before him, brushing the coat which was surely in fine fettle already, straightening his belt, and buttoning the last few buttons up to his collar. 'You look fine, sir,' he said softly. Their eyes

51

met only once, and Crispin read it all in Jack's gaze. The lad knew. He knew this was no mere client. As he had known since receiving the message.

But it didn't make the waiting any easier.

Finally, a step outside the door and the sweep of a trailing gown in the doorway. Crispin turned and only just held in his gasp.

She was as he remembered her. Only . . . there was a new maturity in her features. True, she had been bold and brash even in her youth, but she had lived and weathered these past eight or so years with quiet dignity. At least, *he* hadn't been aware of any further gossip.

She was rounder in the face and hips, but it made her cheeks rosy and her eyes – with that familiar heavy-lidded gaze – that much more appealing. The red tint in her blonde hair had always made him think of brass instead of gold, for she had been a kitchen wench who had married the wealthy merchant and elevated her status beyond what most wagging tongues in London would permit. Yet she had learned the skills of her late husband who turned out to be a fraud . . . and then married Clarence, the brother of the real Nicholas Walcote. There had been murder in this house and great deception, and she had managed to rise above it and hold her head up high. Clarence Walcote had come from a family of mercers, but Crispin suspected that it was Philippa who ran the business, for she had learned much from her erstwhile husband, Nicholas Walcote, even if that had not been the man's true name.

52

'Crispin,' she breathed, a hand at her throat. Her gown, though of rich material, was simple in design. She wasn't a fussy woman. She was plain-speaking and practical, and any gown she wore would be similarly straightforward. Where other women would take advantage of their raised status, she seemed to know how easily it could be stripped away. Hadn't it almost happened that way for her?

The gown's weave and embroidery showed her wealth, but they were working clothes, too, for he had no doubt that she was in the warehouses, checking the cloth herself, examining the wool, and sending the servants scattering to do the household's bidding.

She stepped farther into the room and he only then noticed Clarence Walcote behind her.

Clarence was a broad man of a heftier weight, though his head appeared smaller on those wide shoulders. He was ginger-haired with robust cheeks and a cleft chin. He strode in after his wife and steadied his gaze on Crispin.

'Guest. We appreciate your coming.'

She closed her eyes for a moment, girded herself, and faced him again. 'Aye, thank you, Master Guest, for coming so quickly.' She still tried to hide her lowborn accent with the hint of something higher, pronouncing each word carefully. Was the performance for him? Or was this her usual after all these years?

'Master Walcote. Madam Walcote.' He bowed low, his face schooled to blankness.

She turned to Jack and never tried to stifle her astonishment, and then she lost any hope of a

53

highborn accent when faced with him. 'Is this Jack Tucker?' The artifice fell away and she was the kitchen wench again. Her cheeks glowed with pleasure, and her eyes glittered with excitement. Jack bowed in acknowledgement. 'Well, blind me! You were just a sprig of a lad when I last saw you, and look at you now! You are quite the man.'

Jack couldn't seem to help but blush and smile. He touched his beard as was his habit but dropped his hand quickly.

'Much time has passed,' she said more soberly, before turning back to Crispin. 'Won't you please sit down.'

Crispin crossed to a chair with a cushion and sank into it. She moved to the chair across from it and joined him, arranging her skirts about her. Her face was turned down but her eyes looked up at him with that same sleepy look that had compelled him all those years ago, a look that had held mystery and mischief, and more intelligence than he had first thought. Clarence stood behind her and laid a proprietary hand on her shoulder. But perhaps Crispin was reading too much into it. They had been man and wife these last eight years. And, as far as he knew, Clarence had never known about . . . them.

'Perhaps Master Tucker will serve the wine,' she said, when Clarence said nothing.

'There's no need,' said Crispin with a flick of his wrist. Oh, how he wanted the wine, but his heart was already racing and his agitation screamed in his sinews. He needed to be alert, not to relax. He felt a sense of danger with every

54

one of her movements, and with the lack of them from Clarence.

Jack moved to stand behind Crispin, hands braced behind his back.

'It's been a long time, hasn't it, Guest?' said Clarence pleasantly. 'I've since heard of your doings about London.' He shook a finger at him. 'Can't leave well enough alone, can you? But I suppose that comes with the territory. Being this Tracker and all.'

Philippa glanced down at her hands resting in her lap. 'I am so glad you came. There is turmoil in this house and I fear its outcome. You were the only one . . .' She looked up. 'The only one I thought to call upon. The only one who *could* help us.'

'Yes, Guest.' Clarence sobered. 'It's the damnable truth.'

'Very well. I'm listening.'

Philippa looked up at Clarence, but he deferred to his wife. Crispin had the sense that he deferred to her in most things. He was obviously well-besotted with her. It had happened quickly. Philippa seemed to engender such passion in men, and jealousy in women. 'It's . . . our son. He is being accused of murder.'

'I take it he didn't do it.'

She pressed a knuckle to her plump lips and gnawed on it a moment, even as tears filled her eyes. She blinked them away and dropped her hand back to her lap. 'He is nearly eight years old. He doesn't know what he is saying.'

Crispin leaned forward. 'Madam, does your son say he *did* do it?'

55

She snapped to her feet and wrung her hands as she paced. 'I tell you he don't know what he's saying!'

'My dear.' Clarence stopped her pacing and clasped her in his arms. He glanced over her shoulder toward Crispin. 'We don't know what to do.'

Sitting back, Crispin watched as she slowly extricated herself from Clarence's grasp.

'Has he been arrested?'

'Not yet,' said Clarence. 'But the sheriffs intimated that he would be. Soon. One of the sheriffs is a mercer, a member of my guild. And so . . .'

'Is it possible that he—'

She spun and glared at him. 'Of course it's not possible!'

'An accident?'

She shook her head, looking once to Clarence. 'He will not say. He will not say more than he is responsible. He has always been a stubborn child.'

'Perhaps you would be better off retaining the services of a good lawyer.'

Clarence snorted. 'A lawyer would not be enough. We must prove that someone else killed him.'

'I see.' There was a sour ache in his chest. He had somehow harbored the notion that she had had a desperate need to see *him*, but it was her mother's heart that wanted Crispin only to protect her son. And why not? She only needed Crispin for the one service he could supply. It was his job, after all. And his own idiocy that had carved more out of it than there was.

He resettled, not only his body in the chair,

but his head on his shoulders. This was business. She was a client. He needed clients.

'And yet a lawyer might do you better than I can perform. That's as may be. Tell me what you know.'

She seemed to calm with his taking charge.

Clarence patted her arm and led her back to the chair. 'You tell him, sweeting. You know more than I do.'

She nodded and took her seat once more. 'Our near neighbor, John Horne, was also a merchant in cloth.'

'Was?'

'He was murdered. Madam Horne claims that it was my son who had been trying to steal a family relic, and John caught him in the act.'

'God's blood, another relic,' muttered Jack under his breath.

'But my son would never do such a thing,' she continued. 'Christopher does not steal, nor does he murder. He is only a child, but he knows right from wrong.'

Crispin measured her words. 'Where did the murder take place?'

'At the Horne residence.'

'And what is this relic?'

'A bone from a saint.'

'Blind me,' Jack whispered.

'And when did this all happen, madam?'

'Two nights ago. The sheriffs came, but they did not arrest him because . . . because he is a Walcote. But I fear that his name will not protect him long. John Horne was nearly as prominent a man as my husband.'

'And where were you and your husband during this murder?'

She paused and a bitter smile grew from the shadows on her face. 'We were at home. In the solar.'

'I suppose your servants would corroborate that. How was the mercer killed?'

'He was stabbed.'

'Where?'

'In Horne's bedchamber.'

'No, I mean where on his body?'

She gestured to her abdomen just under the ribs on the left side. 'He died instantly.'

'Did he?' Crispin mulled over that. 'Was Christopher's knife bloody?'

She shook her head. 'I don't know. The sheriffs took it.'

'I shall have to talk to the sheriffs. But first . . .' He rose. 'I shall have to talk to your son.'

'You'll get little out of him,' she said. 'He's stubborn. Like his father.'

'We'll see. Is he here?'

She paused again, squeezing her hands together. She looked up at Clarence.

'Madam?'

'Aye. Yes. He's in his chamber. Shall I . . . shall I have him come down . . .?'

'Would you prefer I go to him?'

'It . . . might be best. He has been through much and much is to come.' She took up a bell on the small table beside her and rang it. A servant came immediately to the door. 'Take Master Guest up to Christopher's chamber.'

The servant bowed and turned to go. Crispin

rose to follow. 'Jack, stay with Madam Walcote and Master Walcote.'

'Aye, sir,' he replied, but he didn't sound happy about it.

Crispin was nearly out the door when she surprised him by laying her hand on his arm. 'You will help him, won't you? If not for his sake, then in the name of God's mercy.'

He gritted his teeth and gently sloughed off her hand. 'I will do what I can, Madam Walcote.'

More quietly, she said, 'It is good to see you, Crispin.'

Clarence was suddenly in the doorway behind her. 'It's damned good to see you again, Guest. I don't mind saying. And I never thought I'd say it.'

Crispin said nothing to that and hurried to follow the servant up the stairs.

He tried to empty his mind, but it was crowded with memories. Her scent brought them all back, especially those private moments she'd spent in his bed. They tapped in his brain like a drumbeat, but he knew he had to concentrate on the problem at hand, not on the ghosts of his past.

Following the servant and checking the inventory of the man's clothing helped. The man was dressed well for the servant of a mercer, as one might expect. The house itself was still the same house in many ways. Arches were familiar, the tapestries were the same, only there were more items here and there, touches that Philippa herself no doubt added, now that she was unquestionably the mistress of her household.

They took the stairs up to the same gallery.

The door to the solar was there; bedchamber doors there and there. They turned to the other side of the gallery and to a room he was unfamiliar with.

The servant stopped before the ornate door of curled iron hinges and carved sheep, and knocked.

'Go away!' came the reply from within, a child's voice, young and high.

'Your mother wishes you to meet Crispin Guest, young sir,' said the servant.

'I said, GO AWAY!'

'I'll proceed on my own,' said Crispin to the man, who seemed happy to leave it to him.

When he opened the door, a dark-haired boy stood staring out the tall window, his back to Crispin. The sunlight fell around him, over his narrow shoulders, striking his black hair and turning the shine blue. He was a child of seven or nearly eight, though Crispin wasn't good at judging children's ages. He wore a fine red tunic of embossed florets with blue hose and long pointed shoes. There were shelves filled with toys of carved wood, a scopperel, a leather ball, a collection of colorful rocks, several wooden tops. A hobby horse leaned against the shelf, its leather reins well worn. A wooden sword and shield lay on the floor where they had been dropped in disinterest, a table of books and candles where he obviously took his tutoring sat in one corner, and a silver basin and jug perched on a sideboard near another window. A bed with curtains stood in its place on a raised platform against one wall, with a mural of a parade of mounted knights with banners behind it. It was the room of a young lord rather than that of a merchant's son, but Crispin supposed Walcote could well afford it.

The boy turned at Crispin's step.

The first thing Crispin noticed was the boy's mouth, twisted in an imperious sneer. The next thing he noted, besides the black hair, was the slate gray of his eyes. Clarence was ginger-haired, and Philippa was blonde. From whence did this changeling come?

Crispin stood a moment longer, merely studying the boy, until an unwitting gasp left his lips.

It was suddenly like peering into a mirror from long ago.

Five

The boy, Christopher, lost his sneer quickly enough when he looked Crispin over. 'Who are you?' he said quietly.

'I am . . . I am Crispin Guest. They call me the Tracker.'

The boy seemed to brighten. 'I've heard of you. They tell all sorts of tales about you. Brave tales. You defied the king once, they said.'

'Yes. It wasn't a very wise thing to do.'

'You were a knight.' He looked back at his wall mural before turning again to Crispin. 'And King Richard took it away. A knight is noble. And honorable.'

'We're not here to talk about me.'

'But what's it like?' He took several steps toward Crispin. The boy was unafraid of strangers. It seemed he *had* been raised like a little prince. 'You've jousted, haven't you?'

Dear God, he screamed in his head. *Could this be?* Christopher was seven. He'd last seen Philippa over eight years ago. The timing was right. Why had she never said?

Of *course* she had never said. She was married to Clarence. It would doom the boy's prospects if Clarence ever suspected . . . but surely the man must. The boy didn't look anything like him.

'You've jousted, haven't you?' the boy said again.

'Er . . . yes. Many a time.'

'Did you win?'

'Often enough.'

Christopher sighed. 'I should like to joust someday.'

'You . . . you're the son of a mercer. I shouldn't think you will have much call to joust.'

He drooped. 'Cloth is boring.'

Crispin straightened, fixing his thumbs in his belt. 'It feeds and houses you. Anything less would be ungrateful.'

Christopher straightened too, as if remembering his tutoring, and parroted, 'I am grateful to God the almighty Father, and to my own father for that which he grants to us.'

'Yes, rightly so.'

'But I should still like to joust,' he muttered.

Crispin got up close to him and studied his face. His skin was creamy white like any child raised with care, and his cheeks were touched with a rosy blush, as were his lips. His brows were as dark as his hair, which was cut in a neat and straight line just to below his ears. He looked healthy and strong, wiry like any boy his age.

And exactly like Crispin, down to the red cote-hardie and blue stockings.

'Do you know why I am here?'

Christopher sighed again and sat in the window seat on his leg, leaning an elbow on the sill and looking out to the courtyard. 'Yes. Because I'm to be arrested.'

'For murder. Do you understand . . .'

'Of *course*, I understand!' he rasped. 'My neighbor Master Horne is dead.'

He still wore his dagger sheath on his belt, and touched it from time to time, no doubt missing the hilt he seemed to want to lean his hand upon. Just as Crispin did.

No! Stop thinking of it. It isn't true.

This was Christopher *Walcote*, the son of a rich mercer. There was scarce anything better than that life.

'Did you kill him?'

Christopher turned such a look of hatred to Crispin he almost took a step back. 'Yes.'

No hesitation. 'Did you try to steal a relic?'

He turned away again. 'No.'

'Can you tell me what happened that night?'

Slowly, the boy shook his head.

'You don't know what happened, or you can't tell me?'

He shook his head again.

Crispin got in close and crouched to be at the same height. 'Master Christopher, do you know your life is in danger? The sheriffs will come and take you to Newgate and lock you in a cell. They might even take you to Fleet Prison.'

The boy shivered. He nodded.

'Do you wish to die?'

'God will save me. I've prayed.'

A deep pang suddenly assailed Crispin's heart. He'd had so many losses in his life. He couldn't lose again. Not again. 'You must help God and his saints to help you.'

The boy's eyes suddenly faced his own. 'Why? Is not God all-powerful?'

'He is. But . . .'

'Then He'll save me.'

'Is there nothing you can tell me?'

He shook his head again.

The boy *was* stubborn. 'Well . . . I will see you again. Perhaps you'll feel you can talk to me then.'

He turned to go but the boy rose and spoke, stopping him. 'It's funny. You look like me.'

'Er . . . there are probably many who . . . who . . .'

'Why? No one else here looks like me. Even my father doesn't.'

He took several strides before he was standing before the boy again. 'There are some things we should not speak aloud, boy. For one's own good. Has your mother never told you?'

'Yes, she has.'

He was slightly surprised but, given the circumstances, maybe he wasn't. 'Then I would listen to that advice.'

He turned on his heel again and left the chamber, closing the door behind him. Leaning his back against the door, he breathed. A son! He had a son. He could not have hoped for better. He thought he would die without progeny. There was Jack, but he wasn't blood. And yet . . . a *bastard* son. Even as his heart lifted, his soul deflated. A son he could never acknowledge. To do so would be to condemn him.

He straightened again, and walked unsteadily down the gallery. He descended the stairs and reached the parlor, where the Walcotes were sitting quietly as Jack stood by.

When Philippa looked up at him he glared.

She lowered her face. Clarence acknowledged nothing by his expression or gestures. Could it be he did not know? The man hadn't been the most intelligent in Crispin's estimation, and denial of the truth had been the hallmark of many a cuckolded husband, but could it truly be so? When Clarence looked at his black-haired son, did he truly think he was his? Yet, he hadn't denied him, and that was a mercy.

Crispin took a moment to compose himself.

'Well, man,' said Clarence. 'Did he tell you anything?'

'No. I shall have to investigate. But he says he did not take the relic.'

Clarence's brows shadowed his eyes. 'Do you believe him?'

'Do you?'

'I always believe my son.'

No, the man wasn't lying. He believed that Christopher was his son. Believed that he would not lie to him.

'I tend to believe him, too,' said Crispin softly.

Jack was studying Crispin's face curiously. He clearly knew there was something just below the surface, and Crispin well knew he'd be interrogated on the walk back. He tried to avoid eye contact with the lad.

'The Horne estate is in mourning,' Clarence reminded them.

'And so was this one when Master Guest came investigating that first time,' said Philippa harshly.

'Investigations are not pleasant,' said Crispin.

'They turn over rocks and find the slime beneath.'

'And you were good at that,' said Clarence. He nodded ruefully. 'I suppose my brother learned that the hard way.'

'If you are prepared for unpleasant truths, I will proceed. My, erm, fee is still sixpence a day.'

Clarence huffed. 'Oh yes. Must pay the Devil his due.' He took a small coin pouch from his scrip and walked across the parlor to hand it to Crispin. 'A sennight's wages. I have no doubt that this might become drawn out. And I know you will do the job, right, Guest?'

Crispin held the weighty pouch in his hand for a moment before handing it to Jack without looking back at the boy. A week's wages! Nearly four shillings. That would keep them well.

He bowed. 'Thank you, Master Walcote. I will endeavor to do my best.'

Clarence nodded. 'It's my son's life, Guest. We've only got him. I'd give my entire business for him, so don't fail us.' His eyes glistened for a moment before he quickly wiped at his nose. 'I must get back to the warehouse. My wife can help you with any further details.' He leaned over and kissed her forehead, gave her a conciliatory nod, and strode out of the parlor.

Jack and Crispin were suddenly alone with Philippa. Crispin felt the sweat trickle down his spine as he stood there, when Jack suddenly announced, 'I'll, er, see to the, erm, the matter, shall I?'

Barely aware of Jack's nattering, Crispin raised his head. 'The matter?'

'Aye, sir. The *matter*. That I'm to see to.' He dithered a moment before he stalked hurriedly out of the door. The sound of a servant opening and shutting the front entrance rang out in the foyer until all fell silent again.

Crispin stood while Philippa sat. He breathed, not knowing what to say, what to do. His hands, restless things, suddenly felt like bulky parcels hanging at the ends of his arms.

'You look well, Crispin.'

He hadn't wanted to look at her any more than necessary, but this time he did. And now that he had, he couldn't stop staring. It was as if it all had been yesterday.

'Philippa . . .'

She was on her feet in an instant. He hadn't seen it coming. But once she was close enough he couldn't help but take her in his arms. When their lips met, the years fell away, and he was in that moment once more. His mouth, his tongue found hers, and the burst of emotions flooded his chest with heat. She was his again.

His one hand cupped the smooth softness of her hair, fingers itching to unbind it. His other clasped her waist and inched down to a plump hip. And his mouth . . . Oh, his mouth tasted and suckled the sweetness of her lips, then tore away and trailed down her throat which she bared for him by throwing back her head.

'Crispin, Crispin . . .'

He growled, not able to form words, only to revel in the fine smoothness of her skin under

68

his lips. He nuzzled her throat with his mouth, nose, cheek. To feel her again, to touch her, smell her! He nearly lost himself in the sensations . . . until all at once he stopped. His senses had been calling to him, screaming at him. And it was only now that he heard that voice. It was Reason, and though he dearly wanted to ignore it, he knew he could not. The pain in his heart was almost too much to bear, but his desires, though even now warring with his honor, told him to gently but firmly push her away.

Her eyes, pupils blown, wildly asked, but he could tell the moment she knew.

'We can't,' he whispered. 'You're married. And that is one sin for which I will not fall.'

She touched trembling fingers to her mouth. 'Aye. You are right, of course. You're right.' She took herself from him then, stepping back, putting a shielding hand to her torso over her gown, as if holding down her beating heart.

Panting, Crispin stood flushed, hard, discontented. 'Christopher,' he rasped when he could speak again.

She turned away and sighed. 'How could I tell you?'

'For God's sake, Philippa!'

Her eyes blazed. 'How could I tell you!'

His anger sustained him for but a moment before it dissipated like a puff of smoke. 'I know.'

'What will you do?'

He ran a hand over his face. A sigh drew his shoulders up then down. 'Nothing. I will do nothing. I would not jeopardize his place in the world. And you must never tell him either.'

'I know.' She sniffed, wiping her nose with her hand. 'So many times I wanted to tell you, send you a message. I must have written so many letters. Letters that I burned.'

He nodded, his throat too hot to speak.

'But you must know this. Clarence has been good to me. And . . . he does not know.'

His skeptical look made her laugh.

'Surely you realize what a . . . a simple man he is. He never questioned it. And he has been good to Christopher. Christopher,' she said with a distant smile. 'I dared not name him after you. But it was as close as I could come.'

'Philippa.'

'And I never would have contacted you again. You must believe me. I never would have torn open that wound if it hadn't been so urgent.' She raised her chin and looked at him, a defiant glint to her eye. Her fisted hand pressed against her thigh. 'But there hasn't been a day gone by that I haven't thought of you. And I am more than gratified that perhaps the same could be said . . . of you.'

'Dammit, woman. What good does it do?'

'Nothing. But it is gratifying nonetheless.'

He straightened his coat. 'I will naturally do all I can for the boy. But if it comes out that he *did* do it . . .'

'Will you tell that to the sheriffs?'

He searched his heart but came up empty. 'I don't know.'

'I trust you, Crispin.'

'Maybe you shouldn't.'

'I trust you. Your Master Tucker will keep you

on the right path. *Strait is the gate, and narrow is the way.*'

'I daresay he will. Jack isn't given to sentimentality.'

'He's grown into a fine man under your tutelage.'

Talk of Jack opened the clouds and allowed a glimpse of light to unburden his soul. 'I have depended upon him these last eight years. He's married now, with a babe on the way, in fact.'

'Oh. Tell him how pleased I am.'

'I shall. And . . . have you . . . are there any other children . . .?'

'No. We tried, but . . . Poor Clarence. I don't think he's . . . able. He was so pleased when Christopher was born right away. He was so disappointed that there were no more. But he believes *he* has a son. A name to carry on.'

'Yes.' He had not meant the word to come out so bitterly.

'And you? Did you ever marry?'

His hands whitened into fists. 'No.'

Her smile waned. The pleasantries were over. 'It wasn't Christopher,' she said. 'No matter what he says. It can't be. Find the killer, Crispin.'

'I will do what I can, madam.'

The pull to her was too strong for him to continue to stay. He jerked his head in a curt bow and strode quickly from the parlor. He was at the entry door before a servant could scramble forward and open it for him.

He hadn't made it more than a few steps on the lane when Jack ran up to him. 'Master Crispin. Is . . . all well, sir?'

71

He scowled at the mud. 'What do *you* think?' he said tightly.

Jack fell in step with him and did not speak. Until, 'To Newgate, sir?'

'Yes,' was all he said.

Six

'Master Crispin,' said Jack softly as they neared Newgate Market. 'Is there something wrong?'

'No. Nothing.'

'But it looks like there's more to it than merely seeing Madam Walcote again.'

'I said there's nothing wrong!'

He sighed and muttered, 'If it's nothing then it shouldn't be so loud.'

Scowling, Crispin glared. 'What did you say?'

'Nothing, sir.'

It wasn't fair to Jack, his foul mood, but there was little to be done. And with Newgate's arch now in sight, that foul mood was likely to get fouler.

Newgate's troublesome bailiffs were nowhere to be seen, and instead the page, Rafe, was stoking the fire in an iron brazier. 'Master Guest and Master Tucker,' he said cheerfully. 'I suppose you'll be wanting me to announce you.'

Rafe was growing from a boy to a young man, though he was still much younger than Jack, but the blond hair draping over his pale gray eyes gave him a more mature appearance.

'If you would, Rafe,' said Crispin, surprised at how civil he sounded.

They followed him up the darkened stair and up into the parlor. Usually the sheriffs' clerk, Hamo Eckington was there, penning his parchments and grumbling at Crispin, but he, too, was absent. Rafe knocked on the sheriffs' chamber door and pushed his way in when there was an answering call. 'Crispin Guest, the Tracker, here to see you, my lords. Master Guest, Henry Vaunere and John Shadworth, sheriffs of London.' He bowed and left the room.

Sheriff Vaunere sat at the desk, poring over a pile of rolled parchments. It was Shadworth who scrambled forward. He was short, stout, and dark-haired, with a dark wide beard lying over the collar of his bright green houppelande. His eager eyes took in Crispin and Jack with almost a hunger. 'So this is Crispin Guest. Oh my! I have heard so much about you. So much, in fact, that I could scarce believe any of it was true. I've been sorely disappointed that you have made no appearance to us till now. And here you are at last. And this must be Jack Tucker if he's anyone. Yes, the ginger beard and curly hair. I've been told about you, too, Master Tucker. The Tracker and his apprentice. In our hall.'

Crispin exchanged a quick glance with Jack, but said nothing. He bowed instead. Jack followed suit.

'There's no need to drool over the man,' muttered Vaunere. The opposite to Shadworth in almost every respect, Sheriff Vaunere was tall, blond, and thin as a rail. His dusky beard was clipped tight to his jawline, and he didn't appear the least bit interested in Crispin's presence.

'Nonsense, Henry. He must be here for a crime. I love tales of his adventures. And now we're to be a part of it.'

74

'So I gathered.' He put down his quill, pushed aside his parchments, and folded his hands together on the table. 'Well, what is it?'

Crispin was about to speak when Shadworth raised his hands. 'Wait! I want to savor the moment.' He went to the sideboard and poured himself some wine. 'Will you drink, Master Guest? The wine is of high spirits from Spain. It is most delectable.'

'I will take a goblet, thank you.'

'How about your man?'

'No,' said Crispin, at the same time that Jack said, 'Aye, sir.'

Sheriff Shadworth looked from one to the other. He laughed and pointed at Jack. 'Aw, now Master Tucker. One must obey one's master. He wants you sharp.' He chuckled as he poured, while Vaunere shook his head and sighed wearily.

Shadworth trotted towards Crispin and handed him a goblet. 'To your good health, Master Tracker,' said the sheriff, raising his cup and taking a long draught. 'Ahhh. It's part of Henry's stock. He's a vintner. A felicitous wine indeed, eh, Master Guest?'

Crispin nodded, lowering the cup.

'So now. Tell us. What is it you are investigating? How can we help?'

Jack made a sound of disbelief, but Crispin ignored it and pushed on. 'I have been called upon to investigate the murder of the mercer John Horne.'

'Oh, indeed,' said Shadworth. 'Nasty business, that. He's in my guild. I, too, am a mercer, did you know? I should say he *was* in my guild.

75

Such a damned shame. And murdered by another mercer's son.'

'Specifically, I was hired by the Walcote household to investigate. They don't believe their son guilty.'

'Well, they wouldn't, would they,' drawled Vaunere. 'The boy likely did it. He confessed, didn't he?'

'He's seven years old,' said Crispin.

'That young?' Shadworth took himself to a chair by the wide hearth and nestled his girth into it, flattening the cushion beneath him. 'How was he able to do it?'

'Stabbed, wasn't he,' said Vaunere. 'It doesn't take much to kill a man with a knife.'

Crispin clutched the silver goblet to his chest. 'Did you examine the body?'

'A cursory look,' said Shadworth, deferring to Vaunere. 'What about you, Henry?'

'Didn't look at all. I considered what the coroner reported.'

Crispin gestured to his torso as Philippa had showed him. 'A stab wound here?'

'Yes, that's the gist of it,' said Vaunere.

'And he supposedly died instantly?'

'That is what the witnesses said.'

'And who are the witnesses?'

Vaunere rose. 'Guest, you aren't going to go about haranguing those poor people? They're in mourning, man.'

'A murder has been committed.'

'By that boy. Is he in our cells?' he asked vaguely of Shadworth.

'No, he isn't. He's a mercer, Henry.'

76

'Doesn't mean he isn't guilty.'

'I know. But I wanted to give them the benefit of the doubt.'

'*I* am the benefit of that doubt,' said Crispin. 'May I see the reports?'

Vaunere leaned over onto the desk, balancing on his fists. 'Now hold, Guest. What makes you think you can come in here and make demands of the office of the Lord Sheriff?'

Shadworth trotted towards the desk and planted himself before the other sheriff. 'He's the Tracker, Henry.'

'I don't give a damn who he is. I don't answer to him. He answers to me.'

'Now Henry. The *Tracker*. He knows what he's about. I'll get the reports.'

'If you go currying to every man who comes to you, you'll disgrace this office.'

'We've held this office since last Michaelmas. We're almost done with this office. Gird yourself, Henry. Admit it. We can use the help. And if he helps with this, might we ask that he help with other cases?'

'Well, that's a good point at least.' He sat again and spread his arms on the messy table. 'How about it, Guest? We let you in on this one and you help with some others?'

He dared not ask for his fee. Instead, he bowed his agreement.

'Well now, see, Henry? It will all work itself out. Let me find those rolls, if that damned Eckington has put them somewhere I can find them.' He retreated to the outer room, where he called out, 'Master Tucker! Assist me.'

Jack glanced at Crispin for acknowledgement and Crispin gave it with a nod.

'I'm coming, Lord Sheriff.'

Crispin found himself alone with Henry Vaunere as they assessed each other.

'So you are this infamous Tracker. You seem old.'

Bristling, Crispin only raised a brow. 'The streets of London can age a man.'

Vaunere scratched his beard. 'So they can.'

'I found it, sir,' said Jack in the other room.

'The devil you did. Give it here, lad. That's fine good work. No wonder the Tracker relies on you so.' They both re-entered through the arched doorway. 'You must tell me some of your adventures sometime. Over supper. I'd be happy to feed the Tracker *and* his apprentice.'

'Oh. Thank you very much, my lord.'

'If we are done with the pleasantries,' said Crispin, 'I should like to see that report.'

Shadworth stared for a moment before he burst out laughing. 'Oh, Master Guest. You are as surly as they say you are.' He offered the scroll.

Surly? Crispin all but snatched it out of his hand and, stepping over to the sideboard, unfurled the scroll. Dated two nights ago, the clerk penned, in a spiky, almost illegible scrip, what was reported: that Christopher Walcote, child, was found in the residence of John Horne, standing over his dead body with a dagger in his hand. The man was stabbed once and bled out and died instantly. That they were alone until the servants came after hearing loud exclamations. It was soon discovered that a relic of great prize owned by John Horne – a saint's

78

bone housed in a reliquary in the shape of a cow – was missing, and the boy was blamed. He was remanded into the custody of his parents until further investigation.

He looked up from the paper. 'The relic was stolen, then?'

'Yes,' said Sheriff Vaunere.

'But the boy didn't have it on him. Wasn't that suspicious?'

'Well . . . he . . . he could have hidden it somewhere.'

'He had the presence of mind to hide it and then deliberately stand over the corpse of the man he supposedly killed?'

'The criminal mind, Guest,' he said, tapping his temple. 'Who can fathom it?'

'I can. It sounds terribly absurd to me.'

'Oh? I suppose you could do better?'

'I intend to.'

'The devil you say.'

'Where is the body now?'

'Lying in state at home, I should imagine. Is that where it is, John?'

Shadworth shrugged, but he was smiling, shaking his head at Crispin. 'Look at the man's mind work. It's a thing to behold, eh, Henry?'

Crispin sighed. 'I would be interested in examining it.'

'That's a ghastly thought,' said Vaunere. 'What, by the Blessed Virgin, would you do that for?'

'You claim the man was stabbed here.' Crispin gestured again to the lower ribs. 'Even if his lung was punctured, it would have taken him days to die.'

'It said he bled out,' said Shadworth, looking over his shoulder at the parchment.

'Was there a great deal of blood?'

Shadworth shrugged. 'Not that I recall.'

'You would have remembered, believe me.'

'Now that's right,' said Shadworth, a finger to his lip. 'Guest here was a lord and knight. He's seen many a battle. Fought well, didn't you, alongside the duke of Lancaster. Glorious, that must have been. I myself have ridden a time or two at tournament, but that was long ago.'

'And several stone ago as well,' muttered Vaunere.

'Eh?'

'Never mind. Guest, are you determined to exonerate your client even against the sheriffs' and coroner's report?'

'Only if the reports are not quite accurate, my lord, which I am not certain they are.'

Vaunere chuckled. 'He's got gall, hasn't he? Some would call it cheek.'

Shadworth sighed happily. 'It's marvelous.'

'Do what you like, Guest. Just leave us alone about it,' said Vaunere.

'Are you going to arrest that boy?'

'I don't see how we can put it off much longer. Walcote or no Walcote. The citizens of London will demand it.'

'Oh Henry. Let's see what Guest can do first. I should very much like to see how he manages this investigation.'

Vaunere leaned back in his chair and began cleaning his nails with his dagger. 'You do know the aldermen of this city elected us to do our jobs.'

'Our jobs involve discretion. And I for one wish to see Guest at his work. It costs us nothing, Henry.'

'That is certainly true. Very well. The boy remains free for a sennight. After that we must do our duty.'

'A sennight?' Crispin stuck his thumbs in his belt. Seven days to exonerate his son. Could he do it? He had to. He glanced at Jack before bowing to the sheriffs. 'Then I must take my leave, my lords.'

'This is exciting,' said Shadworth.

'Good God, John. You'll unman yourself.'

Crispin didn't listen to the rest of their conversation. He hurried down the steps and out of the gatehouse with Jack at his heels.

'Where to now, Master Crispin?' he asked, trotting alongside him. 'To the Horne household?'

'We must.'

'Are you so convinced the boy *didn't* do it . . . or is it because it is Madam Walcote?'

It came over him so quickly and so all-consuming that he was unable to stop himself grabbing Jack by his coat and shoving him hard against the nearest wall. Even before his mind could clear, Jack's expression, the fear in his eyes, the drooping jaw in shock, came up to greet him.

He released him immediately. 'I'm . . . sorry . . . I . . .' He couldn't speak. Taking a step back, he lowered his reddening face. 'I did not mean violence against you, Jack.'

'You . . . must do what you will. You are my master.'

'It is not that way with us. Forgive me.'

'Of course, master. This crime,' he said quietly, 'because of who it involves, must be putting you out of sorts. I know that.'

Crispin wiped his hand down his face. 'You are too understanding.'

'I know about love, sir.'

He grimaced, considering his actions. 'So you do.'

'We go next to the Horne estate, then?'

'Yes. And then we will talk to the boy once more.'

Jack walked beside him with only a brief glance. He squeezed the lad's shoulder to show he meant no harm, and Jack seemed satisfied, his stride growing more eager as they made their way down lane after lane.

They reached Mercery Lane once more but, before getting to the Walcote gatehouse, they turned down a short lane to another manor. Crispin talked to the porter who escorted them to the front entrance and pulled the bell rope, still waiting beside them until the servant answered the door. He introduced Crispin, and Crispin and Jack waited on the step while the servant closed the door again to speak to his masters.

The porter was a stout, grim-faced man in livery, who stood like a wall between the door and Crispin. He fixed his eyes on Crispin and never wavered away. Crispin stared back and didn't so much as move a muscle as their silent duel began.

Presently, the servant returned and opened the door wide. 'You may enter, Master Guest.'

82

He turned away from the porter with a smirk and stepped into the entry. The servant had dark circles around his eyes. No doubt the household was in turmoil now that the master was dead.

'My mistress has granted a *brief* audience with you,' said the servant, 'but I beg you, sir, to be as soft as you can be. She is suffering greatly from this loss.'

Crispin bowed. 'I understand.'

The servant hesitated and Crispin looked him over. He was a man of middle years, and thin, with a balding head and clean-shaven face. 'You have served in the Horne household for a number of years?'

'Yes. Nearly twenty-five years. I am the steward here, Robert Hull.'

'Did you see anything of this murder, Master Hull?'

His eyelids fluttered. His lashes were moist and those reddened eyes seemed susceptible to weeping again. 'No. By all the saints, I wish that I had. I wish I could have stopped it.'

'And the boy. Christopher Walcote.' The name threatened to stopper his throat. 'Did you see anything of him?'

'He frequented this household. He was a friend to Master Horne's apprentice, Martin Chigwell.'

'So it was common to see the boy here?'

'Yes. He . . . he usually meant no harm. He was a lad like any other, full of mischief and laughter. He was most often cheerful and courteous.'

Crispin took a moment to mull his words. 'Master Hull, do you believe Christopher Walcote stole the household relic?'

83

'I . . . I don't know.'

'Do you believe he killed John Horne?'

The steward stilled, eyes fixed on Crispin's. 'It is not for me to say,' he said at last. 'I will take you to my mistress now.'

He and Jack followed the steward up a wide staircase and to a room that turned out to be a bedchamber. The lady of the house was standing before the window, bathed in its light. It was nearly the mirror of how he had found Christopher.

'Madam,' said the steward with a bow. 'I present to you Crispin Guest, the Tracker.'

She didn't acknowledge them when the steward bowed again and retreated to the door. But by the position of his shadow, Crispin noted that he hadn't gone far.

Jack stood silently behind him, surreptitiously surveying the room.

'Madam,' Crispin began, bowing deeply. 'My sincerest condolences to you and your household for this unfortunate event.'

Slowly she turned her head. 'Unfortunate event,' she said. 'Strange how a life snuffed out can be described thus.'

He took a step closer. 'A feeble description, surely.'

'Yes. An entire life chipped down to a platitude. What is a "tracker", Master Guest?'

'It . . . is a title that the citizens of London have bestowed upon me. I investigate lost objects, solve crimes . . .'

Her face, a pale, lifeless entity, scoured his. 'Are you here to "solve" a crime? But the crime is already solved. That boy from next door, that

84

Walcote boy, killed my husband and stole a valuable relic.'

'Tell me about it, madam.'

'There is little to tell. There was a commotion of raised voices and then silence. When I went to investigate I saw him standing over my John. He had a bloody dagger in his hand. When will he hang, do you think?'

Crispin swallowed. 'The circumstances *seem* indisputable.'

'I thought as much, too. Has he returned my relic?'

'He claims he never took it.'

'He's a boy. He lies.'

'Some boys do not lie.'

She snorted at that.

'Do you have any children, madam?'

Her face fell again. 'Sorrow upon sorrow. We had no children that lived beyond a month or two. I have no sons to care for me, and now no husband. What's to be done?'

Crispin wanted to leave but he had to ask his questions before the steward tossed him out. 'These voices you heard. Was it the boy and your husband? Was anyone else in the room?'

'I . . . I don't know.' She dropped her face in her hand. 'I can't answer any more. Please leave.'

The steward was quick to re-enter the room. 'I shall escort you out, Master Guest.' He all but took Crispin's arm, using the bulk of his body to intimidate, and glared at Jack.

Crispin wasn't cowed, but he did comply. As he and Jack walked across the hall to the front

85

entry, Crispin asked, 'Do you know if anyone else was in that room, Master Hull?'

'I don't know. There might have been.'

'Might have been? What is it you are not telling me?'

'It is time for you to leave.'

'Hold. What is this relic? What did it look like and where was it kept?'

Hull sighed impatiently. 'It looked like a bone inside a little carved wooden cow. The whole was thus.' He gestured with his hands something six inches in length. 'A little red cow, as I said, with its paint peeling off. It was kept in the family solar.'

He glanced up the stairs to a room at the top with a closed door.

Crispin studied it from below. 'Is your master in the solar now?'

He nodded, wiping at his nose.

'I know it is an imposition, sir, but may we see it?'

He looked toward the bedchamber they had exited, and then down at his feet. 'The funeral is later today, sir.'

'Master Hull, it is my business to make certain a child does not hang for a crime that he may not have committed. A *child*, sir.'

Wavering, the steward finally nodded. 'Very well. I will take you there.' They climbed the stairs once more and the steward pointed. It seemed he did not want to enter, and Crispin was just as happy that he didn't.

But as Crispin opened the door, the wimpled faces of six women turned to glare at him. *God's*

86

Blood, they're sitting vigil. While Crispin was thinking of a logical way to get them out of the room, Jack was already stepping forward.

'Madams, please come and receive refreshment. The steward will lead you out.'

'But we've only just arrived,' said one, whose face was scored with tiny lines.

'This is to fortify you on your holy cause. Come now. Let me help you.' He hoisted two women to their feet by grabbing their arms.

'Here now!' said a hefty woman in a scarlet cote-hardie, waving her rosary like a weapon. 'You're too rough.'

'My apologies.' He opened the door and gently ushered them through, closing it smartly behind them.

'That was very enterprising, Jack.'

'That steward will be none too happy with us after this.'

Crispin turned at last to the body laid out on a bier, around which the women had been kneeling. Horne was starting to smell. It was best he was buried soon.

'Help me, Jack. We won't have much time.'

'Help you with what? Oh, blessed Virgin, you aren't going to—'

But Crispin was already rucking up the man's shift, exposing the man's privities. All of him was pale white. Even the hair on his legs and barrel torso seemed less vivid. His genitals lay limp and shriveled at his legs' juncture.

'Christ,' muttered Jack, grimacing as he looked away from Horne's lower extremities.

'Here is the fatal wound, Jack.'

The lad moved forward, doing all but holding his nose. He looked where Crispin pointed. 'Would that be fatal, sir?'

'That's the question. Help me turn him.'

'Master!'

'Come, Jack. I haven't all day. Do you imagine I like touching corpses any more than you do?'

'Aye, sir.'

They pushed. His heavy corpse yielded as they rested him on his other side. 'What is this?' Crispin ran his finger down another two slices at the man's back, around kidney height. Though they had been cleaned they were raised tears and darkly discolored. 'Surely these would be a deathblow. Why was this never mentioned?'

'So he died from these wounds, then?'

'Most assuredly, though the one through his ribs didn't help matters. It might have hastened them. These two here might have harmed his organs, bled him from within but surely caused greater blood loss. He would have lingered for days with a collapsed lung, but with pierced organs here, he would have died quickly.'

He pulled the body onto its back once more and affixed his shift into place, covering him again with the shroud.

He turned his attention to the room. There was a niche framed by gilt molding where a candle hung above it on a chain, but the niche was empty. Crispin touched the plaster but saw nothing else. This must have been where the reliquary was kept.

He made sure Jack noted it too before he trotted down the stairs and met Hull before the front entry. 'I don't know what you said to those women . . .' Hull began.

'I apologize for that,' said Crispin hastily. 'The coroner's report said that servants first found Master Walcote with the dagger. May I speak with them?'

Exasperated, Hull did not look at first as if he would comply. But after a moment of consideration, he pressed his lips tightly together and nodded. 'The two chambermaids are in the kitchens, down those stairs. I'll take you.'

'Thank you. Oh, one thing more. Where is the funeral to be?'

'St Modwen's,' he said over his shoulder. 'He was a longtime patron.'

That's a coincidence, thought Crispin, suddenly remembering his rendezvous there tonight. *Perhaps John Horne will walk the fields this night.*

He did not need to glance at Jack to sense the boy thinking the same thing.

They followed the steward to the kitchens by a narrow stair.

Two women and two men were chattering together before the main hearth. One man in a cote-hardie, gray with age, sat before the hearth, peeling turnips. Another older man stood above a great cauldron and held a stirring spoon in his hand. Two women, better dressed than the two cooks, bent close as they talked. None of them noticed Crispin and Jack until Crispin cleared his throat.

They started and whipped around. They all bowed and curtseyed, eyeing him warily.

89

'This is Master Crispin Guest, the Tracker of London,' said Jack by way of introduction, 'and he's come to ask questions about the death of your master.'

They took on solemn faces. The man with the spoon folded his arms and tilted his head back. The linen cap on his head framed his face. The one sitting with the turnips clutched the sides of the wooden bowl in his lap and bit his lips, eyes wide with wonder.

Crispin soon ignored them in favor of the women. Their kerchiefs were clean, their aprons equally so. Their clothes were in better form so he assumed they were chambermaids. 'You two. Did either of you witness Master Horne's murder?'

They looked at each other and seemed to take courage. One of them, the blonde one on the right, clutched at her apron. 'I saw it. I saw that boy.'

'Just what exactly is it that you saw?'

'There was a fierce row. Everyone heard it.'

'A row between Master Horne and whom?'

She looked again at her dark-haired companion, who nudged her with her elbow. 'Go on, Nesta. Tell him. You saw more than the rest of us.'

'Well, I sent Clarice to fetch the steward. It's not that any of us could interfere, mind, but there was always cleaning up to do afterwards.'

'These rows happened often?'

She gnawed on her finger. 'I don't like to say, sir. My master and mistress . . .'

'You heard them arguing?'

'Not this time. It was the master and Master Chigwell, his apprentice.'

90

'And what happened when you fetched the steward?'

'I wasn't exactly in the room, sir, but outside it. And the steward waited with me.'

'And the boy, Christopher Walcote. Was he there?'

'No. He was in the solar.'

Crispin glanced at Jack. Could it be? Could the boy have been in the solar stealing the relic after all? He didn't want to believe it of his own flesh and blood, but the boy certainly could have lied to him. And, what's more, he might very well have killed Horne as well.

'Why was he in the solar?'

She shrugged. 'He had the run of the house. Master Chigwell took a fancy to him. And Master Horne didn't mind.'

'Did young Master Walcote take a fancy to Master Horne?'

She stared down at the floor, biting her lip. 'Master Horne . . . was not easy to like, sir.'

'Oh?'

'I shouldn't say.' She glanced worriedly at the stoic Hull. 'I shouldn't speak ill of the dead, him being upstairs and all. And the funeral soon to happen.'

'But you must speak. This is a murder investigation.'

She glanced past Crispin's shoulder toward the steward. 'Master Hull? Must I say?'

'Speak your mind, Nesta,' said Hull. 'You might be compelled to by the law court.'

'At the trial? I don't want to speak at the trial.'

'Then speak now,' said Crispin, edging closer.

91

She nodded. 'My master was not . . . well loved. He was sometimes cruel to Master Chigwell and my mistress. He . . . he toyed with the maids and my mistress didn't like it.'

'And so when did Master Christopher return to the room with Master Horne?'

'I . . . don't know.'

'You said you were nigh when the arguments ensued.'

'Yes, but he came out and told us to go away after my mistress left him. And we did.'

'Then you did not witness Master Christopher and Master Horne argue as you at first claimed you did.'

'No, sir. We do not know whether they argued or not.'

He sighed. 'Very well. Thank you.'

They scurried off and Crispin turned to Hull. 'We have no choice but to talk to Master Chigwell.'

'I have sent pages to find him, but so far he has not been found.'

'Indeed. Then rest assured I will return.'

Hull bowed and fidgeted by the door, seemingly itching to escort them out. Crispin let the man stew for another moment more before he gestured for him to do so.

They left the Horne residence and stalked past the gatehouse, only to glance across the way to the Walcote manor.

'Funny, Chigwell missing and all,' said Jack.

'Yes, funny.'

'Do you think he is at the heart of it, sir?'

'I do. At least . . . he will have more interesting answers. Let us go, Jack.'

'St Modwen's?'

'Two birds with one stone. Later. But for now, we must go back to the Walcote house.'

'Are we to talk to Christopher Walcote again?'

'Inevitably. There are now several unanswered questions.'

'Maybe he won't talk to you.'

'That's why you're coming. You're younger. He might . . . see a kindred spirit.'

He needed Jack to see the boy, to understand, for he could not open his mouth to tell Jack himself.

They passed through the gatehouse again, the porter waving him on. Jack rang the bell rope and the same steward opened the door, surprised to see Crispin again so soon after departing.

'No, I don't want to see the master or mistress. Just Master Christopher.' The steward hesitated. 'You do know why I am here, Master Steward?'

The steward glanced at Jack. 'You investigate murders.'

'I intend to exonerate your young master.'

His lips tightened to a thin line. He nodded curtly. 'Yes. Come, then.'

Seven

This time, Jack accompanied him up the stairs to the carved door. The steward knocked and announced Crispin. When Crispin opened the door this time, the boy was waiting for him.

'You're back,' said Christopher with an eager face. 'Does that mean it's over?'

'I'm afraid not. It merely means I have more questions.'

When Jack walked in after his master, he gasped. 'Master!'

'Not now, Jack.' He gestured toward Jack. 'This is my apprentice, Jack Tucker.'

'You have an apprentice?' said the boy, studying Jack curiously.

'Yes. And you had a friend at the Horne residence who was also an apprentice, did you not?'

The boy frowned. 'They probably won't let me see him anymore.' He folded his arms over his chest. 'It's not fair.'

'Can you tell me about him? I'm sure Jack would like to hear, too.'

The boy smiled at Jack. 'Is being an apprentice fun? I should like to be an apprentice. Though Father says I'm his, it doesn't feel like it. And cloth is boring.'

Crispin elbowed Jack, and, catching on, Jack knelt next to Christopher. 'Well, young master, it isn't always fun. An apprentice must work

94

hard. He's to learn his master's work so that he can take it on someday. When you apprentice with your father, it's so you can be a mercer when you're of age.'

'Martin wants his own shop. That's why he apprentices with Master Horne, but Master Horne was—' He stopped, biting his lip. 'I mustn't say.'

'Why?' asked Jack in the same soft tone. 'Did . . . did someone tell you not to say?'

'I mustn't say. When will all this be over? I don't like being a prisoner in my room. I want to get down to the vats. That's interesting, at least. And maybe Martin will be there.'

'Martin Chigwell,' said Crispin.

'That's right. He sometimes comes here to talk to our apprentices, but it's not allowed. Why isn't it allowed?'

'Your . . . your father and Master Horne are competitors. Do you know what that means?'

Christopher slid off his stool and walked to the heavy curtains hanging on either side of his window. He clutched them, stroked the nap. 'It means we have a business and they have a business and we must fight for every customer we get.' It sounded like something Clarence would say. Of course it was. He must have told this to his son many a time, possibly scolding him for spending so much time with a rival's apprentice.

He showed Crispin and Jack the curtain material. 'My father imported this from Flanders,' he said. 'I don't know where Flanders is.'

'It's across the sea to the Continent,' said Crispin.

95

'Have you ever been there?'

'Yes. Many times.'

'They say the people speak funny there. I've met men my father says are from Flanders and they speak funny. I didn't understand them.'

'People from distant places speak differently from you or me.'

'It's because of the Tower of Babel, isn't it?' He let the drapery drop and scuffed along the wooden floor to his books. Crispin coveted the number of them. Christopher toyed with the edge of a leather-bound tome, flicking his finger at the corner. 'I like Scripture. It tells you things. Things about life and how God protects us, even in adversity.'

'Yes. It tells us to love our enemies.'

Christopher frowned. 'I don't understand that one. Our enemies aren't lovable. Else they'd be our friends.'

'Was Master Horne an enemy?'

'He was no friend,' he said with a scowl.

'Master Christopher,' said Jack, telling Crispin with his expression to back off. 'Did you argue with Master Horne that day?'

'Yes.' His answer was clipped, and he shut his mouth, keeping the rest closed.

'Was anyone else in the room with you?'

His cheeks reddened. 'I don't want to talk about it anymore. Everyone wants to talk about it and I don't want to!'

'You must,' said Crispin, stepping forward and standing over him. 'Don't you understand? If you don't tell us what really happened, you will hang. The sheriffs will have you executed.'

Strangely, the boy seemed calm, except for his reddened face. 'They'll kill me, I know. But *greater love hath no man than this, that a man lay down his life for his friends.*'

Taken aback at the boy's calm and his words, Crispin exchanged a look with Jack. 'Are you protecting a friend, Christopher?'

'You have to leave now.'

Jack rose and sucked on his teeth a moment. 'Can we come back another time? There's a game I'd like to teach you.'

The boy brightened. 'Yes, please. I'd like to learn a new game.'

'Then we will.' It seemed that he couldn't help reaching over and rubbing the boy's head, tousling his hair. The boy didn't seem to mind. 'Good day, little master.'

'Farewell, Master Tucker. Come back soon.' His wide gray eyes looked up hopefully.

'We will. Come, Master Crispin,' he said softly, poking Crispin in the ribs. They said nothing along the gallery. Crispin's heart was hopeful of catching another glimpse of Philippa, but his mind scolded him for such a foolish thought. Down the steps they went and across the court-yard, saying nothing to one another, even as the gray skies started a light sprinkling. But once they reached Mercery, Jack rounded on Crispin.

'How long have you known?' he demanded.

Crispin frowned and fidgeted at his belt. 'Only the moment I saw him. Philippa never hinted, never sent a message . . .'

Jack paced before him. 'Oh, Master Crispin, we are in the kettle now.'

'I know. But we mustn't say anything. No one must know.'

That stopped the lad's pacing, and he stared, slack-jawed. Until understanding slowly passed over his eyes and his stiff posture slackened. 'Oh, master . . .'

Crispin couldn't stand his expression anymore and turned away, stalking up the lane. 'It doesn't matter. We must proceed as if we had never known, as if it wasn't . . . what it was. At any rate, I'm not convinced the boy is guilty.'

'Neither am I. Someone else *had* to be in that room. And why didn't the coroner note the other wounds? Someone is lying. Where to now, sir?'

'Home. I would think on this before I proceed further. And then we have these revenants to think of tonight.'

'Shall we . . . shall we go to the funeral of John Horne this afternoon?'

'Might as well. We can survey the churchyard. Since this will be the newest grave . . .'

'Do you think *he* will walk, sir?'

'There's no accounting for any of it. I should like to see if he does.'

'But sir!'

'If you've no stomach for it, then stay at home.' He hadn't meant for his tone to be so sharp, but his nerves were on a knife-edge as it was.

Jack didn't seem to notice. 'I've no stomach for it and that's a fact. But I am an apprentice Tracker and so . . . and *so* I must needs gird m'self.'

They returned to the Shambles. Isabel fed them, and they argued across the table as if she weren't there.

'I think he was protecting his friend, Martin Chigwell,' said Jack.

'I agree. So we must find cause of Chigwell to be alone with his master in that room. We must speak with him and soon. Unless he has fled.'

'And Christopher had gone to the solar where the relic was kept. Do you suppose he truly *did* take it?'

'Unknown. He's a stubborn boy.'

'Like his father.'

Crispin raised his face to Jack. Jack smiled sheepishly. 'He does look hearty and hale . . . like you, sir.'

Crispin crushed his hands into fists and stared down at the worn tablecloth. Small repairs in careful stitches was the work of Isabel.

Why had this had to happen? It always seemed that when everything was going tolerably well, something always came along to throw a caltrop into it. He would have been happier never knowing he had a bastard son. Or would he?

Isabel waddled toward him, leaning over and pouring him more wine. Seeming to read his sour thoughts, she softly said, 'It's better to know he is there, Master Crispin.' Apparently, Jack wasn't about to keep such a secret from his wife. Crispin's scowl deepened. 'Someday you might even tell him. He might wish to know.'

'I doubt very much that he would wish to know he was the son of a traitor, a pauper living on the Shambles.'

'No. He will be proud to know his heritage comes from mighty warriors and lords. That in his blood runs the blue of nobility, of history. He might be glad to know his father was a knight—'

'And is a knight no more?' He snapped to his feet. He didn't offer excuses or his leave when he stomped up the stairs and slammed the door to his chamber.

He sat hard on his bed and planted his forehead to his hands. The boy was much, much better off not knowing. He could be a wealthy mercer. What was wrong with that? It was an honorable profession. He'd be a town alderman. Maybe even Lord Mayor someday. Though, according to the law, he had to first serve as Lord Sheriff. 'Oh God.' How would Crispin cope with that? He shook his head and grunted a laugh. Crispin might be dead by the time that happened, and it would be Jack's problem.

Though there were . . . *things* . . . he wanted to tell him. Wisdom he wanted to impart. And dammit, yes, his family history. He should know. He should be told about the proud heritage he came from.

He threw himself back on the bed, and stared up at the worn canopy of muslin above.

A timid knock at the door before it squealed open. 'Master?'

'Come in, Jack.'

'I rounded on my wife, sir. She doesn't know when to keep her mouth shut sometimes.'

'You mustn't scold her for that. It was the truth. But I can't in good conscience tell the boy. Surely, if she thought about it, she would realize the wisdom of it.'

'She does, sir. She just hates to see you unhappy, as do I.'

'I'm not unhappy, Jack. It is merely yet another stumble in the road. I have a son, but he must carry another man's name. And, as it is, it's better for him that he does. Carrying the name of a traitor? I would not wish that on my worst enemy.' He thought of his family motto *'His Own Worst Enemy'* and chuckled. 'But I do have a son. And that was something I had already put aside, something I assumed would never happen. And so I should be rejoicing. That I have family at last.'

'But you do have family, sir. Me and Isabel and the little one when he's born. And Gilbert and Eleanor. And even John Rykener and Nigellus Cobmartin. We are all your family now.'

He stared at the lad a long time before he rolled to his feet. Clapping Jack on the shoulder, he smiled a genuine smile. 'You are worth ten apprentices, Master Tucker.'

'Does that mean you'll raise my salary?' He laughed at Crispin's widened eyes. 'I jest, sir.' He ducked out of the way of Crispin's clout. 'I truly came to tell you that the abbot is here.'

Crispin felt his cheeks grow cold. 'Abbot William? Now? He's early.'

'Aye, sir. Never fear. Isabel has given him a chair and is feeding him wine. All is well. I thought you needed a moment.'

He allowed his stuttering heart to beat its slow rhythm again. 'So I did. Let me go down to greet our guest.'

* * *

101

'I must apologize for being so early, Crispin.' Abbot William seemed at ease, and not the least discommoded by his surroundings. Crispin sat beside him, taking up the cup Isabel pushed at him. 'But I'm afraid impatience got the better of me.'

'You?'

'I know it is uncharacteristic, but I was anxious to discuss this whole matter with you. But here. You have a grave look about you . . . if I can say as much without meaning a jest.'

'It is another client, my lord. A child is accused of murdering a mercer.'

'A child? How can a child be responsible?'

'It is my contention that he is not. But the new widow swears that he did, and stole a family relic as well, a bone of a saint housed in a reliquary in the shape of a cow, or so it is said.'

'A cow, you say? What could that be, do you think?'

'I'm no expert.'

'Ever the skeptic,' he muttered. 'It wasn't a *red* cow by any chance?'

'I do believe that red was mentioned.'

Abbot William nodded. 'Then I should associate that with St Modwen as well. She is often depicted with a red cow and a staff. Are you familiar with the life of Saint Modwen?'

'No, my lord. I confess that I am not. Only that which you have already told us.'

'She was an Irish noblewoman, back in the seventh century. She was an abbess and founded Burton Abbey, performing many miracles—'

102

'Yes,' said Crispin. 'We have been acquainted with one in particular.'

'Of course. The cow . . . well. There are several stories of her dealing with cows in various ways. A wolf that ate a calf and then she admonished that wolf to protect the mother cow for the rest of its days; the cows stolen by thieves, but who by her miracle were unable to cross the river and escape with them; the calf killed and brought back to life—'

'Why would someone bring a cow back to life?' asked Jack, scratching his head.

Abbot William stuffed his hands in his sleeves. 'One does not always understand the ways of God's holiest, Master Tucker.'

'No. Of course not, my lord.'

The abbot's mouth curled into a brief smile. 'At any rate, her staff is said to help women in labor, and it is much sought after in Burton for that purpose.'

'Oh!' Jack couldn't have cared less about resurrected cows, but he perked up at the mention of the staff.

'My apprentice is soon to be a father,' said Crispin in explanation. Isabel turned from the fire standing in profile, her obvious physical condition unmistakable. Jack blushed.

'So I noticed. Congratulations again, Master Tucker. I grieve that Burton upon Trent is so far away that your wife may not partake of the healing power of the staff. But perhaps this bone of St Modwen will do.'

'Were it not stolen,' put in Crispin.

Abbot William shrugged. 'And so this mercer

103

had a most coveted object of veneration. I'd be interested to hear the tale of how it arrived at his door.'

'I don't know that the widow would be particularly eager to discuss its history, only its return. She still thinks the boy has it.'

'Does he?'

'I don't think so. But of course, you can ask her yourself. We will be attending the funeral in a matter of hours . . . at St Modwen's.'

'You're jesting.'

'Would I be so careless with you, my lord? It seems our mercer was a great patron of this church. No doubt the relic was bestowed upon him for his charity to the parish.'

The abbot drank his wine with relish. 'You do lead a fascinating life, Crispin.'

'Sometimes too fascinating,' he muttered into his goblet.

'When is the funeral to be?'

'Soon. I was planning on leaving now so as not to miss it.'

The abbot set his goblet on the table and rose. 'Then shall we be off? The three of us, like pilgrims upon the road!' He actually slapped Jack on the back, the latter stumbling forward with surprise on his face.

Eight

The abbot rode his horse while Crispin and Jack walked beside him. They reached St Modwen's in little time. The afternoon sun branded the face of the church with radiant light, sharpening the relief of carved statue and stone blocks, some of which were said to be from Roman times when the city was called Londinium. Already the Horne household had gathered for the funeral, with many wealthy friends and business acquaintances. Crispin recognized the mourning vigil ladies from earlier. Horses, carriages, and footmen awaited outside the walls of the churchyard. The abbot dismounted and Jack served as his groom, holding the horse's bridle and tying it to a nearby post.

Father Bulthius bustled among the mourners and, when he glanced Crispin's way, he did it again in quick succession, taking in Abbot William. He excused himself from whomever it was he was talking to and hurried over. 'Master Crispin. It isn't nightfall.'

'I am here for this funeral, good Father. May I present to you Abbot William de Colchester of Westminster Abbey? Father Bulthius of St Modwen's Church.'

Father Bulthius bowed and dithered with his hands. 'I am honored by your presence, my Lord Abbot.'

'I am honored to be in your parish, Father Bulthius.'

'Will you do me the further honor of celebrating the funeral mass with me?'

'Of course. We are brothers in the Lord, Father. It is my privilege.'

The priest and the abbot took their leave and Crispin hung back as the assembled made their way into the little church.

'Jack, I want you to keep a sharp eye out here. Examine the hole that was dug for his coffin. And mark if anyone suspicious draws nigh.'

'Aye, sir.' He bit his lip, glanced toward the rectangular hole and pile of dirt, and crossed himself.

Crispin entered the church last, dipped his hand into the font and sketched a cross over his person. He took up a place standing in the back corner away from the font, arms folded over his chest. The church was small enough – more like a chapel – that he could see down the short nave through the modest crowd toward the altar that was raised up on a dais. The priest and Abbot William worked in concert, intoning the Latin prayers, their backs to the assembled, their prayers for God's ears. Finally, the priest stepped forward to face the mourners and the flower-draped coffin that stood below the altar, and preached of death, the inevitable journey for all, of sin and redemption. The usual platitudes, Crispin thought with a jaundiced eye. At least it was likely the priest knew the man, being that he was a patron. Who would keep the roof from leaking now?

An old man Crispin took to be a sexton, Father Bulthius, and Abbot William walked around the coffin, the priest sprinkling holy water upon the wooden box, the sexton swinging a smoking censer, its perfume shimmering over the mourners. The cloud of incense, like the bowers of Heaven itself, lingered in the air like a fragrant mist.

It certainly smelled better than John Horne.

Crispin changed his weight from one foot to the other. It was a long ceremony and he was relieved when it finished at last. Only a few received the holy bread of communion. Like Crispin, many had likely not shrived themselves prior.

The man with the censer led the procession, the priest and Abbot William walking behind him. Four men stepped forward to heave the coffin to their shoulders. The widow followed immediately. She was veiled, but Crispin could plainly see that she hadn't been crying. Her mouth was set firmly, her eyes stared straight ahead. She had wept when he had talked to her, but she had been speaking of her immediate difficulties. 'Who would care for me now?' she had bemoaned, having no children. Now she looked bitter but determined. Maybe she had found a way to care for herself after all.

A young man with hair almost as red as Jack's moved slowly after her. Unlike his mistress, this youth was distraught. His face was red and anguished. Tears marred his cheeks and he kept pushing the heel of his hand against his nose. Perhaps this was the apprentice, Martin Chigwell, friend to Christopher Walcote. He was twelve, maybe even thirteen. Likely he was realizing he had big shoes to fill – or wondering if he would be kept on as an apprentice. Was he master enough at this point in his training? He was young yet to take over a business, though Crispin had known lords who took possession at a younger age. He himself had been seven years old, in fact, when he inherited his own estates in Sheen. The same age as young Christopher, he thought with some irony. But Crispin had been a much more serious child than Christopher. He couldn't recall the playthings he had owned, except for the dapple-gray wooden horse. He vaguely wondered what had happened to it. But then, when he was a young man, he had purchased a real dapple-gray stallion he had named Hippocrates. A strong horse with a good heart that could turn on the spot with just the slightest pressure from Crispin's knee. He dared not think what had happened to him.

Lancaster had been there in his life to see to his estates until he came of age. That was the moment he had moved into the duke's household, where he was raised to think of Lancaster, only a mere ten years his senior, as a father, for his own father was often gone to war and he seldom saw or remembered him.

Then his mind went inexorably to King Richard, who had taken the throne at ten. Crispin had objected to it by treason, which, of course, had led to his being disseized and degraded. It was only in the last few years that Crispin had been proven right, that the Duke of Lancaster would have been the better choice to be king. But there was bitter joy in that revelation.

He shook himself free of his past and looked up just as the last person exited the church. He followed them out to the churchyard, where a grave had been dug, and found his place next to Jack. 'What have you found out?' he whispered, leaning close.

'Naught much, sir. The grave was dug like any grave, I suppose. Naught special about it.'

Crispin gestured surreptitiously toward the apprentice. 'I believe, but am not certain, that yon lad is Martin Chigwell. He looks to be more upset than the widow.'

Jack frowned, but he wasn't looking at Chigwell. 'God's blood,' he swore. 'The sheriff.'

Crispin looked over his shoulder. Sheriff John Shadworth had just dismounted and was striding toward the funeral party. After all, he was a mercer, too, but instead of going directly to the widow or the graveside, he made straight for Crispin.

'Master Guest,' he said in a loud whisper, so loud that the widow turned her head to look.

'Lord Sheriff,' said Crispin as quietly as he could, taking several steps back. The sheriff followed. 'Here to pay your respects?'

'Well . . . in truth, I'm here to watch you do whatever it is you do.'

Give me strength, he prayed. 'At the moment, I am giving my due to the deceased.' He tipped a finger to his lips in hope of quieting the man.

'Oh. Quite right.' Shadworth lowered his head

in prayer, but he was also bouncing on his heels, as if eager to spring forward.

Father Bulthius sprinkled the coffin again, droned his Latin over it, and nodded to the gravediggers, Tom and Hal, who lowered the coffin in by hauling on two sets of ropes. Crispin eyed the widow, whose face was stern under her veil but not distraught.

Martin Chigwell – if apprentice he was – sniffed and grimaced in his tears as he watched the coffin descend. Each threw in a clod of earth. The priest sang psalm after psalm.

'*But unto the wicked God saith,*' intoned Bulthius. '*What hast thou to do to declare my statutes, or that thou shouldest take my covenant in thy mouth? When thou sawest a thief, then thou consentedst with him, and hast been partaker with adulterers. Thou givest thy mouth to evil, and thy tongue frameth deceit. These things hast thou done, and I kept silence. Now consider this, ye that forget God, lest I tear you in pieces, and there be none to deliver. Whoso offereth praise glorifieth me: and to him that ordereth his conversation aright will I shew the salvation of God.*'

The assembled solemnly watched as the coffin was carefully covered by the soil, and as the mourners slowly walked away, the gravediggers got down to it, and spaded the earth over the grave with more vigor and more speed than was strictly necessary.

Widow Horne made her way to her barrel-shaped carriage. Crispin hurried to catch up to the grieving lad at her side. 'Martin Chigwell?'

He turned. His red face was streaked with tears. 'Yes? I am Chigwell.'

'I would speak with you a moment.'

He frowned and paused to study Crispin before he turned to his mistress. 'I must accompany my mistress on this horrific day.'

'That's all right, Martin,' she said, barely glancing at him. 'You may talk to Master Guest. I'll see you back at the manor.'

She turned abruptly and, barely allowing a servant to help her into the carriage, dismissed him.

Martin wiped his face and straightened his cote-hardie. 'She called you Master Guest. Would that be Crispin Guest, the Tracker of London?'

'It is. You are a hard man to find, Master Chigwell.'

He shook his head. 'No, I'm not. I've been busy, is all.'

'Covering the tracks of a murderer, perhaps?'

'Oh, you've got him there, Master Guest.'

Crispin slowly turned to face the sheriff. 'Lord Sheriff, perhaps my apprentice can show you something interesting about the church.'

Sheriff Shadworth looked back toward the frowsy building and shrugged. 'Something interesting about *this* church?'

Jack stepped forward. 'Aye, my lord. Over here. Something . . . er . . . *interesting*.' He took hold of the sheriff's arm and dragged him back.

Crispin sighed. But Chigwell was still stewing over Crispin's last comment to him. 'I'm not covering anything.'

111

'You know your friend, Christopher Walcote, is being blamed for the murder of your master. He confessed it. What have you to say to that?'

The lad's indignant expression fell away and concern took its place. His eyes shifted, darted among the tombstones and twisted trees, perhaps seeking him out. When they had searched the graveyard, finding no trace of his friend, his gaze settled none too steadily on Crispin. 'I don't . . . I don't know anything about that.'

Crispin raised a brow. 'You don't?'

'No. I . . . I wasn't there . . .'

'The maids say you were.'

His lips trembled. 'The maids are a gaggle of scolds and should hold their vicious tongues.'

'This is an investigation into a murder, Master Chigwell. All witnesses are admonished to tell the truth. And, so far, the truth seems to be that Master Christopher is guilty of theft and murder.'

'Theft?'

'The relic of St Modwen, Chigwell. The relic has been stolen and Master Christopher is charged with stealing it.'

'But . . . he'd never do that. He just wouldn't.'

'Nor would he kill, I presume.'

Chigwell stared, mouth firming like a locked gate.

Crispin's heart gave a jolt as the boy's expression made itself known to him. Martin Chigwell *did* think the boy was guilty. It was written all over his face. *God's blood!*

'Is . . . is that all you wanted, Master Guest?'

'No.' Over the lad's shoulder he saw Jack and Sheriff Shadworth returning. It looked as if Jack

112

was doing his best to discourage the sheriff, but the man was marching toward him anyway. He had to move quickly. 'Tell me, Master Chigwell, what did you argue with Master Horne about?'

He shrugged. 'I often argued with him. He was sometimes disagreeable about this and that.'

'Disagreeable? And what was he disagreeable about this time?'

He shook his head curtly. 'He was just . . . disagreeable.'

'Did you see him argue with Christopher Walcote?'

'I . . . I don't know.'

'It's a simple question, man. Did you or did you not see or hear him argue with Master Horne?'

'I heard him, all right! I heard him. And then I left. I have to go.'

'One more thing.'

Chigwell halted, but trembled with the need to leave.

'I noticed that you are aggrieved. You say Master Horne was disagreeable, yet you mourn him. Did you like Master Horne?'

'No. But . . .' He wiped his face and straightened. 'It's a death, isn't it? Shouldn't all men be aggrieved at that?'

'Not that aggrieved.'

'I must go,' he said again, bowed quickly and hurried away, trotting after his mistress's rocking carriage.

Shadworth arrived and turned his head to watch Chigwell grab onto the side of the carriage and hold on. 'Looks like you were giving that lad a grilling. What was that about, then?'

113

'Oh, the usual. One must ask many questions before one draws a conclusion.'

'Oh come now, Master Guest. Do you really believe that boy isn't guilty of murder? He was caught with the dagger in his hand.'

'*Law is order, and good law is good order*, Lord Sheriff.'

'And what is that supposed to mean?'

'That's Aristotle,' said Jack. 'I think Master Crispin is trying to say that just because the boy was caught with the dagger, doesn't mean that he's guilty. It's up to the law to prove it.'

Shadworth gave Jack a withering look. 'I *know* what he means. And I disagree, for it is very much up to *him* to prove he's innocent. But clearly in this instance it seems a waste of time to assume his innocence merely because he is a child.'

That ache in Crispin's heart grew. The sheriff, much as it pained him, could be right. Was Crispin giving him the benefit of the doubt merely because he was Crispin's son?

But no! Chigwell was clearly disturbed, and the widow was hiding something in her contempt of . . . of what? Or of whom?

'The evidence,' said Crispin, 'is likely somewhat misleading.'

'Oh truly, Master Guest! Is this how you actually conduct yourself? You throw out all evidence in favor of something more *interesting*?'

'I assure you I do not. But in talking with the witnesses I find that their testimonies dispute one another. And there is a great deal that seems to be kept hidden. I am further assured that the

Walcote boy had little to do with it, but I am not certain why he feels he needs to confess to it, and the others skirt around it. There is a great lie here, Lord Sheriff. I consider it my sworn duty to ferret it out.'

The sheriff stared for a moment before his face burst into a huge smile. 'Oh Master Guest, you do not disappoint!'

Crispin barely refrained from rolling his eyes. 'Did *you* know John Horne, Lord Sheriff?'

'Only in the faintest of ways. We had a nodding acquaintance, as they say.'

'And did you find him disagreeable?'

The sheriff blinked dumbly at him and then that bright smile appeared again. 'You're *interrogating* me! How extraordinary. Well, ask away, Master Crispin, ask away! Oh! I may call you Crispin, may I not?'

'If it suits you, Lord Sheriff.'

'How extraordinary,' he chuckled. 'Well now, getting back to the business of it.' He schooled his face into something soberer. 'I myself had little occasion to speak with the man, but I had heard from others what a whoreson he could be. Especially with other men's wives.'

'Oh?'

'He was a dallier . . . so they say. And boorish. It's little wonder he was murdered. We just never expected it to be a boy who did it.' Crispin's pointed gaze seemed to stir the sheriff. 'Oh! I see what you mean, Master Crispin. So I see. You are clever, aren't you.'

'Just observant, my lord. This concludes my investigation into the Horne matter for the day.

If you will excuse me, Abbot William of Westminster has asked for a conference with me.' He bowed, motioned for Jack to follow, and walked away.

When Crispin glanced back at the man, Shadworth drooped. He screwed up his face, ready for a rejoinder, but Crispin was too far away from him at this point. He seemed to change his mind and got his horse, fussed with the bridle before he mounted, and rode back, presumably, toward Newgate.

'That was a lie, wasn't it?' said Jack.

'I'm certain God will forgive it. He has forgiven so much from me as it is, one more won't strain Him.'

'You shouldn't blaspheme, sir.'

'We have work to do, Jack.'

They both looked toward the sun making its long trek toward the western horizon. But there were still some hours to pass before sunset.

Crispin crossed his arms over his chest and stared at the newly covered grave. Tom the grave-digger leaned the spade over his shoulder, and with his dirty hand resting on Hal's shoulder, they both lumbered away to a rickety shed at the other end of the yard. As soon as they disappeared, Crispin hurried to the newly made mound of dirt.

He stooped, examining it, looking for any clues that would give him some idea of why a corpse would rise. It looked like any other grave he had ever seen. And he had noticed the prodigious use of holy water both at the funeral mass inside the church, and over the coffin and dirt outside it. If holy water were not enough to stop a revenant . . .

'I noticed the gardeners . . . er . . . gravediggers,' said Jack, 'made extra certain that they tamped down the soil over it, sir. They don't want Horne walking any more than we do.'

'But I do want him to walk, Jack.'

'What? That's blasphemy, too!'

'I'm fairly certain that he will. For, as I have said many a time, you must not always believe your eyes. At least at first glance.'

'You still think it's a trick?'

'I hope to God it is.'

'And if it isn't?'

'Then thank God Abbot William is with us.' He brushed the dirt off his hands and straightened. He looked toward the sun again. 'There is time for us to make our way to an alehouse.'

'I thought an alehouse would get into it at some point,' Jack muttered.

Abbot William boarded his horse since they didn't want the beast to be tied up all day and night. The abbot was content to sit in the alehouse, watching the rabble. He filled his horn cup several times with the aromatic ale, while Crispin sipped at his wine.

'So that was the bereaved family,' said the abbot. 'I have seen many a funeral, Crispin, as you can imagine. Presided over almost that many more. One can't help but observe the family undercurrents.'

'And this one?'

The abbot shrugged. 'Not all widows wail

117

over their husbands' coffins. Some are reserved by nature. And some, well . . . Theirs was a marriage of partnership, of alliances, and though we priests assure both parties that love will come in time . . . sometimes it does not. We might have the same situation here with Madam Horne.' He took another drink and set the cup down. 'Who was the grieving youth? Their son?'

'No. He was Master Horne's apprentice.'

'I see. Perhaps he fears for his situation now. He isn't likely to be of an age and experience to take over the business, is he? Or perhaps he had a special fondness for his master. It sometimes happens that apprentices grow very fond of their masters, thinking of them like a father.' He glanced at Jack over his cup.

'That was not the case with Martin Chigwell. He said that John Horne was disagreeable most of the time. Even the sheriff admitted as much. In fact, the sheriff intimated that Horne was a cuckolder and not well liked by his community of mercers. If I may quote the sheriff: "*It's little wonder he was murdered. We just never expected it to be a boy who did it.*"'

'Now that *is* interesting,' said the abbot. 'What do you think on the matter, Master Tucker?'

Jack jerked in his seat, not expecting to be addressed. 'Aye, Lord Abbot?'

'You're an apprentice. What do you think is Martin Chigwell's motivation for his actions today?'

'He's worried about something, my lord. But I don't think it's his master. I think it's something

118

else, but I can't put my finger on it. Sir,' he said to Crispin, 'if we could put Martin and Christopher in the same room and let them talk, I'm certain we can make much of it, especially if they thought they were alone.'

'That's good thinking, Jack,' he said, running a finger thoughtfully over his lower lip. 'As soon as this business tonight is done, then we can concentrate more fully on the matter.'

'You think it will be done tonight?'

'Yes. We will discover what the truth of the matter is before the night is out. I'm certain of it.'

'Bold words, Crispin,' said Abbot William.

'It's not pride, Lord Abbot, but mere sure-footedness. Father Bulthius is unaware of what could be behind it, but I suspect something more mundane than demonic.'

Abbot William leaned forward. 'Like what?'

Crispin sat back and crossed his arms over his chest. 'The most obvious might be to simply lure him away from the rectory at night in order for an accomplice to steal from the church. Last night there were silver candlesticks on the altar. Today they were missing.'

Jack pushed at him. 'Why didn't you say so before, master?'

'We shall have to ask him if other items have gone missing,' he said with a lopsided grin. 'I tell you we can clear this up quickly.'

'I'd look no further than the gravediggers' cottage. Them two could easily dig up graves and steal from them. And take what they like out of the church without the priest knowing

119

what's happened.' He nodded toward Abbot William. 'Nimble fingers, my lord, can do much mischief.'

'I understand that this is something you know about well, Master Tucker.'

'Oh, er, well—'

'That was a long time ago,' cut in Crispin. 'I'm certain you do not wish to embarrass the boy by bringing up a history long past.'

'But our history is what makes us, wouldn't you agree, Crispin? For instance, if you had not had the temerity to commit treason, then perhaps you wouldn't be quite as interesting or noble a person as you turned out to be.'

So casually spoken, it took Crispin aback. 'I . . .'

'I don't mind talking of my life as a cutpurse.' Now it was Jack's turn to rescue him. Crispin appreciated the gesture.

'You were an orphan, were you not?'

'Aye, m'lord. Not a soul on this earth to care for me. It was do the deed or starve. And what does the Church say about this moral dilemma, sir? Should I have starved to death for the good of my soul? For I was later reformed and now I do good in the world.'

'That is an interesting point you make. Certainly the seventh commandment forbids theft. Snatching another's property against the will of the owner. However, is it truly theft if consent can be presumed?'

'I assure you, Abbot William, consent was the last thing on their minds.'

'Ah, but as St Thomas Aquinas tells us, the

120

starving man's need makes the other man's bread his possession.'

'How does coin figure into it, sir? For it was often more expedient to simply steal men's purses.'

'And what, pray, did you buy with these ill-gotten gains?'

'Well . . . food, sir.'

'Then, in this case, the coins are as good as bread. Now, if your determination to steal had been to aggrandize yourself, to purchase baubles and entertainments to commit more sin, it cannot be assumed that your needs were great.'

'I never did that, m'lord. My only concerns were food and shelter. I was only a lad, after all. I hadn't any other sins to add to me mind yet. I mean, I knew it was wrong, but who would take in a lad like me?'

'Only me,' said Crispin into his cup.

'Your charity was great, Crispin,' said the abbot. 'For I'll wager you had nothing to offer the lad but said food and shelter, and he gladly worked for the privilege. These are great signifiers of grace.'

He and Jack exchanged glances. 'I didn't do it for charity,' said Crispin softly. 'I simply couldn't get rid of the boy.'

Jack laughed. 'Aye, I was persistent, that's a certainty.'

Crispin snorted. '"Persistent"? Is that what you call it? I called you a nuisance.'

'I was that too, sir.' Jack grinned.

Abbot William downed his cup. 'And how well it turned out. Well, we should not keep poor

Father Bulthius waiting.' He rose and straightened his robes. 'I'm certain he's already agitated enough.'

Crispin rose and Jack followed suit, and soon they had paid the alewife and made their way to the street again.

Abbot William chuckled. 'It feels like a fair day when I was a child.'

'Were you ever a child, my lord?'

'Tut, Crispin, I could say the same of you. You are so serious. True, your predicament is a serious matter, but you seem to have risen above it and recovered your honor, in a fashion.'

Blunt as always. Abbot William didn't mince words, though Crispin sometimes hoped he might. He said nothing to that but he saw Jack bristle for him.

The golden-yellow light from the horizon streaked across the lane and painted the church walls, stealthily crawling up to the top of the bell tower, tipping each crenellation with gold. Until the sun suddenly dipped too far and the light was only like a mist upon the rocky face of the structure. The graveyard was falling into shadows, first gray, then blue, then darkest black. The moon was already up, a gold moon, but it was low yet, just peering over the rooftops of London.

They ventured first into the church by the side door closest to the rectory building.

'Father Bulthius!' Crispin called. No answer. 'Jack, go take a look around. See if our priest isn't doing his rounds or some such.'

'Aye, master.' Jack hurried back through the church and called out for the priest.

Crispin turned to Abbot William who had at last put a solemn face to the proceedings. 'What now, Crispin? This is your territory.'

'Well, it is best we go into the churchyard and keep watch of the newest grave. And then we—'

'Master! Master Crispin!'

Jack clung to the doorway, his usually pale face shining even whiter. 'What is it, Jack?'

'Come quick, master!' He tore out of the door and disappeared into the gloom.

Crispin took one look at Abbot William and pelted after his apprentice. He followed his tall, dark figure through the headstones to the mercer's new grave and stopped dead. The coffin was sitting upright on a pile of newly unearthed soil. 'What the devil?'

Abbot William's heavy footfalls padded after as he came to a stop beside Crispin. His breath was heaving. No doubt the abbot wasn't used to such vigorous activity as running through churchyards.

'What is it, Crispin?' But he stopped when he saw the coffin. 'Blessed Lord.' He crossed himself.

Crispin came around to the front, turning to see what Jack was pointing to.

The coffin lay open, its lid cast aside. But inside the casket . . . The gown was bloody, and no wonder. His head had been severed from its neck and placed neatly between his legs at his feet. But it was that face that Crispin knew would haunt his dreams for years to come. It was bloody and beaten, mouth open and twisted in an eternal silenced scream.

'It's horrific, Crispin,' gasped Abbot William. 'Who could have done that to poor John Horne?'

'It isn't John Horne,' said Crispin. '*That* is Father Bulthius.'

Nine

The abbot intoned prayers over the corpse, hands clasped and pressed to his lips.

'Where's John Horne?' whispered Jack desperately.

Crispin couldn't help himself and spun around, looking into the distance, expecting to see the man's corpse walking into the rising mist.

'I don't know. We should fan out. Search for it.'

Jack pulled his dagger free. And, with a deep breath, he turned and headed south.

Abbot William was staring at Crispin with a pale countenance. 'Am I to search as well?'

'It would be very much appreciated, my lord.'

The abbot seemed to gird himself and compose his face. He took up the metal cross that hung over his chest and raised it aloft. 'I'll go that way,' and he pointed north.

Crispin felt foolish, but he still thought it the best course to draw his blade, stretching the sharp dagger before him. He moved away from the church, roughly in an easterly direction. Oh how the darkness could give rise to wild imaginings! Any ordinary night would simply be the relief at the end of a long day. But in graveyards, the dark thrust upon a wary mind all the ghosts of one's past, of every fear and nightmare from one's childhood bed. Crispin tried to shake it off, but he couldn't help the hairs on the back of his neck from rising, or the ripple of discomfort from slithering up his spine.

Footfalls.

Crispin stilled and listened. Was it Jack or Abbot William? No, they had gone in the opposite direction. He cocked his head, listening hard.

The tread was steady and slow, as if someone were carrying a burden. When he looked past the trees he thought he saw movement. Stalking carefully forward, he caught sight of the tail end of a gown . . . or was it a trailing shroud?

Crispin ran. He slid through the trees and out to the expanse of meadow and saw . . . nothing.

Had it been the moonlight playing tricks with his eyes? But he had heard the footsteps, hadn't he?

A whisper of a sound on the wind. A moan? His hand readjusted his grip on the dagger hilt.

A rustling behind him made him spin to look. That trailing hem. He paused just that long before he dove through the brambles for it, but it eluded him again. Especially when a cloud passed over the rising moon at just that moment.

With the darkness complete, he could see nothing. He strained his eyes and ears and saw in the distance in the meadow a faint bouncing light. It flickered and bobbed and, as he watched it, it grew fainter. He hurried toward it and was startled by an animal scream.

Stopping, he listened again. A fox? But it wasn't repeated and suddenly the light winked out. He stood a long time, scanning the dark meadow, listening carefully, and soon gave up.

Keeping a sharp eye out, and glancing over his shoulder now and again, he made for the church. He stumbled once and saw what looked like twine – threads twisted together. Likely a snare. He brushed off his cote-hardie and returned to the churchyard and the grave, staring at the ghastly corpse now within the coffin. Had the corpse of John Horne done the deed? The Devil himself?

Crispin shook his head curtly, as if convincing the voices warring in his head. And then he glanced for only an eye-blink into the dark grave itself and caught a glimpse of something white.

The cloud passed away from the moon, allowing the disc's light to shine forth, and a white shroud was illuminated below. And then a white leg from beneath the shroud and that unmistakable stench of the dead.

'Jack! Abbot William! Come here!'

Crispin stepped to the side of the grave and leapt in. That shiver up his spine returned, for he had escaped death by a hairsbreadth too many times to count. No need to court it by stepping into a grave on his own.

It smelled strongly of the corpse and the deep, earthy smell of newly turned soil. Roots sprang from the grave's walls, curling back toward themselves, as if not wishing to touch the body.

He knelt and pulled the face cloth away from the corpse's countenance . . . it was Horne. And on the cloth, specks of blood just where his mouth had been. What had the corpse got up to?

'Master Crispin! Where are you?' called Jack.

He popped his head from the grave and said, 'Here!'

'God's blood!' Jack screamed and fell back on his tail. He laid a hand to his heart. 'God's teeth and bones! What did you go and do a thing like that for, master? I nearly shat me braies.'

'Sorry. But I have found Master Horne. He is here. In his own grave. Help me out.' He reached out a hand and Jack grabbed hold of it, while Crispin used that leverage to haul himself out.

He brushed off the grave soil, grimacing in distaste, and looked down into the hole. Abbot William ran up, joining them, and the three of them stood on the edge of the grave and peered down.

'He was there all this time,' said the abbot.

Crispin grunted. 'Was he? I didn't notice the shroud before. And look at his face cloth.'

They did. The two on either side of Crispin gasped as they recognized the blood.

Jack took a step back. 'Did *he* do this to Father Bulthius?'

Crispin shook his head. 'I refuse to believe it.'

'Crispin!' cried the abbot. 'You see it with your own eyes.'

'I see a corpse dumped into a grave. I see a decapitated man thrust into his unearthed coffin. I see foul play.'

'But surely . . . surely it is the Devil at work?'

'The Devil in someone, perhaps. But mayhem was done and now I must see to this murder. Jack, go to Newgate and have them fetch the sheriffs.'

* * *

They waited. Abbot William knelt beside the grave and chanted his Latin over the corpse lying at the bottom of the grave, and Crispin paced before it, keeping half an ear open to the graveyard, and the other half on the road for the sheriffs.

The sheriffs' horses arrived first.

He approached them and laid his hand on Shadworth's horse's bridle. 'My lords,' he said to them with a bow.

'I was at my supper, Guest,' said Vaunere with a scowl. 'And I don't like being interrupted when I'm eating.'

'I assure you, Lord Sheriff, that I would not have had my man interrupt you if it hadn't been of the utmost importance.'

Just then, Jack popped up. He'd been following behind the sheriffs along with the bailiffs. He gave a nod to Crispin and got out of the bailiffs' way. The men bore burning coals in cresset cages dangling from poles, illuminating everyone's faces with mere glances of light.

'See here, Henry,' said Shadworth. 'It *must* be important if Master Guest declares it so. And look! There is the Abbot of Westminster.' He climbed off his horse and ambled toward Crispin, before Crispin stepped aside so he could see. The sheriff gasped when he beheld the casket.

'Bless us with all of God's saints! Henry! *Henry!* Come look.'

'I'm coming. Good grief, John. You do let Master Guest ruffle you.' He approached and looked where Shadworth pointed. 'Holy Christ.'

'Wh-who is that?' asked Shadworth, squinting

and crooking his head this way and that. He gestured to a bailiff to bring the light closer, but it only threw more shadows onto his twisted features.

Crispin stood with his hands behind his back. 'It is Father Bulthius, the priest of this parish.'

'What a dreadful thing!' Shadworth could not seem to look away.

Vaunere was not so enamored. He turned immediately and took several paces back, covering his mouth with his hand. He clearly hadn't the stomach for such a job. 'Have you . . . have you any suspects, Guest?' he muttered to his horse's flank.

'Do you wish me to investigate, my lord? I have a fee.'

'Pay his fee,' Shadworth rushed to say.

'I will not. Should I go filling the money pouches of every man who claims he can help? He's the first finder in a murder. I should charge *him*.'

'But this is what he does, Henry. I'll pay him myself.' He dug into his scrip and pulled out a money pouch, one far thicker with coins than Crispin expected. The sheriff seemed anxious to hand it over.

Crispin took it but, with a flourishing gesture more suited to court than a graveyard said, 'My fee is only sixpence a day, my lord.'

'Keep it,' said Shadworth with a careless wave of his hand. 'I wager it will take many days and you will earn that.'

He thanked the sheriff with a courtly bow, and stuffed the pouch quickly away. He felt slightly

guilty that his pleasure at the coin pouch inter-
fered with his somber thoughts of the brutal
murder. But all he had to do was glance at the
corpse again and he was back to pondering it.

'If I may ask,' said Vaunere, standing near the
horses and away from the spectacle inside the
casket, 'just what are you doing here, Guest . . .
and in such august company?' He nodded toward
the abbot.

Abbot William, with wide eyes, deferred to
Crispin. So it was Crispin who was required
to lie, was it? He stuck his thumbs in his belt.
'My Lord Sheriff, Abbot William, here, was
meeting us at this parish to speak to Father
Bulthius about some missing church endowments,
when we found him thus.' There. That wasn't
even too much of a lie. When he glanced at the
abbot he could tell that the man was satisfied.

'When did this happen?'

'Well, Sheriff Vaunere, all of us attended a
funeral he had given just this afternoon.'

'Odd, though,' said Shadworth, leaning close
to the head sitting at the body's feet. 'Why should
he be beheaded, do you think? Seems a lot of
trouble.'

Crispin stood beside him and studied the corpse
objectively this time. 'Yes, Lord Sheriff. I would
agree. It does seem a lot of trouble.'

Shadworth raised his face. He wore a beatific
expression. 'You don't mean to say that *I* gave
you an idea, Master Guest?'

'John, for God's sake!' chaffed Vaunere. 'Quit
fawning over the man. Let him get on with it.
You paid him enough. Guest, you might as well

131

wait for the coroner. Else you'll be fined all that money you just got.'

Crispin bowed to the sheriffs. Shadworth seemed reluctant to leave, but he was probably more reluctant to let Vaunere get the better of him. They both mounted. The sheriffs instructed the bailiffs to remain, which was a blessing, for they were carrying lights.

Instead of waiting outside, Crispin directed his party back toward the church and rectory, while the unhappy bailiffs awaited the arrival of the coroner outside.

Jack entered the rectory cottage first and stoked the fire. Crispin admonished his companions from moving further into the room before he had a chance to look around. Jack cautiously followed him with a lit candle.

'There is a conspicuous absence of blood,' said Crispin.

'Aye, sir. I was about to say. I also think that maybe he was beheaded after the fact.'

'And why do you say that?'

'Just so, sir. An absence of blood on the corpse. Oh, there was some, but it seems to me that the heart stopped beating before the head left the body. Else the coffin would be filled with it.'

'Correct, Jack. I predict it would have happened outside on the grass somewhere, allowing the blood to be soaked up in the turf.'

'We shall have to find that in the morning.'

'Yes. Firelight is notoriously bad for such an examination.'

Abbot William sat slowly in a chair, arranging his robes around him. 'I have to agree with

Sheriff John Shadworth. You are a most interesting man to follow. And the two of you
together, why . . .' He shook his head.

'It's all a matter of practice, m'lord,' said Jack.
'Master Crispin and me, we've seen a lot of
corpses. A *lot*.' Jack placated him after observing
Abbot William's horrified expression. 'Not that
that's a good thing, sir. Of course not. God bless
them, sir.' He crossed himself vigorously.

'The abbot gets your meaning, Jack.' Crispin
rubbed his chin. He had expected the room to be
in a state and was surprised to find it as if the
priest had just stepped out. The fire in the hearth
had been banked with ash and had come back to
life easily. There was a loaf of broken bread on
the table on a wooden plank. A silver candlestick
sat on the table, which was covered in a fine
linen cloth. But there was nothing on the mantel
but the tinderbox. Crispin noted circles untouched
by dust where two somethings had been. He
suspected more candlesticks. So at least he
hadn't really lied. Church goods *were* missing.
The question was when had they disappeared?

'I need to examine the body,' he said suddenly,
and before the others could object, he hurried
out the door again and into the chill night. The
bailiffs were momentarily startled but Crispin
announced himself and knelt by the corpse to
have a look at the head.

He'd been beaten. It was hardly recognizable
as Father Bulthius. If not for his clothes and
luxurious dark hair, Crispin might not have
known him at all. Had he been beaten to death?
Perhaps the head had sustained a blow. He

133

reached into the casket and grabbed the top of his head, even as the bailiffs gasped. He slowly turned the heavy object, grimacing in distaste for the squelching sound it made as raw, bloody flesh and bone scraped on the coffin's wood. But even as he moved it, he did not see any sort of indentation; any other bloody show that would indicate a blow.

He stood and looked at the body. It was hard to see it at first, what with the ragged flesh and blood on the neck, but there looked to be a wound that wasn't accounted for with a beheading. He surmised by the flushed nature of the skin around it that this was the fatal blow – a slash – and Jack was right. The head was taken off after the blood stopped flowing.

He examined the priest's gown. As expected there was blood present, but on closer inspection it appeared to have been deliberately smeared there, instead of being the result of a flow from his throat being slit. He delicately pulled the gown away from the ragged flesh of the headless neck. It should have been soaking with it, but there was no blood to speak of on the collar. Had the murderer been sorry there hadn't been more blood on show? Why else add blood where there had been none?

But, more importantly, when his throat was slit, there would have been blood on the collar of the gown and on the shift beneath.

He couldn't help it. He hated to leave it for later. 'May I borrow one of your torches?' he asked the bailiffs. They exchanged glances, and one of them handed over the pole.

134

'Bring it back,' said the bailiff forlornly, looking about the dark churchyard.

'I shall. Much thanks.'

He held it aloft and scoured the grass like a hound on a scent. It wouldn't have been near the grave, he thought. The grave was visible from the road. It would have been behind the church between the church and the rectory, where all was sheltered. He turned the corner of the stubby little church and held the burning coals as close to the ground as he dared. There. A patch of grass, bent and dark and wet. He reached down and swept his finger through it and pulled it back to look at it properly under the light.

Red.

Glancing over his shoulder, he looked toward the gravediggers' shed. 'Where have they got off to?' Leaving the gore behind, he hastened toward the shed. It was all dark within. He pounded on the door. 'Ho there!' He knocked again.

The bailiffs peered around the corner of the church at him.

With no answer, Crispin worried that someone had also dispatched the gravediggers when he heard a shuffling within. The door creaked open and the older man, Tom, hair in disarray and eyes squinting, looked up. 'Aye?' A strong smell of drink came with that breath.

'Did I wake you?' asked Crispin.

The man rubbed his hair. His eyes were groggy and unfocused. 'Aye. 'Tis night.'

And you've been drinking to excess, he mused. There was a time not too long ago that Crispin did so himself, trying to forget his ills. 'Did you hear anything earlier? Anything that might have sounded like an altercation?'

'Oi, you're that Tracker fellow.'

'Yes, Crispin Guest.'

'I remember you. Hear anything? No, no. I had me ale and then went off to bed. Digging graves is hard work for an old man.'

'And where is your younger companion?'

'Off with some maid, no doubt. He comes back late. Long as the priest don't see him and give him a hiding, I don't make no nevermind what a lad gets up to.'

'And you both dug the grave for Master Horne this afternoon?'

'Aye. And helped to bury him in it.'

'A usual burial?'

His eyes widened. 'He . . . he didn't go off and walk out of his grave, did he? Oh Lord!'

'It's worse than that.'

They both turned, just as the sound of the coroner's cart came up the road.

Ten

The coroner, John Charneye, glared at Crispin as if the corpse were his fault. Crispin stoically accepted the coroner's unrelenting scrutiny, but he made certain that Charneye was aware of the slash to the corpse's neck.

'Are you gainsaying me, Guest?' he sneered.

'Not at all, my lord. Simply making you aware of something that your assistants might miss. Such a cut would be easy to overlook under the circumstances.'

'And before you say anything, I had my clerk mark where you pointed out the blood in the grass.'

'Of course, my lord.'

Charneye stewed for a moment longer before he asked, gruffly, 'Any ideas, Guest?'

Crispin had settled in to think about the problem. And he was damned if he was to consider a walking corpse as the murderer. 'I do not yet have all the facts, my lord.'

'I didn't ask for facts, I asked for ideas.'

'No ideas . . . as of yet.'

'What of those gravediggers? They look to be a menacing duo.'

'One was drunk and asleep, and the other was absent, purportedly engaged in immoral pursuits. Either would have been covered in considerable blood had they been involved.'

137

'Are you certain that they had nothing to do with it?'

'No. But killing the priest would most certainly result in their being unemployed. It doesn't seem a wise course.'

'Men have engaged in such before without a view to the consequences of the hangman's knot.'

'True. But such an endeavor as to beheading the man seems somewhat more advanced for these two.'

The coroner turned and ran his gaze over them again. 'Yes, I see what you mean.' He folded his arms over his chest. 'Well then, what's to be done? This is intolerable.'

'Yes. It shall be a challenge.'

He slid his gaze toward Crispin and clucked his tongue. 'By the saints, you enjoy this, don't you?'

'"Enjoy", my lord? I would not go so far as to say that. But the challenge is . . . an exercise for the mind.'

'The devil it is. Well, I've enough of this. I've got your statement. You can go.'

'What of the other matter, my lord? That of the wounds on John Horne's back.'

'If I were a suspicious man, I would say you engineered this whole scene just so I could take a second look at your corpse.' His brow was raised high. 'But since I am not, let us call it a convenient happenstance. I'll amend my report. That doesn't mean that boy didn't stab him in the back as well.'

'No, but it adds to the tale.'

'What's that Walcote situation to you, Guest? Hired you, did they?'

'Yes, my lord. And I would not see a child hang.'

'Even if he's guilty?'

'I do not believe him guilty.'

The coroner huffed. 'It's too late in the evening to argue.' He yawned. 'I'm tired. I'm going home. I recommend you do the same thing.'

Crispin was more than happy to comply. He bowed as Charneye turned his back on him. Crispin moved to gather Jack and Abbot William. 'I have something to check before we depart.'

'Check?' said Jack.

'Out in the meadow.'

'Then I'm going, too!'

'What of Abbot William? Would you leave him alone?'

'Well, I . . .'

The abbot shook his head, a placid expression fixed on his face. 'I need no guarding, Crispin. I am content in the Lord that His shield shall guard me.'

Crispin exchanged a look with his apprentice, and they headed out toward the meadow, Crispin picturing in his mind where he had seen glowing lights before. He was certain there had been a cottage of some sort at the farthest edge, but he could see no lights now, no smoke reflecting moonlight.

'Where are we going, master?'

'There is a house out there.'

'Out *there*?'

'I have seen it in the daytime.'

139

'What has it to do with this business?'

'Maybe nothing. But I saw bobbing lights out here and thought they might have something to do with it.'

'Unless them lights are spirits.'

Crispin didn't answer. He moved on, stepping over knolls and skirting brambles. He paused when he stepped on a patch of sticks. Kneeling, he examined them, their position, their broken ends, the swaying stalks of the bushes beside them. One stem appeared to be deliberately stripped of its leaves.

'What is it, master?'

'Not certain.' Rising, he moved on until they reached the cottage. All was dark. As Crispin suspected, no smoke rose from its chimney. He pressed his face to the seam of the shutter and peered in. No one there.

'What's this?' said Jack, lifting the edge of a white rag tied to the front door latch.

Crispin joined him and looked it over. 'No idea.'

Jack shivered and rubbed his arms over his coat sleeves. 'I'd like to return home, master. If you've seen all you need to.'

'Yes. Let us gather Abbot William.'

They returned from the meadow and joined the abbot, who seemed to be standing immobile, perhaps in contemplation of a prayer.

'May I offer you lodgings with us tonight, my Lord Abbot?'

He blinked and glanced up at him. 'That would be most obliging, Crispin. I'm afraid I've forsaken all my prayers this night. I must

140

rise especially early to do my utmost to amend that.'

'You will find comfort in my chamber,' said Crispin, walking between the abbot and Jack.

'Then you shall have mine, master.'

'Don't be absurd, Jack. And leave your wife lying on the floor? No. I can make myself comfortable downstairs in the hall.'

'But sir!'

'Don't argue with me, boy.'

Jack fell silent. In fact, none of them spoke as they made their way through London's dark streets back to the Shambles. It had been a long day and a longer night.

When they got in, Isabel was waiting for them by the fire. She, too, tried to insist that Crispin take their bed. And, at another time in his life, he wouldn't have thought twice about accepting it. *I've grown soft*, he thought with a huff. Instead, he motioned for Jack to help the abbot and ready his chamber, while Isabel pushed his chair before the fire. She made sure his footstool was there, the one Jack had acquired for him, and got him a woolen blanket from the ambry.

She offered to help him off with his cotehardie, but he somehow felt ill at ease with the suggestion and waved her off.

'Go to bed, woman. You've a babe to care for. Get some sleep. The abbot says he'll be up early for his prayers and you'll need to heat the water and such.'

'Yes, Master Crispin. Goodnight, sir. God rest you.'

She slowly ascended the stairs and closed her

chamber door. Jack peered down from the top of the landing. 'Is all well, sir?'

'Go to bed, Jack.'

'Aye, sir.'

The chamber door closed him in, and Crispin listened to the soft murmurings of their conversation, no doubt discussing the strangeness of their unusual master.

Crispin rose and unbuttoned his cote-hardie, laying it across the chairs at the table. In his stocking feet, he rested them on the footstool and tucked the blanket about him. Had it all really happened in one day? Had he met with Philippa once again, held her in his arms, kissed her . . . and met her son . . . *their* son? His body was weary but his mind raced.

She loved him still. Even after all he had seen and heard today, it was that single thought that pushed away everything else. She loved him. And she had borne his child and named him to something as close to his name as she dared. She loved him.

He lay his head back and sighed into the rafters. And, dammit, he loved her. And if he were any other kind of man, he would steal into her chamber when the husband was away, and do his will on her. And how he wanted to.

But . . . he wasn't that kind of man.

Sleep, Crispin, he admonished himself. It took a while, but even while reliving the moments of kissing her, he must have found his rest sometime in the night, for when he opened his eyes again, there was sun streaming in from the shutter and Isabel was creeping about as

142

quietly as she could, warming water and slicing cold meat.

He stretched and yawned, and when he rubbed the sleep crust from his eyes, she was looking at him with a kind expression. 'Good morn, Master Crispin.'

'And good morn to you, Isabel. Is Jack awake?'

'He's attending to Abbot William. I'm sorry if I woke you.'

'No apologies necessary. It was time I got into the day.'

He rose and stretched again. But when he turned to grab his cote-hardie, he didn't see it.

Isabel held it out for him. 'I brushed and cleaned it for you, sir. It had dirt on it. And a little blood.'

'I can assure you it was not my blood.'

She wrinkled her nose and held it out for him to slide his arms into. 'I'm not certain I *am* assured by that.'

He chuckled and shrugged it over his shoulders before he began to button the many closures. She had prepared his shaving water and supplies, and he set about shaving without his brass mirror.

Once done, he rolled down his sleeves, buttoned them, and felt prepared as Abbot William trudged down the stairs at last to join him.

He sat heavily in the chair by the fire. 'Crispin, I fear I am getting old.'

The monk's silvered barley-colored hair was curled at his ears. The top of his head was, of course, shaved, denoting his clerical status, but it hadn't been re-shaved in some time and was fuzzed with a nap of downy hair.

143

'What shall you do in the light of day, Crispin?' he asked, accepting a cup from Isabel. 'What have you decided regarding walking corpses and murder?'

'I do not believe it was a corpse who did the murdering, my lord. Else why be concerned where you beheaded someone? It should have been done in the coffin. No, that particular act was done at a place to hide it and was not the method of execution.'

'No?'

'No. His throat was slit first. That's what killed him. And then beheaded for . . . for what purpose?'

'Don't forget that he was beaten about the face,' said Jack, striding down the stairs.

'Yes.' Crispin rubbed his newly shaved chin. 'It was plain he was in a fight for his life.'

'I saw his hands, sir,' Jack went on. 'He fought back. Hard. His knuckles was all bruised.'

'Were they?' asked the abbot. 'And Bulthius seemed so tame a man.'

'He was young yet, sir. Maybe all that religion hadn't wrung all the life out of him yet. Oh. Begging your mercy, m'lord,' he said with a bow.

Abbot William hid his amusement in his cup of warmed wine. 'I have no idea what you are talking about, young man.'

'We must return to the parish church,' said Crispin. 'I don't know who else to speak to about the missing items or who will take over the parish now that he's gone.'

'The Bishop of London, I should think,' said

144

the abbot. 'Though as Bulthius was a Benedictine, as I am, perhaps there is something *I* can do.'

'Get a message to the bishop, sir. Tell him . . . well.' Crispin shook his head. 'I don't exactly know what you are to tell him.'

'Perhaps he will meet us at the church.'

'Do you think he will?'

'I shall couch my phrases carefully. I think he might. Do you have ink and quill?'

Crispin saluted the abbot with his cup. 'I look forward to it.'

Robert Braybrooke, Bishop of London, arrived with his retinue to St Modwen's parish church near noon. The abbot and Crispin had busied themselves going over the books and inventory with an old sacristan called Stephen, who was so feeble that he was of little help in the matter.

Crispin had sent Jack to survey the grave, but Horne had been reburied in his casket and the grave covered up again. The gravediggers covered the turned earth with a large slab of flagstone, likely in the hopes of keeping the corpse from roaming. Crispin thought the gesture was amusing, though his apprentice did not share in his humor.

The tall bishop put his hand out for Abbot William to kiss his ring. When he turned and spied Crispin, his long face frowned. 'Aren't you Crispin Guest . . . the traitor?'

Standing stock still, Crispin answered stiffly, 'I am.' Braybrooke was Richard's man. The bishop had stood by the king in all his missteps and had been handsomely rewarded for it.

'And what are you doing here?'

'Master Guest investigates crimes, Your Excellency,' the abbot interjected, 'as you know.'

'I have been so hired by the sheriffs to investigate the death of Father Bulthius.'

'Have you? I wish you luck.'

'And God's grace?'

The bishop raised his brow and his lip in a sneer. He turned pointedly away to address the abbot.

It was just as well. The bishop wouldn't be helpful to him, but he had yet to speak with the gravediggers again.

'What of a replacement for poor Father Bulthius?' the abbot was saying. 'And of course, to reconsecrate the churchyard after blood has been spilt.'

'It's a very small parish, of little importance. And Father Bulthius . . . a foolish man. He came to me with some story about the dead arising. What nonsense. Rumors like that certainly didn't help gain parishioners. As far as I can tell, it kept them all away. I dislike speaking ill of the dead, but, well, perhaps it was best that Father Bulthius left this world.'

'Surely you don't mean that he deserved to be murdered?'

'Did I say anything of the kind? You put words into my mouth, Abbot William. And I thought you had such a care with your own words and comportment. My fellow bishops were given to understand that you have a gift of discretion.'

'And so I do, Your Excellency,' he said with a bow. 'Else I could not have performed my duties as Archdeacon of Westminster for those many years.'

The bishop only acknowledged it with the slight cock to his head. 'Of course, we are aggrieved that one of our own died in such horrific circumstances. And we are gratified that he is now in the arms of our Lord, but as far as St Modwen's is concerned, it matters little, for I've been in consultation for some time about this parish, as a matter of fact. Our council has decided that the church will be absorbed by the closest parish and the church itself closed, deconsecrated. There will be no reconsecration of the churchyard.'

'Closed? But my dear bishop!'

'It has no income. The one feeble patron it did have . . . well. He's dead and buried in this very yard, isn't he? And I see that you've gone over the books. There is no income. No relic, no pilgrims, no endowments. I daresay this Horne didn't see fit to endow the church with much. A pity it wasn't his birth parish, else his mortuary fees might have accounted for more.'

The bishop suddenly turned and scowled at Crispin who had been lingering nearby. 'Haven't you got somewhere to go, Guest?'

Without another word, he bowed and took his leave, heading toward the hut with Jack in tow. Crispin stopped and put his hand on his apprentice's shoulder.

'Jack, stay with the abbot. He hasn't got a retainer and I expect you to serve him for now, as you serve me.'

'It's an honor, sir.' He slipped a gaze toward

147

the shed, and one toward the bishop's bored retainers standing with the horses along the lane.

'And Jack?'

'Aye, sir?'

'Do keep your ears open.'

Jack smiled. 'I will indeed, sir.' He trotted back toward the abbot and stayed a respectful distance behind the cleric and the bishop.

Crispin continued toward the shed and knocked smartly upon the door.

Hal came from around the other side just as Tom opened the door, as bleary-eyed as Crispin had seen him before, with the smell of beer on his breath.

'It's that Tracker again, Tom,' said Hal, leaning a rake alongside the shed wall.

'I can see that,' he grumbled. 'What do you want now?'

'Some answers. Did either of you see anything of the night before?'

'The coroner asked us that,' said Tom.

'And now *I'm* asking.'

'No one believes us when we tell it, so we don't say naught.'

'Believes you? As in walking corpses?'

'Aye, that's just what I mean,' said Tom, getting in so close his stale breath pelted Crispin's face.

Hal wrung the hem of his tunic. 'It's a terrible sight, sir. I never want to see it again. I seen it too much as it is in this damnable churchyard. I'd leave now, but I need me situation.'

Should he tell them that their situation was likely to change, and soon? He mulled over it for only a moment.

'Have the dead walked often in the last sennight?'

'Was it four times, Hal?'

'Aye, I think it was.'

'And was it the same corpse to walk?'

'Oh no, sir,' said Hal, stepping closer. 'Each time was a different one. It's horrible.'

'And you truly believe that the dead walked abroad?'

'We seen it.'

'Aye,' said Tom. 'We seen it. And in the morning, the turned earth and the disturbed coffins.'

'Was there a noise?'

Tom sniffed and hacked a phlegmy cough. 'A noise, sir?'

'Yes. A noise of earth being dug up, or, I suppose, heaved up, and the coffin torn open?'

He exchanged glances with the boy. 'No, sir. Never heard a thing.'

'And you were here, in the churchyard, during all this?'

'Aye.'

'And if it was twilight – supper time – why did you come outside at all?'

Their faces went through various gyrations. 'Well . . . we . . . we . . .'

'I went once to the privy and saw something queer,' said Hal.

'And I stepped outside to get a bit of air.'

'Father Bulthius told me that you were tending to the garden when he warned you to get inside.'

Tom pointed to Crispin and nodded. 'He said that. He told me.'

149

'But you didn't believe him at first.'

''Course not. But now . . .'

'I see.' Crispin looked out toward the meadow. He thought he saw smoke coming from the small cottage at its outskirts. 'Have you ever seen strange lights out there?'

Tom peered around Crispin and stared at the meadow. 'Out . . . there?'

'Yes. At night. Strange lights.'

Tom exchanged a glance with Hal. 'I never seen anything like that. Have you, Hal?'

'I dunno. At night, I try not to look out there. It makes me come all over queer. Sick-like.'

'Do you know who lives in yon cottage at the edge of the meadow?'

Both men silently shook their heads.

'And what of anything of animal killings?'

Hal looked aghast. 'Animal killings? Like what, sir?'

'Geese being killed and left to rot. Goats sucked of their blood.'

Both gravediggers looked horrified. 'Bloodsuckers?' gasped Hal. 'Them walking corpses! I knew it! I told you!' He pounded on Tom's shoulder and Tom, now appearing more annoyed than horrified, grabbed Hal. 'Don't get excited, Hal. We . . . we should go to our prayers, that's what.'

'I don't like it.'

'Who does? Let us inside to ask God's mercy.' He glared suddenly at Crispin, pushing Hal before him inside the little hut where he slammed the door shut.

Crispin let his gaze roam over the gravediggers'

hut, and then turned to cast his gaze over the meadow. Now that he looked carefully, there was not even a string of smoke escaping from that lone cottage's chimney, and no movement from man or animal, at least that he could see.

He left the churchyard, walking up the lane to town. He was thinking about what he'd seen and what it could mean when he found himself on Mercery Lane, standing at the corner with a view of both Walcote and Horne manors.

Though his mind was thinking to talk to Madam Horne, his eyes kept roving toward the Walcote home, and all thoughts of walking corpses vanished. Would she be there? Would she welcome him?

His feet took him toward the gatehouse, up to the porter, who didn't even ask him, and escorted him without a word to the door.

The steward opened it and explained that Master Clarence was somewhere in the other end of town on business, but would he like to speak with Madam Philippa?

He nodded stiffly and was led again into the parlor.

He paced. There was no fire in the hearth but the room was warm. Too warm. His back was facing the door when it opened. He stilled, waiting to hear her step, and only once he had, did he turn.

She was framed in the light from the outer hall and stood with hands folded together. The lidded eyes – which could be interpreted as modesty as much as mystery – gazed up at him through her lashes. Her brassy hair, which seemed to be

151

longing to escape, was instead discreetly encased in golden netting and veil.

She shut the door behind her without turning, leaning back against it as if to secure the heavy wood. She looked him over. Hungrily? Was it only his wishful thinking that thought so? But no. For when her tongue wetted her lips, he could not help but stride forward, and didn't stop until his arms encaged her where she stood, braced against the door.

'Philippa.'

She raised her glistening eyes to his and whispered, 'Crispin.'

He was lost again. His hands slid from the door to her shoulders and he dragged her in, covering her mouth with his. He kissed her hard, trying to take, but he soon succumbed to the soft gentleness he instead wanted to bestow.

She melted into his arms. Her hands traveled up his back and dug in, gripping him tightly. He kissed her again and again, peppering his lips over her face, her greedy mouth, her throat. He longed to take her up against the door, and would have, when his senses abruptly returned to him. He drew on enough strength from within to stop himself, to simply hold her tight, resting his chin on the top of her head, fitting her against him as he had done all those years ago. He kissed her brow, for he could not help but touch his lips to her skin and hair.

'My love,' he murmured, closing his eyes, wishing this moment never had to end.

Of course it did. But neither of them moved for a long time.

She sighed, squeezing him once before she lowered her face and stepped back out of his arms. 'You are honey to this she-bear.'

He almost chuckled at that. 'I am just as drawn.'

'So I see.' She touched her finger to her kiss-swollen lip. 'As much as it pains me to say, I hope you have not come to see me . . . but to give me news.'

'I will not lie. I did come to see you . . . and to ask more questions.'

'Oh *Jesu*, Crispin. Tell me you have found John Horne's killer so that my son will be free of suspicion.'

Our son, he wanted to say, but refrained. 'There is still much to discover.'

'But the sheriffs—'

'Have given me a sennight to discover the truth.'

'Can you do it in that time?'

'Yes, of course.' He walked toward the cold hearth, staring at the blackened stones.

'You don't sound so certain.'

'I am. I will do it, woman. Your . . . your son is stubborn.'

'Little wonder.'

He rested his hand on the mantel and kept his eyes averted, bluntly aware of her presence behind him. She didn't try for a palace accent when she was with him. He preferred her this way. 'Will you . . . will you tell me about him?' he said quietly.

She sighed again and brushed down her serviceable gown, toying with the buttons running

153

down its length. 'He was always a clever child. Eager to learn. And happy. He wanted for nothing.'

'You spoiled him,' he said gruffly.

'I did. I could not help myself. Clarence was always good and patient with him. But I confess, when I looked at the child, I saw you.'

He picked at a splinter on the mantel with his fingernail. 'Has he learned anything of arms?'

'I suggested as much to Clarence, but he said time and again, "What does a mercer's son need with arms?" Christopher wants to, though. He adores knights so.'

He whipped around. 'You didn't tell him—'

'Of course not. But he loves horses and the pageantry of tournaments. He has his own horse and he took to riding immediately.'

Crispin smiled, puffing a little. 'Likes horses, does he?'

Philippa's dimpled grin ached his heart. 'He's mad for them. I don't know that he is suited to being a mercer.' The grin faded. 'But that *is* what he is.'

He frowned. 'Does he . . . sing? Dance? Other courtly pursuits?'

'He is being tutored. He can dance well enough. But as for singing . . .'

'I'm a terrible singer as well.'

'Are you?' She touched his arm lightly but briefly. 'I've never heard you sing.'

'There is little enough cause.' Still, his frown faded. 'But in your presence, I feel I could sing now.' He dared gaze at her then, and her sad smile tore at his already aching chest. He took

154

a deep breath and looked away. 'I came here to speak with him again.'

She seemed reluctant to move from their frozen tableau: he standing at the hearth, she beside him. So very domestic. He moved first, stalking away from the cold fireplace to stand in the middle of the room. 'I will go to him.'

But still he paused. He set his mind to the business at hand, tamping down his ardor. 'Do you know anything of Madam Horne?'

She followed suit, stopped looking at him as if she would enfold him in a soft blanket. 'I've met her, briefly socialized at the guild gatherings, but little more than that. Her christened name is Clementia.'

'Is she kind; put upon; strong; spoiled?'

'Ah, I see. You would know her character. Well, as I said, I know her little. But of what I have heard . . . she is stern, religious, not given to flights of fancy . . . not like her humble neighbor who rose from the kitchens.'

He gave her a heart-warmed smile. 'Who has made much of herself and has everything to be proud of.'

Her brows rose for a moment before she looked down at her hands. 'Thank you for that.'

He knew he had to leave before he made a complete fool of himself. He strode toward the door with every intention of passing through it before he said too much, but it was she who stopped him this time.

'Crispin, maybe we could . . . meet.'

He paused. He couldn't remember why they hesitated before. Maybe they could. Maybe . . .

But then he watched her face fade from hopeful to resigned. 'No,' she said with a sigh. 'We couldn't. Clarence, for all his faults, has been a good man. He's been good to me when he didn't have to be. I had married his brother, after all . . . or so we had all thought. Poor Nicholas, as I still think of him. For we shall never know that imposter's true name, will we? As far as the rest of the guild knew, as far as all London knows, I married my brother-in-law.' She wrung her hands, stared at Crispin's boots. 'He was dishonored enough when his own brother Lionel killed Nicholas. I cannot dishonor him further.'

'And neither can I. Though . . . my honor seems but a weak thing now as I stand before you. I almost forgot it.'

She gave a rueful smile. 'You, forget your honor? And yet it was that very honor that kept us apart and put me into Clarence's arms.'

What could he say to that? It was the truth. His stubborn honor that he wore like armor. What had he been protecting himself from? Marrying a kitchen wench? That was what he had told himself all those years ago, but what had it got him? He wasn't a lord, never would be. He could have had her . . .

He wiped it all away with a brush of his hand across his brow. 'I . . . I will not bid my farewells once I've talked to . . . to your son. It's better that way.'

'Yes, I agree. You are too dangerous to me, Master Guest.'

'And you to me.' He bowed and, without looking at her again, dashed out the parlor door.

He took the stairs two at a time, the better to get it over with.

When he neared Christopher's door, he heard voices. The young, high voice of the child, and an older boy's voice, just coming into its rich tones. A servant? But it sounded like an argument. Crispin approached and rapped on the door. The voices stopped and there was a scramble. Something was knocked to the ground and Crispin didn't hesitate. He pushed open the door.

Christopher turned his wide-eyed face toward him. And Martin Chigwell, tangled in the curtains, was halfway out the window.

Eleven

Crispin was in the room in an instant, grabbing Martin and hauling him back, tearing the curtains from their rings as he did so.

'What are you doing here?'

'He came to see me!' cried Christopher. 'Let him alone!'

'I'm talking to Chigwell, if you don't mind. What have you to say for yourself, Chigwell?'

'Nothing. I'm saying nothing.'

'I can make you talk.' He lifted him higher and shook him.

Suddenly, little fists were pounding at his back.

'Leave him alone! Put him down. You're cruel, just like Master Horne. I don't like you very much, Master Guest.'

The words pierced his chest like a dagger thrust. He released Martin and swiveled toward Christopher. 'Can't you see that I'm trying to save you?'

'I don't want you to save me. I want you to leave him alone.'

The boy had a stubborn curl to his lip. It was most familiar. He turned away from the boy and fastened his gaze on Martin. 'Well?'

Martin blinked rapidly and glanced at Christopher. 'He's my friend. And they wouldn't let me see him. So I climbed through the window.'

'Who wouldn't let you see him? Madam Walcote?'

158

'No. Madam Horne. Doesn't want me here anymore. But I don't know that she . . . well. She might not be my mistress anymore either.'

'Has she let you go?'

He shrugged petulantly.

Christopher grabbed his arm and clung to him. 'You can work here, Martin. I'll see to it. My father will have you.'

'He's already got an apprentice. Many of them.'

'He'll make room for you. I'll tell him to.'

'You're a good friend, Chris.'

Christopher raised his face to Crispin and frowned. 'I want you to go.'

But Crispin stood his ground. 'Now both of you, shut your mouths and listen to me. This isn't a game. The sheriffs mean to hang you and I am trying to stop it. You both *must* talk to me.'

Two solemn faces stared back at him. They were silent and still.

'Now. I heard you two arguing just now before I came in. What were you arguing about?'

'Nothing,' cut in Christopher.

'For the love of God, boy, close your mouth. I want Chigwell to answer me.'

But Martin kept looking at Christopher and the boy pleaded with his eyes. Martin hung his head. 'We argued over . . . a game. A game we play.'

'It was a game,' said Christopher hastily.

Crispin folded his arms over his chest. 'Is that so?' Christopher stared at him defiantly, while Martin looked at the floor. 'Very well. We'll leave that for now. Tell me about that day. You first, Martin. And before you say anything, the

159

maids Nesta and Clarice saw you both there, one after the other, talking to Master Horne. And they saw *you*, Christopher, in the solar . . . where the relic was kept.'

'It was a red cow,' said Christopher. 'I always liked that cow. I didn't know why they kept it there or thought so much of it.'

'Because a saint's bone was inside it. And it's very valuable.'

Christopher wiped his nose. 'That's what Nesta always told me. I mustn't touch it. It's valuable.'

'And did you?'

'Once. But I didn't mean any harm. My mother would have given me a hiding had she known. But Nesta said she wouldn't tell.'

'When was that?'

'Ages ago. When I was a child.'

Crispin raised a brow. Why was everything the boy said reminding him of his own early years with Lancaster? A memory suddenly came rushing forth, from a time when he had not been much older than Christopher was now. He had first come to live with the duke when Crispin was newly orphaned. Crispin had touched something in the parlor he had been told not to touch and had broken it. A glass beaker made in Italy. At first, he had lied about it, but when a servant was being blamed he had spoken up and confessed it. The duke, a mere seventeen years old at the time, had called him into the parlor.

'I am told you have something to say to me, young Baron Guest,' he had said in his sternest voice. The duke seemed tall in those days, and

160

had begun styling himself with a dark, trimmed beard. He wasn't yet a duke. That was to come four years later, but he was still a mighty lord and third in line to the throne, and Crispin had been made aware of that fact time and again by stewards and governors.

Crispin remembered how he had felt. He had been terrified that his Lord of Gaunt would beat him; that he'd be thrown into a cell in the darkest hold in the house – as other servants had been threatened.

But, more than any of that, he had thought he might be sent away, and that was most frightening of all.

Yet even as afraid as he was, he had stood as tall as he could and faced the man. 'I do, my lord,' he had said, his voice high and sweet. 'For *I* have broken the beaker. I was told not to touch it and I did. I was afraid to say. Afraid you would send me away. But I could not let Roger be punished for something I did.'

Gaunt had gazed down at him for only a moment before he crouched low to look Crispin in the eye. And it was only then that Crispin realized he had been crying, for Gaunt reached out and wiped his tears with his thumb. 'Well,' he said, 'that was very brave of you. Even afraid as you were for being sent away. You spoke up and saved an innocent man. You mustn't ever be afraid to tell the truth, Crispin. You shan't be punished for that.'

His lip trembled but he did not look away from those intense eyes. 'Will you send me away?'

'You foolish boy.' He enclosed Crispin in his

161

arms then and rose, hoisting him to his chest. 'I'll not send you away. You are my squire. What would I do without you? And now I know you are a man who will always be loyal and tell me the truth, even if it frightens you.'

'I will, sir! Always! I promise!'

Gaunt laughed then, and Crispin hugged him around the neck, and he knew that it was going to be all right.

The duke had always protected him . . . especially years later in his greatest hour of need.

Would that he could return the favor to this boy, *his* boy, and take him up and reassure him. But he couldn't. He didn't yet know what the truth was, or if he truly could shield this boy from harm.

Instead, he slowly crouched to look him in the eye. 'Christopher,' he said, his image of a young Lancaster fading in his mind. 'No matter how it frightens you, no matter who you think you are shielding, you must tell me the truth. For Jesus himself would always wish that you tell the truth.'

'I know,' he said softly. He looked at his feet. 'But . . . I have nothing to say.'

Crispin looked up to Chigwell, standing over Christopher's shoulder. 'You understand the seriousness of this, Master Chigwell. Tell me. What happened on that day?'

'I . . . I . . .' He breathed hard. 'I told you before. My master could be disagreeable. He . . . says things. About . . . about women. He said something unkind about Madam Walcote and I told him that I didn't think it right he say it. He

162

struck me.' He placed his hand to his smooth cheek in remembrance. His cheek was unmarked now. 'I know it is not the place of an apprentice to speak against his master, but I told him that Christopher was here and that I didn't think he should hear such talk, but he didn't care.'

'Where *was* Christopher at the time?'

'He was in the solar.'

'Alone?'

'Yes. But he didn't take the relic. Why would he? He had no interest in it.'

'He said he liked the red cow.'

'But he didn't need it. If he had asked, Madam Walcote would have got him one just like it.'

Crispin knew that to be true. 'Could he have heard you arguing?'

'I'm standing right here,' said Christopher with an indignant stomp of his foot.

'Then tell me. *Did* you hear Master Horne and Master Chigwell?'

'Yes. He was a stupid man who deserved to be whipped for the things he said. If I were older, I would have.'

'And rightly so. Though the better course would be to challenge him to a duel.'

'And I would have!' he said, hand on his empty sheath. 'But I haven't learned enough about arms yet. But I will.'

'And did you raise your voice to him?'

'I did. And I'm not sorry.'

'Did you take your knife to him?'

He opened his mouth to answer but quickly closed it. 'He's dead, isn't he?'

'He certainly is. But a man must never be

stabbed in the back when you are defending your honor or that of a loved one.'

'I didn't! I'd never. No knight ever would.'

Crispin rose and stared hard at the boy. He didn't know. Christopher had no idea that Horne was stabbed in the back. Crispin was immeasurably cheered by that.

But then he glanced at Martin. His face was as unreadable as before.

'Then what happened, Christopher? You argued. Was Martin there?'

'No, he'd left after Master Horne slapped him. And I yelled at Horne. And then I ran out.'

'You did? Then where did you go?'

'I went to look for Martin but I couldn't find him. So I went back upstairs, because I had forgotten my book – I had a book I was showing Martin – and Master Horne was holding his side. There was a knife on the floor and I picked it up. It was mine. It must have fallen out of my sheath when Master Horne shook me earlier—'

'He laid his hands on you?'

'Told me I was a stupid boy and to keep my mouth closed and he would say what he liked about my mother. I kicked him in the shin.'

Good. Crispin was more and more convinced that Horne was a man who deserved to be murdered . . . but that was not a Christian thought. *I'll think my Christian thoughts later*, he mused. 'What happened when you found the bloody knife? What did you think happened?'

'I didn't know it was blood at first. I thought it might be berries or some such. And why was he using *my* knife? But he was clutching his side and breathing funny. He didn't notice I was there. And then he fell over.'

'What did you do?'

'I don't know. I stood there. I didn't do anything. And then Madam Horne just appeared there and screamed. She said, "You killed him!" and then I knew what happened.'

'So you didn't kill him like you told everyone?'

He stopped. His eyes rounded with alarm and he threw his hand over his mouth. Those wide eyes suddenly filled with tears. 'I shouldn't have said,' he sobbed. He turned to Martin, and the apprentice suddenly hugged him. Chigwell had a faraway look in his eye.

'You must never be afraid to tell the truth, Christopher. No matter the outcome.'

'You can't tell anyone,' he cried, snuffling.

There is no greater love than this, thought Crispin, the quotation the boy had used earlier. He certainly knew his scriptures and had taken them to heart. But it was misguided. He was protecting someone.

He was protecting Martin Chigwell.

Twelve

Crispin wanted to get the apprentice alone to talk with him and he grabbed his arm.

'Where are you taking him?' cried Christopher.

'Not far. But I must speak with him. And smuggle him out of here.'

'Oh. Then you're still my friend?'

Crispin released Martin long enough to take a knee before the child and touched his arm. 'I will always be a loyal friend to you, Christopher. Never doubt it.'

'You were a knight,' he said, thoughtfully. 'But you aren't one now. Why?'

He swallowed. 'Because my loyalty was to my lord, the Duke of Lancaster. And when his brother died and then his father, I thought that *he* should have been king instead of his nephew Richard, who was only a few years older than you are now.'

Wide-eyed, Christopher's gaze tracked over Crispin's face. 'But that's . . . treason.'

'Yes. It was. And I should have died. I should have been executed most horribly, as traitors deserve. But the duke stood up for me, saved my life. And now I am not allowed at court or to own my lands anymore.'

'And you can't be a knight?' His voice sounded forlorn, and Crispin warmed at the innocent sympathy there.

166

'No. But I still live as a knight, by my honor, and doing what I can to protect the innocent and punish the guilty. This I have sworn.'

'But you still have a sword.'

Crispin drew it and showed the Latin engraving on the blade. 'You see this? I did a service for the Duke of Lancaster's son, Henry Bolingbroke, and *he* gave me this sword. I use it only when necessary.' The light reflected on the blade and shone in the boy's eyes. Crispin quickly sheathed it again.

'So . . . *you're* going to protect me?'

Crispin pressed his fist to his heart. 'I so swear, Master Walcote.'

His rosy mouth fell open breathlessly. 'Then you're *my* knight . . . aren't you?'

'Yes.' Crispin rose. 'Do you trust me now?'

'Yes, Sir Crispin.'

He offered the boy a lopsided grin and bowed. He jerked his head toward Chigwell, and the boy followed him to the window. He passed a shelf full of toys. He did not know why it caught his eye, but it suddenly had. Tucked behind a leather ball and a discarded hood . . . was a red cow.

Slowly, he walked toward the shelf, reached out, and pulled it forth. Wooden, carved in the shape of a cow, its red paint was peeling off, rubbed down with age. There was a crystal in the middle of its flank, and Crispin could just see a white chip of something within.

He turned with it toward Christopher.

The boy's eyes widened. 'That's it!'

'You lied to me.'

167

'No! I didn't. I didn't take it. I don't know what it's doing here.'

Crispin took two strides to grab the boy by his arm. 'You lied to me.'

'No! I swear, Master Crispin. I swear by my honor!'

Crispin released his arm and took in the boy's expression. He was clearly staring at the cow in wonder.

He whirled on Chigwell. 'You. What do you know of this?'

Martin shook his head. 'I don't know. I don't know how it got here. I *know* Christopher would never have taken it.'

Crispin glared at each in turn. 'One of you is lying to me, and I don't like being lied to.'

The more he glared at each boy, the more they looked at each other. 'Bah!' he said at last, and shoved it into his scrip. He leaned over the sill and looked down. It was high, but there were vines and trees close enough to the wall. 'You're a squirrel, boy,' he said to Martin. 'Let us go down to the courtyard below and from there we will talk.'

Martin nodded shakily. He waved his farewell to Christopher, and straddled the sill before slipping down the other side by grabbing onto the vines clinging to the wall. Crispin let him get down a few paces before he followed, glancing once more at the suddenly small figure of his son, standing forlornly in the center of his chamber.

He turned away quickly, and climbed down, landing on the gravel walkway where Martin

168

Chigwell meekly waited for him. He grabbed the boy's elbow and ran with him to a secluded corner near the wall.

'Had to get you away from the windows,' said Crispin in explanation. 'Now. Tell me about this relic. And I warn you. I do not take kindly to liars.' *Or murderers*, but he did not say the last aloud.

'But I didn't lie, sir. I don't know how it got into Chris's room, but I know – I *know* he didn't take it.'

Crispin glared at him for another moment before he turned away and paced. 'Dammit, boy. You must be lying.' He turned to look at him again, but his smooth, youthful face was nothing if not innocent. Either they were both extraordinary storytellers or . . .

He sighed and stopped, gazing up to the unhelpful heavens. 'Then only God knows how it got there.'

The boy said nothing. He only glanced forlornly toward Christopher's window.

'Tell me truthfully, Martin. You didn't expect what Christopher had to say, did you?'

'No, but God be praised.'

'Why?'

'Because . . . because . . .' He lowered his face and whispered, 'I truly thought *he'd* done it.'

Crispin sighed again and rubbed his forehead. 'And he thought *you'd* done it. *Did* you do it, Martin?'

'No. I swear by Almighty God. I wanted to, but I didn't.'

'Christopher was willing to take the blame. *To give up one's life for one's friends.*'

169

'No! He never!'

'He did. But I don't think he truly understood the consequences.'

'Oh God!' Tears flowed freely from the boy's eyes. But, even as he wept, he laughed, shaking his head. His fists screwed into his cheeks and wiped the tears away. 'He's such a knight, is that boy. He loves the "honorable thing".'

Crispin stiffened. 'And what's wrong with that?'

'Nothing. If you can afford it. But he is no great lord. They *will* hang him, even if they put it off for now. Oh, what will happen, Master Guest?'

'He will recant his confession, but well before that, I shall find the real culprit.'

'I didn't do it, Master Guest. I didn't. No matter how much I may have wanted to.'

Crispin sighed. 'Tell me of the relic.'

He shook his head, biting his lip. 'No one really bothered much with it. I never saw the bone myself. To tell you the truth, I never paid much attention to it at all.'

'But such a holy object, present in the household. Would it not be the focus of private masses and prayers?'

'It wasn't. I saw madam praying in front of it many a time, but hardly anyone else did . . . least of all *Master* Horne.'

'He wasn't a praying man.'

'No, sir. But he could blaspheme with the best of them with oaths.'

Crispin took it out of the scrip and turned it over in his hands.

'It isn't much, is it?' said Martin.

'No. But it does contain the bone of a holy saint.'

The boy peered into the cloudy crystal. 'By God's wounds.' He pointed. 'Is that it?'

'Yes.' Crispin could feel a familiar tingle in his hands. He soon enough longed to rid himself of the thing.

'I swear I don't know how it got into his room. Do you think . . . do you think it was a miracle?'

The tingle was growing more unpleasant so he dropped it into his scrip and held down the flap. 'I doubt it. Stolen goods are not miracles.'

'But maybe the saint, St Modwen, is trying to comfort Christopher in his hour of need.'

How could Crispin dispute it? It wasn't for him to say. Instead, he stayed silent.

'Can I go now, sir?'

'Yes.'

He started to climb the wall, and Crispin gave him a leg up, pushing him up higher until he was on the top and dropped down on the other side. Crispin recalled when he and Jack had climbed over that very wall some eight years ago . . .

Come to think of it, it was the easiest way out, since he didn't want to walk through the house again. He grabbed hold of the sun-warmed stone, and hoisted himself up.

Crispin brushed down his cote-hardie as he walked down the lane, but stopped when he glanced up at the Horne residence. It seemed like a good idea to talk once more to the

171

maidservants before he rescued Jack, and return the relic to Madam Horne, but what to tell her about it?

He was let inside again and the steward, Robert Hull, looked none too pleased to see him again. 'Master Guest, I thought your investigation was at an end.'

'Only for that day, Master Hull. But I am interested in speaking with the maidservants Clarice and Nesta once more.'

'Oh. They are at their duties within the house. Cleaning the chambers.' He stood immobile, as if in challenge.

'And which rooms are those, Master Hull?' Crispin raised his head to glance up the stairs.

'But those are private chambers.'

'Indeed. I have no interest in those. Only the maidservants.'

'If you are so insistent, then I will accompany you.'

Crispin nodded and gestured for him to lead the way. This did not seem to make him any happier, but he bowed and stepped forward toward the stairway.

As they ascended the stairs, Crispin looked back and spied Madam Horne glaring up at him from the shadow of a doorway. He felt obliged to speak with her first.

'Wait, Master Hull. I must speak with your mistress.'

'This is inexcusable. She has only just buried her husband.'

'I have a duty to perform and you will not stop me.' He pushed Hull aside firmly, but gently,

172

and walked past him toward Madam Horne, who had not moved from the spot.

'Forgive me, madam,' said Crispin with a bow. 'But I must return this to you.' He reached into his bag and his fingers touched . . . nothing. He pulled the bag against his chest and opened it wide. His coin pouch, some lint, and a thorn. But nothing else.

'I . . .' He looked up, trying to think. Could he have dropped it going over the wall? But the damned scrip had been latched closed. He had to unlatch it just now to open it. He couldn't imagine it slipping out, even if he were turned upside down.

'I . . . apologize, madam. I . . . was mistaken.'

Now her glare was tinged with skepticism. 'Are you sure you know what you're doing?' she growled.

At the moment, he wasn't too sure himself. He said nothing, bowed again, and pushed aside Hull to reach the stairs once more.

The whole way up the steps he tried to recount where he could have lost the thing, but there was no reasoning it out. He groped the scrip, running his fingers over the bottom seam, looking for holes that weren't there.

When they reached the first chamber, the maids were absent, and Crispin reluctantly turned to the problem at hand.

At the second chamber, Clarice was there, sweeping the floors. She seemed surprised at first to see Crispin again, but then she pushed her brown hair into her kerchief and brushed down her gown.

173

Crispin nodded his head in an abbreviated bow. 'Clarice. I would take another moment of your time to ask about the day Master Horne was killed.'

She curtseyed and waited, eyes wide, moistening her lips with her tongue. She was flirting with him. At any other time, he might have flirted back, but his thoughts were still on Philippa . . . and the damned relic.

'You said you heard Master Horne arguing with Martin Chigwell.'

'That was Nesta. She heard them more than I did.'

'And where is Nesta?'

'I don't know. She wasn't in our room when I woke this morning. I thought she'd got up early to tend to the fires, but she hadn't – left all the work to me.'

Hull frowned. 'You haven't seen her all morning?'

Clarice shook her head. 'She's made me cross with her, what with all her coming and going.'

'She leaves the premises?' asked Crispin.

She put a hand to her mouth and bit at her nail, glancing out of the corner of her eye at Hull. 'I . . . shouldn't say.'

'You'd better, girl,' scolded Hull.

'It isn't my fault. She goes to see that Oliver, down by All Hallows.'

Crispin frowned. 'And you think she is there now?'

'I suppose. If you want to know anything, you'll have to speak to her. I told you all I know.'

He rubbed his chin. 'Did either of you pay much heed to the relic of St Modwen?'

174

Clarice glanced at Hull. 'No one did, for all the mistress's admonishments that it was worth so much. It didn't look like anything so grand. There were no jewels on the cow, after all.'

'Is that true, Master Hull?'

He fidgeted with a garland of keys hanging from his belt. 'Yes. I would have thought that such a thing would be made of gold and silver and embellished with jewels and such. But this one wasn't. I think because St Modwen was a humble woman and abbess. It was the carving of the cow that meant more. I suppose.'

'What sort of bone was it?'

'Well, my mistress said it was but a fragment. From the arm, I thought she said. But as Clarice said, none of us paid it much heed. It was just a red cow.'

And so should all relics be thus venerated, he thought with a scowl. 'And when was it noticed missing?'

Hull and Clarice conferred silently. 'It was after we discovered Master Horne,' said the steward. 'There was a lot of confusion.'

Which might well have been used for cover. Crispin wondered if there had been a connection, but he was inclined to believe that the relic was stolen because the moment was opportune.

'Horne was found in his chamber?'

They both nodded.

'And does – how shall I say this? – does Madam Horne share that chamber?'

Hull exchanged a look with Clarice. He also glanced over his shoulder. 'Not for many a year. She has her own chamber.'

175

'I see. Thank you, Master Hull, Clarice. I'll be back to talk with Nesta, if I may.'

Hull didn't seem to like that idea but he said nothing. Only led Crispin back down the stairwell and to the door, closing it sharply behind him.

Crispin stood for a long moment in the courtyard, gathering himself. The sun warmed his face and he watched the trees at the edge of the courtyard rustle from a breeze. The air smelled of summer, of the sun on wool coats, of fruit from the harvest warming in the summer light, of freshly mown grass, and roasted meat and baking bread on the wind. The clouds above were starched white and hovered in ranging groups, like a herd of sheep meandering in a deep blue sky.

All should be well. All should be in its right order. But it couldn't be, even on a day such as this. Not with murder in the background. And relics.

His hand went to his empty scrip again, and he narrowed his eyes at the garden wall across the lane. He hurried toward it and leapt up, grabbing the top and hauling himself up. He sat astride on the wall, searching the grounds. It was here that he had scrambled over it. Could it have been Martin Chigwell? Was he as adept with his fingers as Jack Tucker was?

He leapt to the ground in the garden, and stayed in the shadows of an over-arching tree, surveying the grass, the gravel paths, the patches of flowers, the garden benches. He crouched low and made his way back over the path he had taken before, eyes sharp. He *must* have dropped it here. There was no other explanation. None he was willing to entertain.

He got near the house, the place where he and Martin had climbed down from the window, and looked around. When he straightened again, he glanced toward the ground-floor window; Philippa was staring at him with her head cocked to one side. No doubt she had caught sight of his strange antics.

He offered her a sheepish smile. There was nothing for it. He bowed to her, and hastened to escape again over the garden wall.

With thoughts in his head of relics, Christopher, and Philippa, he wandered up the lanes until he arrived once more at St Modwen's parish church.

It appeared so small and dingy on its perch on a slight incline at the edge of a meadow. Its gravestones and carved crosses stood in haphazard rows: some tilting, some covered in lichen and spotted from time and weather, their chiseled names and dates wearing away as their inhabitants disappeared from memory. A grave was always a sad and final place, thought Crispin. How many would be left to remember the deceased? How many years would it take until all memory was wiped away, where even the names of those souls buried there would be wiped clean from the stone marking their places, a stone that was supposed to be a monument for the ages? It was a dreadful thought, to be so forgotten. That is, until the final judgment, when all in their graves would be called forth by the Almighty. But it was the now he was concerned with. Who would remember him in the decades to follow? Who would ever talk of Crispin Guest, the disgraced knight? Maybe he *was* best forgotten.

'Master!' Jack came running forward, a grim look on his face. He straightened his cote-hardie and glanced back over his shoulder. 'Abbot William was not happy, but mostly he listened as the bishop told him this and that, about the goings-on of court and the politics of the Church. The parish must go, it seems, and there is no argument for it.'

Crispin cast back to the graveyard and the decaying stones. 'So now the church will be even more forgotten, its buried only a scant memory.'

'Eh? Oh, right. The poor souls. What's to become of the graves, sir?'

'Indeed. What? I suppose there are those buried on the battlefields under the tread of their horses, and still more in distant places to be plucked clean by uncaring predators. What does it matter unless the dead walk to claim back their own?'

'But the dead *do* walk,' said Jack quietly. 'At least in this graveyard they do.'

'Yes, they do. And we still have not reckoned how or why.'

'Will . . . will Father Bulthius walk, do you think? His head was cut off. Isn't that supposed to stop them?'

'But his heart was not removed and burned at a crossroads.' He smiled grimly when he said it but Jack did not look appeased.

'Blind me. Do we have to—'

'I have no desire for such surgery, Jack.'

178

'Thank Christ for that.'

'But it does seem that we shall have to keep vigil again tonight in order to ascertain that Father Bulthius does not walk. I assume that we will inter him today.'

'The bishop has already done it. Seems he wants to hurry along the proceedings.'

'It does seem rather hurried . . . and slightly sacrilegious, being that the man was a priest.'

'Aye, that's what I thought. Abbot William objected but he's spent the better part of the day red-faced and stone-lipped. He always seemed like such a sedate man to me, but today . . . oooh, Master Crispin. He's fit to be tied.'

'I'd better—'

But before he could do anything, the bishop appeared again and scowled severely when he spied Crispin. He marched toward him and Crispin stood at attention, bowing when the cleric stood directly before him.

'Guest, why are you still here?'

'I am attending Abbot de Colchester, Your Excellency.'

'I doubt very much that he needs nor wants the attendance of your like.'

'I can speak for myself very well,' said the abbot, striding up behind Bishop Braybrooke.

The bishop offered him the merest eyelash flick before he waved to his attendants. 'Thank God this business is done. And fitting, too, that the last priest of the parish should depart this world before his parish was unconsecrated. It is the way of things.'

'I beg your mercy, Your Excellency,' said

179

Crispin, trying not to furrow his brow, 'but there is nothing fitting in murder.'

Straightening his gloves, the bishop deigned to glance his way. 'Murder? Oh, yes, yes, yes. Troublesome, isn't it? Well, I understand you're to see to it, so, Guest . . . do so.'

Crispin bowed to prevent himself from saying what he wished to say. Even Jack laid a hand to his arm to remind him not to. When Crispin straightened, the bishop was blessedly out of earshot.

'What an insufferable man,' huffed Abbot William, crossing himself. 'I shall do penance for such a grievous thought, but by St Sebastian he makes a man suffer so!'

'Why . . . my Lord Abbot. I have never seen you so out of sorts.'

'You heard him. And you heard the brunt of it, did you not, Master Tucker?'

'Aye, my lord, I regret to say that I did.'

'He doesn't give a damn for this parish. Pardon my language.' He adjusted his cassock and his cloak, which he suddenly peeled off. 'It's too hot for this.' He jammed it into Jack's hands. 'And for my hot blood. How I envy you, Crispin, your ability to swear!'

'Is it not a sin for me to do so, my lord?'

Abbot William sketched a messy cross over him with a finger. 'And I so absolve you for now and always.'

Crispin grinned. 'Thank you, my lord.'

Abbot William squinted at him, seemingly only now realizing what he had done. 'I think I am in need of a cup of ale. Shall we?' He led the way back to the alehouse they had gone to the night before, while Jack and Crispin followed.

Crispin licked the foam from his lips and sat back, watching the room with one eye and his agitated friend the abbot with the other.

'He has no interest whatsoever working for the parish to grow it. Those poor few who remain! What of the mortuary fees paid by them? What will they do now? I don't suppose they'll be getting any remittance for all they have paid. And to bury poor Father Bulthius in unconsecrated earth. It's appalling.'

'I agree.'

'Ah, Crispin.' He took a sip of his beer. 'I do apologize. You have done nothing for the last half an hour and more but listen to my complaints.'

'I have never seen you thus before, my lord. I thought it best to simply let you tire yourself out.'

His eyes widened before he burst into laughter. 'Well, bless me. Perhaps it is old age catching up to me. I find I cannot suffer fools as I did in my youth. Is it a sin, I wonder? I was a placid man in those days, I can tell you. I could sit for hours at a time, waiting my turn to speak with cardinals and popes. Oh yes. I waited in silence, in contemplation of a prayer. But now? I am like any ruffian in an alehouse.'

'I shouldn't express that particular opinion too loudly, my lord,' muttered Crispin into his beaker.

Abbot William looked around. A few faces were turned their way, but soon enough they lost interest. 'I daresay,' he said, quaffing more.

181

Jack had a bemused expression that he turned from Crispin to Abbot William and back again.

'My apprentice is learning much this day,' he said under his breath.

Abbot William rested his hand on Jack's shoulder. 'Your young Master Tucker was a comfort to me. He made his presence known when necessary, and slipped away when that, too, was necessary. You should be proud of him.'

'I am. And constantly surprised.'

'I don't know why you should be, sir. I learned all me talents from my days as a cutpurse. Talk about patience.'

Abbot William howled his laughter. He slapped his thigh. 'Master Tucker, I do admire you, sir.'

Jack's expression was priceless. Yes, he well knew that look. It meant that he had sussed that Abbot William was a bit into his cups. 'My lord,' said Crispin, rising. 'I think we should be escorting you back to Westminster.'

'Oh? Are we done investigating revenants?'

'Well . . .'

'Are you not going to see if Father Bulthius rises?'

'I had planned on doing so. But you don't wish to—'

'But of course I do!' He jumped to his feet. 'Jack, my boy, get a message to Westminster, and tell them I will be delayed another day and night. If it is all right with you, Crispin, I should like to take advantage of your hospitality further. Here, Jack, before you go . . .' He reached into his pouch and pulled out some silver coins. 'I am eating all your fare, Master Guest. Have your man refurbish the larder. Get some lamb for tonight's dinner, and some fruit from the stalls. I'm sure your wife can prepare some figs in cream, and perhaps a savory galette and a cheese pie.'

Jack stared at the coins filling his hand and blinked at the abbot. 'I will, sir. Thank you, my lord. I shall do as you bid.' He nodded once to Crispin before he whooshed out of the tavern.

'I feel you are neglecting your duties to play with us,' said Crispin seriously.

'I must confess that perhaps I am. But it isn't every day that a man goes in pursuit of the walking dead.'

'Do you truly believe that this is what we are witnessing?'

'I have the feeling that you don't believe it.'

'I don't. I think it is something considerably more prosaic than that.'

'And why do you say so?'

Crispin rose. Maybe the abbot would sleep the day away and leave the investigating to Crispin. 'Because it is convenient, Father Bulthius being killed. It gets him out of the way.'

'He was the one who hired you.' He led the way through the tables and Crispin followed him outside into the sunshine. 'Those with evil intent clearly wanted to stop him.'

'Yes, but just what is that evil intent?'

'To prevent the blessings of Christ to stop their evil and the encroachment of the Devil.'

'That could certainly be part of it. But I think there is something else to it. I just don't have any idea yet what that could be. And I am still

183

concerned with the murder of the mercer John Horne.'

'And why so concerned, Crispin?'

'It's the accused that concerns me – a seven-year-old boy.'

'Oh?' They walked side by side down the lane toward London, walking in under the shadows of tall shops and houses. 'Do you think the boy innocent, then?'

'Unquestionably. But if he is not guilty, someone else is. And the sheriffs have only given me a week to discover who it was.'

'Have you considered that it is a case of Occam's razor?'

'No, it isn't,' he rasped.

'Oh ho! This boy has got under your skin. Is it somehow personal?'

Crispin stopped and glared at the abbot and priest. He didn't look as tipsy as he had earlier, and he aimed a blue eye at Crispin.

'Got it, did I?'

'It's not . . . personal. You well know how I cannot stand an injustice.'

'Injustice. I see.'

Should he tell him? If he made it a true confession, then the abbot would be under the seal and unable to speak of it. But he didn't want to burden the abbot so. Or was it because of Philippa? If he spoke of it, that door would be closed for good, and maybe he still wanted that door . . . ajar.

They passed through the lanes and alleys until they reached the Shambles, and made it to the poulterer's. Crispin opened the door, wiped his

184

feet on the granite step outside, and offered the threshold to the abbot.

Isabel was working a broom across the floor when she stopped and curtseyed to the abbot, who took a chair by the hearth and settled in.

'Isabel, Abbot William will partake again of our hospitality. Jack has been given coins for shopping. Our friend the abbot has expressed a desire for a savory galette and a cheese pie.'

'That is easily done, my lord,' she said to the cleric. 'As soon as Jack returns with the shopping, I can hasten it for you.'

'Don't go to any trouble,' said the abbot, scrutinizing his surroundings again, and perhaps taking stock.

'It's no trouble at all. I used to do a lot of cooking in my father's house. God rest his soul.'

The abbot crossed himself. 'And he would be proud indeed of such a dutiful daughter.'

'Yes, my lord.'

She set about getting flour and a wooden mixing trough, something that had been added to Crispin's household inventory of which he knew very little. But she seemed to know what she was doing, preparing a dough of some kind. Then she picked flowers from the window box and set about chopping up the blossoms.

'Wine, Abbot William, and perhaps a game of chess?'

They sat in the window with the shutters wide open, enjoying the summer air breeze through, each concentrating over the chessboard when Jack arrived, bundles piled high in his arms. He

185

greeted Crispin and the abbot, and kissed Isabel's cheek as she took in all that he had brought.

Soon, there was lamb roasting over the fire, with leeks and shallots sizzling in a pan, a galette baking on the hob, and a gillyflower cheese pie cooling on the sill.

All was calming and domestic, thought Crispin, and it bestowed upon his heart the ease and contentment it had long desired.

Until he spied the red cow sitting on a shelf.

Thirteen

'God's blood!' cried Crispin, shooting to his feet, knocking his chair over. 'Where did this come from? Jack?'

Crispin snatched it from the shelf and shoved it toward his apprentice. Jack stared at it. 'I dunno, sir. Isabel?'

She looked at it curiously. 'I found it lying on the floor, Master Crispin. I thought it was something you had brought in. I put it on yon shelf.'

Clutching it in his fingers, he sank slowly to a chair. He placed it carefully on the table. 'This is the missing relic of St Modwen,' he said breathlessly. 'I first found it in Christopher Walcote's room this morning.'

Abbot William knelt beside the table, grabbing its edge to steady himself. 'Then what's it doing here?'

'I asked again of Christopher if he had stolen it, presented with the evidence, but he seemed just as surprised as Martin Chigwell to see it.'

'What was Martin Chigwell doing there?' asked Jack.

Crispin glared at him. 'Take aim on the more important part of my story, Jack. This relic!' He gestured at it. 'I was convinced that neither of them had taken it, and with the idea to further investigate it, I put it there in my scrip' – he pointed to the obviously empty bag hanging by

187

the door – 'with the intention of returning it to Madam Horne, and when I was standing before the woman, it wasn't in my scrip at all. I thought it must have fallen out, so I went back to the Walcote's courtyard garden.'

'And . . . did you find it there?' asked the abbot.

'No. I returned to you, Jack, with an empty scrip.'

'Surely you must be mistaken.' The abbot gestured to the cow. 'For here it is.'

'It must have been in your scrip all this time,' said Isabel. 'You just didn't see it.'

Jack curved his arm around Isabel. 'It's them relics,' said Jack in a hushed tone.

Crispin grabbed it again, ignoring the abbot's gasp, and stared hard at it. 'Very well, St Modwen. What have you to say for yourself?'

Everyone stilled . . . until a spark exploded in the fire and they all yelled.

'God have mercy!' cried Isabel. 'Maybe, Master Crispin, you should return it then.'

'Jack, fetch me my scrip.'

'In all haste, sir.' Jack hurried in stumbling steps to the bag and handed it over with a shaky hand.

Without a pause, Crispin shoved it deep within the leather satchel, and closed the flap, tying it down. He draped it across his chest, over his shoulder and stood. 'My Lord Abbot, Jack: will you accompany me to the Horne household?'

They both nodded warily, and gave Crispin a wide berth.

* * *

188

They walked through the quieting streets of London. The day was still with them, being summer, but business obeyed a different sweep of the gnomon. Shops were being shuttered, drovers were returning to their fields, and weary shopkeepers were joining their families in a late supper.

Crispin's band made it to Mercery and the porter simply waved Crispin through. When he knocked on the door, Hull answered and pressed his lips tight upon seeing Crispin. 'What is it now, Master Guest?'

Before he spoke, Crispin felt the bulging scrip. 'I have something to give to Madam Horne.'

The expression on his face seemed to say, *Are you certain this time?* But he said nothing. Instead, he let them in but, instead of leading them to the parlor, had them wait in the entryway.

They waited for what seemed like an hour. Crispin slipped his hand inside the scrip with his fingers resting on the reliquary.

Madam Horne came striding from a shadowed doorway, her hands pressed tightly together before her. 'Master Guest. And a cleric?'

Hull stumbled over the introductions and Crispin came to the rescue. 'This is the Abbot of Westminster, William de Colchester.'

She curtseyed and returned her stern gaze to Crispin. 'What is it, Master Guest? It must be important to disturb the household's meal.'

'It is. I thought that you would at least be contented with the return of your relic.' He pulled free the red cow and presented it to her with a bow.

Gasping, she took it with trembling hands. 'You finally got it out of that boy!'

'No, madam. It was found . . . er, near the house.'

'Well, I don't care. It is back. My Lord Abbot, will you have the honor of placing it back where it belongs?'

'Well, I . . .' Looking toward Crispin, he seemed to decide on his own. 'Yes, certainly.' He shook out his sleeves to cover his hands, took the small reliquary and held it before him. 'Where . . .?'

'Up the stairs to the solar. Robert! Gather the household. We will place it back in the solar with celebration.'

'Yes, madam.' Hull hurried to comply.

In the meantime, Abbot William slowly progressed toward the stairs. Jack was moving forward before Crispin put his arm across his chest and held him back. Madam Horne followed the abbot and then the household slowly gathered, following them. From below, Crispin counted and assessed the number of people, seeing Clarice but not Nesta.

'Are we not to go up?' asked Jack.

'Not unless you want to.'

Jack shuddered. 'Not particularly.'

They waited. It seemed that the full complement of the Horne household was now in attendance in and outside the solar, for there were so many – both servant and apprentice – that not all could fit in the modest room.

'While the others are occupied,' said Crispin quietly, 'let us look at the place where Master Horne was killed.'

190

'But sir,' said Jack, following after Crispin's stealthy advance. 'We don't know which is his bedchamber.'

'I think I can make an educated guess.'

Up the stairs they went and stood on the gallery. Abbot William began to intone some prayer that they all responded to with bowed heads. Crispin moved to the left of the assembled household and found a large room with an equally large four-poster bed with resplendent curtains around it.

'Blind me,' cooed Jack. 'Now that's a bedchamber.'

'Indeed.'

'You'll probably tell me it's still smaller than the one you used to have.'

Crispin sneered. 'I wasn't going to say anything of the kind.'

'Is it, though?'

With a world-weary sigh, he nodded.

Jack smiled. 'Good. I'm glad yours was bigger.'

Crispin couldn't help but paint a lopsided smile on his face. 'You have the strangest sense of humor, Tucker.'

The room was like any other bedchamber, with a tall window of glass, a table with a rug over it, chairs with cushions, a sturdy stone fireplace, a curtained alcove for a servant, candelabras, an ambry, two coffers. Every stick of furniture was carved and made of fine, dark wood. A tapestry hung on one wall, a painted mural covered the other. A cabinet with a stool, no doubt, and other decorative pieces here and there, including a silver ewer and basin, and a silver wine decanter and carved horn goblets. The floor was painted in a chequy pattern.

Crispin crossed to the window and looked down. A stone courtyard below and beyond that the garden. The drapery was heavy and embroidered. He moved to the bed and looked beneath it. No truckle. That led his eye to the alcove. He walked to the niche and tossed the curtains aside. A small ledge where a bedroll was curled into its corner. The servant, if servant there was, certainly served elsewhere during the day. There was a door in the back of it. Crispin pushed on it but it was locked. It likely led through a passage putting it at the end of the gallery or down a stairwell toward the kitchens. It was very much like a lord's chamber. The rich styled themselves so. It would not be out of place in an alderman's house.

Jack peered into the alcove. 'Blind me, Master Crispin. Could the killer have used this?'

'Very likely.'

'How are we to discover *that*?'

'Carefully, I should think.'

Jack planted his hands at his hips. 'You don't know, do you?'

Crispin merely raised a brow.

Jack smacked his own forehead. 'That's how you appear so clever. You let everyone think you know, but you really don't.'

'That's not entirely true.' He smiled. 'But it is mostly true.'

'Well, then. I, too, can easily be a Tracker.' He raised his chin and caricatured one of Crispin's inscrutable facial configurations.

192

Crispin playfully flicked the boy's temple. 'As long as you keep a neutral expression, Jack. It works wonders.'

Grinning, Jack commenced examining the rest of the room, looking for more secret portals and hiding places. 'I don't suppose it matters where exactly he fell.'

'It might.'

'Martin Chigwell likely knows all the passages, sir. Any young man would have explored them.'

'I am aware of that, Jack.'

'You haven't ruled him out, then?'

'No.'

'But you said that he was relieved that Christopher Walcote didn't do it.'

'Jack, men have lied to me before. Frequently.'

'That's certainly true. And he is the likeliest. *Plausible impossibilities should be preferred to unconvincing possibilities . . .*'

'What are you doing in here?'

They both turned to find the red-faced Madam Horne in the doorway.

Crispin bowed and Jack followed suit. 'I hoped to examine the room where Master Horne was killed.'

'Get out.'

'This is the room, is it not?'

'I said get out!'

But Crispin stood his ground. He could feel Jack's agitation behind him. 'And where, madam, was he found?'

She strode into the room, hauled back her arm, and slapped his face. It only slightly turned his head but he returned it forward to gaze at her squarely. 'Perhaps you don't understand me, madam.'

She wound up to strike him again when he caught it. Bosom heaving, face as red as a crab apple, she opened her mouth in astonishment. He tightened his grip and she stared at her wrist, purpling under his fingers. 'I do not like to be struck, madam. Especially in the course of my serious work. I will ask again. Where was it that he fell?'

She yanked her wrist free of him and rubbed it. With her mouth tightly shut, she pointed with the reddened wrist toward the place before the bed, almost the middle of the room.

Crispin bowed. 'Thank you, madam. And where did you find Christopher Walcote?'

Without a word, she pointed to a spot before the place where Horne had died near the chamber door.

'Was he facing the door?'

'Yes.' The word was clipped, her attitude stony. 'Master Guest,' she said stiffly. 'You are not welcomed into this house further.'

'Noted. And yet, I *will* have to return to investigate.'

'I forbid it.'

'I have the leave of the sheriffs, Madam Horne. This is a murder, after all.'

'But the boy did it!'

'No, he didn't. Someone else did. And I have every reason to believe it is someone in this household. So you will not bar me. Is that understood?'

She said nothing, but her eyes bulged with unspoken frustration.

Crispin whirled away from her and strode out of the room without looking back. Jack ran to catch up.

'You've made an enemy,' he whispered to Crispin's back as they stomped down the stairs.

'She's just another in a long line of them.'

They waited at the foot of the stairs as the servants filed past him, each giving him and Jack a lengthy stare.

Clarice hurried past but was unable to escape Crispin's darting hand. He grabbed her arm even as she tried to squirm out of his grip.

'Clarice. Has Nesta returned? I need to speak with her most urgently.'

'I haven't seen her.'

'Interesting. She is most truantly in her duties. Does Master Hull know?'

'Shhhh!' she hissed. 'Please don't tell him. He'll be just as cross with me. He thinks I'm trying to cover for her, but I'm not. I'm just as angry she isn't here.'

'You said she was seeing someone near All Hallows. Who is it?'

'His name is Oliver. But I don't trust him. He never shows his face around here. Maybe there is no one. Maybe she's lying.'

'Then what other reason would she have to sneak away?'

'I don't know. It's always a man, isn't it? I wish I had a man to sneak off to.' She eyed Jack suddenly. Jack straightened and fidgeted with his knife sheath.

Crispin made an incremental step in front of him. 'Does she have family in London?'

Clarice shook her head. 'None left. She's been in service here almost as long as I have. Since we were children.'

'If you see her, tell her that she must come to me. I'm on the Shambles—'

'At an old poulterer's,' she said sullenly. 'Everyone knows that.'

She nodded and curtseyed, and hurried away under the stern eye of Hull. He gave Crispin a dismissive turn of his shoulder, before Crispin decided that they'd best leave as soon as possible.

They waited outside for the abbot, and he shuffled hastily across the courtyard toward them. 'This is all very strange,' he said, pulling his cowl up over his head. 'I have seen many household shrines but this one . . . struck me as odd.'

'In what way?' said Crispin, leading the way beyond the mercer's gate. He couldn't help but glance toward the Walcote house. His stomach was growling and he wanted to return home to the supper that Isabel had laid out.

'The people usually have great reverence for such a thing. It is a very great gift to have a saint's relic in one's house.' He wagged a finger at Crispin. 'As much as you might despise the very thought.'

'I have never used such a harsh term, Abbot William.'

'Well . . . the sentiment is certainly there. Never mind. What I wish to say is that it was not the occasion it was meant to be. Such an object and it was lost and suddenly returned. One would think there would be much rejoicing. But that was simply not the case. Oh, the mistress

196

of the house was much overjoyed at its return, but the others . . . It seemed more that it was taking up their time.'

'A servant's lot,' said Jack, speaking carefully. 'We don't always have the time to take, Lord Abbot. When something must be prepared or done as the master wished it, he don't want to hear any excuses.'

The abbot patted Jack's arm as they turned the corner at the Shambles. 'I quite understand, Master Tucker. Yet even servants are glad at the presence of one of the Lord's favored. These were not. Ah, it is just a feeling. A small observation.'

'Perhaps an important one,' said Crispin. 'I will think on it.'

They arrived at the poulterer's and greeted Isabel, who had kept warming cloths over the dishes.

Later, they left the warm and homey companionship of Crispin's household for the little church in All Hallows. Crispin was quiet and thoughtful as they walked, gravel crunching under his boots. Even as he lifted his face to the twilit sky, inhaled the fresh breeze that blew through London's streets and bore away the smells of the Shambles, he pondered. Two murders occupied his thoughts. The one certainly had nothing to do with the other. Yet for the one, there was a time limit, for he was worried about Christopher. He had confessed to murder, and that was something not easily forgotten. The judges would not forget it; neither would any jury, who were likely already deciding even before the trial. Would he lose his son having only just found him?

He glanced toward Abbot William. Should he tell the abbot about these tidings? It wouldn't likely help, and it would change nothing. For Clarence Walcote acknowledged the boy as his own, and that was the best course, the only course. There were always bastards being born to nobility. It wasn't an uncommon thing. Lancaster had them. His longtime mistress Katherine Swynford bore the duke's bastards, but she was widowed when they were born. He could acknowledge them and they lived well because of it. But this was a merchant's son, a London alderman. What could Crispin offer? Only shame to the boy and his mother. The lad might even be disinherited. It wasn't worth the cost. And the boy wouldn't thank him.

No. It was better he kept silent. Jack knew. Isabel knew only because Jack was keen not to keep such secrets from his wife, but he didn't fear they would say anything. It was only his own vanity that made him want to speak of it, to show the world he could father a son.

Yet every dog could do as much.

And as far as Philippa was concerned, he dared not be in the same room with her, for he burned, and so did she. Any further congress would lead to sin and they both vowed not to indulge. For the first time in his life, he questioned the need to satisfy his honor.

He'd burn that little portrait of her he coveted. It had been foolish to keep it this long. Now it was dangerous to have it in his possession.

'Sir?'

He suddenly realized Jack had been speaking to him. 'What was that, Jack?'

'I said what are we to do when we reach the church?'

'Same as before. We shall find a place to hide and watch his grave. And we'd best keep an eye on Horne's grave as well.'

'But what of the holy water? The bishop locked the church door, said it was unconsecrated.'

'Holy water is holy water, Jack. Er . . . is that not so, Abbot William?'

'Holy water is a sacramental and remains forever in that state. Its blessing cannot "expire". Just as a rosary remains a sacred object, as well as a . . . reliquary.'

'And yet a church *can* expire,' said Jack bitterly. Crispin smiled indulgently at his apprentice. Even after all he had seen, all he had experienced in his life, Jack was a staunchly devout man. Jack was not tainted by his thieving past, nor by his brief time in a brothel as a child. Crispin knew that while *he* languished in Purgatory with all his sins, he'd have to wait till Jack came along to get him out.

'It is a loathly thing,' said the abbot, shaking his head, not for the first time today. 'All those souls awaiting resurrection in what was once sacred ground . . . It is just as bad a crime as murder, for their souls seem to have been murdered as well. And for what? So the church can sell the land for profit? *For what shall it profit a man if he shall gain the whole world and lose his own soul?*'

199

'But what can one do, my lord?' said Crispin. 'I have a feeling there is no arguing with the bishop if he is determined.'

'Oh, determined he is. I have dealt with his like all the years of my adult life while serving God. I have conversed with cardinals of a like mind, with clerics from Rome to the edge of civilization. When men reach a certain rank . . .' He stopped himself and suddenly stared at Crispin. 'Well . . . you well know it, don't you, Master Guest? Sometimes to be so high is to forget where you came from, and its purpose. You yourself forswore your oaths to commit treason—'

'It was no light decision, my lord, I assure you,' he rasped. 'I knew well what I was doing, and considered the very matter you assume I had forgotten. For I was only thinking of my tenants, my fellow citizens of London, of all England. It was not for me and my vanity, though well you may think it. If you must constantly throw it in my face, at least know the truth of it.'

Breathing hard, he scowled at the abbot a long time before he swung his face away. Damn Abbot William for incessantly bringing it up, and damn Crispin himself for ever contemplating treason in the first place.

'I see I have been too flippant and too quick to judge,' said the abbot calmly, though there was an edge to his voice this time. 'I had always assumed that to put Lancaster on the throne would be advantageous to you. And so it would have been. But perhaps I have mistaken your motives. And I am sorry if I have done so.'

Crispin grunted his reply.

'And I also see how you have taken your disgrace to heart, for indeed, you could very well have left London, left England itself for its enemies abroad, and in your thirst for vengeance, fought against your homeland. But you did none of those things, and I must conclude that your motives were as you say they were. I myself cannot fathom doing as you did . . . but then again, I have not put myself in your shoes as our Lord urged us to do, and for that, I do heartily beg your mercy.'

Nodding, Crispin glanced his way. 'Even a confessor cannot know entirely what is in a man's heart. If you wondered if I do penance, I do it every day just by being alive . . . in London.'

'I shall never underestimate you again.'

Softening, Crispin offered him a smile. 'Only at your peril, my lord. Especially at the chessboard.'

The abbot's face, so solemn in his confession, brightened marginally. He nodded, and turned toward the road again. There was just one curve before they spied the darkened church. Even the sanctuary lamp was now dark.

Except there *was* a light within. And it was moving.

Fourteen

Crispin motioned for the others to halt. He gestured to Jack and each took an opposite direction to surround the church. Crispin crept in from the north door, expecting it to be locked, but it opened silently. He drew his dagger.

The church was nearly pitch-dark and, cocking his head, he listened. Whatever light he had initially seen had been snuffed out. He could still smell the smoke.

He stepped carefully into the nave. His boots scraped against the stone and he cursed himself in his head for making the noise. Stopping again, he listened.

A shadow passed over him. He turned. Something made him raise an arm in defense and whatever it was that was poised to strike him in the back of the head glanced off his temple instead. It still took him down to a knee, and there was a scramble, and a door flung wide. He caught a hazy glimpse of a figure in the doorway before it disappeared and then there were hands on him. He struggled for only a moment before a familiar voice at his ear said, 'Hold, master, it's only me!'

Crispin fell limp in his arms, closing his eyes to the double vision, swallowing down the bile.

'Did you see who hit you, sir?'

'No. But I doubt very much that it was a revenant.'

'Well, you never know.'

Footsteps, and they both turned.

Abbot William's white face in its hood stared at them. 'What's happened?'

'Master Crispin's been struck on the head.'

'Good God. Are you all right?'

'Getting better,' he said, his stomach still woozy. He rubbed at his temple, felt a lump, and cursed under his breath.

'Can you rise, sir?'

'I had better try.' Leaning on Jack, he got unsteadily to his feet and looked around the dark church, but he could see nothing but shadowy arches and black windows. 'You saw nothing, Jack?'

'I wish that I had, but I regret to say that I did not.'

'And you, Abbot William?'

'No. Nothing.'

'They obviously left the church once they struck me. It's possible they doubled around the other side.' Jack started to move but Crispin held him back. 'There's no point now.'

'I'm going to look for footprints, master.'

'You won't find any. It's been dry, and the bishop and his retinue have been all over the place . . . taking inventory, no doubt.' He glanced toward the altar when he said it and noticed that there were no candlesticks there at all. 'My Lord Abbot, did the bishop's men, by any chance, take away that inventory?'

'No, Crispin. That was for another day.'

'Then our burglar was here again.' He pointed and they both looked.

'Blind me! Oh . . . sorry, my lord.'

'Not a bit of it, Jack. Would that *I* could swear an oath or two.'

Jack heaved a sigh. 'Well . . . are we to stay, Master Crispin? Have we scared off the ghosts and resurrected?'

'As long as we're here, we might as well stay. Let us find a quiet spot to watch the graves of Father Bulthius and John Horne.'

He winced as he walked toward the open door, rubbing his head as he went. 'I wonder what it was they hit me with.'

Jack closed the door after them. 'Probably a stolen candlestick.'

Crispin nodded. 'You're probably right.' He scanned the now dark and lonely churchyard. There the cottage of the gravediggers, with a small candle flame in the open window. And there the edge of the low wall, beyond which the meadow lay. Looking in the other direction was London, whose cressets and candles shone in the night, with sluggish smoke from chimneys rambling over rooftops like so many sleepy sheep.

'Let us investigate the graves of our most recently interred.'

They went first to John Horne's grave where it appeared to be undisturbed, stone slab and all. They tromped over the softened earth toward Father Bulthius's grave, where the earth was mounded over his casket.

Crispin stood over it for a moment, staring at

it, daring it to heave open. 'Forgive me, good priest, for not being able to stop this and for not being vigilant enough to prevent your untimely death.'

'It's not your fault, sir, that he got himself beheaded.'

'I wonder.'

'It was the revenants,' muttered Abbot William.

Crispin huffed. 'I have my doubts about that, my lord.'

'Then what?'

'Remember that his throat was cut . . . before it was hidden by his decapitation. Someone wanted us to believe it was these doings in the churchyard that killed him.'

'So *are* these bodies going about walking out of their graves or not, Master Crispin?'

'What do you think, Jack?'

He rubbed his hand over his head, ruffling the wild ginger curls. He studied his master, amber eyes roving over the neutral face Crispin presented. 'I *thought* it was the dead rising and causing mischief . . . but I see that this is not what you believe at all, is it?'

Crispin said nothing, but he couldn't help one brow from rising.

'Blind me,' he muttered, now moving his hand over his beard. 'You take everything I've ever believed and turn it upside down. Very well. Let us use logic.'

Crispin snatched a glance at Abbot William, who was now smiling with folded arms and an enquiring expression.

'If it is *not* the dead rising, then it is someone

or many someones trying to make it look so. And if *that* were the case – and I'm not saying it is for certain – then these horrible someones are doing it for a purpose. But, master, what could that purpose possibly be? Murder?'

'Well, they've accomplished that. But I can't believe that was the final desired outcome of it.'

'No, that wouldn't make sense. But . . . it is a distraction.'

'Quite. Now you're using your logic, Tucker.'

'Aye, but a distraction from what?'

'From the thievery going on in the church?'

Jack snapped his fingers. 'And that's why they killed Father Bulthius.'

'Wait,' said Abbot William, frowning. 'Do you mean to say that the dead are not walking?'

'You needn't look so disappointed, my lord.'

'I am nothing of the kind, Crispin. How indelicate of you to suggest it.'

'Of course, my lord.'

'It is just that . . . well. To witness a super-natural event—'

'But surely the Devil having his say. Would you not rather witness one of God's miracles?'

The abbot huffed and dug his hands into his sleeves.

'There is the timely appearance – and disappearance – of the relic of St Modwen.'

The abbot appeared cheered by that. Crispin was relieved the relic was out of his hands at last.

'If the dead are not walking,' said Jack in a shaky voice, 'then what is *that*?'

Crispin turned to where he was pointing. Out in the misty meadow, lights bobbed.

'What *is* that?' enquired the abbot. 'Souls!'

Crispin squinted, trying to ignore the flash of gooseflesh running up his arms. 'I don't know. Let us find out.'

He bolted for the meadow. Behind him, he heard Jack swear and then the sound of his footfalls as he belatedly tried to catch up. The faint steps after *him* must have been Abbot William.

The glowing lights seemed to have a mind of their own; bobbing, weaving, floating just above the tall grasses, like lost souls wandering the countryside. Revenants? Was Crispin wrong? *Were* they souls wandering free, looking to suck the blood of the innocent?

With renewed courage, he surged forward into the meadow. The grass tugged at his stockings, and the hem of his cloak snagged on brambles, but he pushed through. But no matter how far into the meadow he went, the lights seemed just as far away . . . until they suddenly winked out.

He stopped, the abbot and Jack crashing through the brambles and may bushes behind him with their clumsy gaits.

'Where'd they go?' hissed Jack, coming to a stop beside Crispin.

He scanned the dark meadow. 'I can see nothing now.'

'That was most extraordinary,' huffed the abbot, clearly out of breath.

'Was it the revenants?' asked Jack. He straightened, seeming to gird himself. 'Or . . . those that would make us *think* it was revenants?'

Crispin looked back at the now distant church, a black silhouette against the still faded blue horizon. 'Dammit!' He hit the ground running again, back toward the church. He'd fallen for it. Even as he had explained to Jack, he'd still fallen for it.

The church door lay wide open, but it was the door to the cottage near the church, the rectory where the priest had lived, that also stood open. He slammed into the rectory's doorway, panting, scanning the room. Whatever goods had been in there were surely gone now. There had been plate, and some small table goods worth little, but those, too, were missing.

'Dammit!' He whirled on the sound behind him, but it was only Jack.

'Sir? What's wrong?'

'While we idled in the meadow, following fairy lights, someone has robbed the priest of his household goods.'

'The whoresons!'

Abbot William huffed and puffed as he arrived, then bent over his thighs, wheezing. 'Ho, Crispin! Let me catch my breath.'

'There's no need to hurry. The damage has been done.'

'Damage? What damage?'

Jack gestured toward the open door. 'Thievery, my lord. We were lured away. Again.'

'This is diabolical!'

'Yes,' said Crispin. He walked into the modest room and looked around. There was still streaks of light enough to see by, but it was getting darker. From what he could tell, the room was stripped. Even the bed no longer had linens.

'Perhaps it is time to speak to the gravediggers,' he said.

'I'll go with you, sir,' said Jack, pushing up his sleeves.

The abbot grabbed the only thing left: a fire poker. 'I'll stay here.' He was still breathing hard. 'I won't let them return.'

'Don't do anything rash,' Crispin warned before he marched toward the small cottage. He could see candlelight behind the shutters and smoke puffing from the chimney. If they were the culprits – and he was becoming more certain with every stride that they must be – they wouldn't have much opportunity to hide their booty.

He and Jack came up to their door, and it was Jack who pounded on it. 'Open up! The Tracker is here to talk to you two.'

They waited. Crispin listened for any sort of scrambling inside – a window opening or perhaps even an undercroft trapdoor lifting – but there was only silence.

'Try the door,' he said.

Jack grabbed the latch and it opened easily. He took one step in and gave a shout of surprise. Crispin pushed him aside and couldn't help but gasp.

They were both sitting at their single table, bodies lying limply back against the chairs, their throats exposed, showing very clearly where a blade had sliced each one.

Fifteen

Such blood. Their chests were covered with it. It pooled on the floor beneath them, still dripping from the chairs, and smelled sharply of metal. Crispin reached forward and touched their faces.

'God's blood,' he murmured. 'This was very recent. They are still warm. The blood has not separated. This might even have happened while we were distracted in the meadow.'

Jack turned a white face to Crispin. 'I'll go check on Abbot William.'

'Go!'

Jack fled from the doorway. Crispin glanced about the small, one-room cottage. He knew that thieves were not all like the gentle Jack Tucker, innocently taking only what they needed to survive. Most were bloodthirsty, for the penalty if caught was steep, and their greed was never sated, no matter how much they stole. How much had the church goods amounted to? Well, the chalice, paten, and ciborium were likely silver, as were the candlesticks. They would be quite valuable and portable enough. And worth killing for, he supposed. But if that were the case, why this dragging it out over many days? And why so brutal a dispatching of Father Bulthius? Had he caught the thieves in the act?

Of course, Crispin had suspected the thieves

were the gravediggers, but their own slit throats belied that.

Something more cruel and dark was going on than just robbery.

And the graves were opened, and many bodies of the saints which slept arose. But those were not saints who arose, he thought. They were demons who murdered and sucked the blood from animals and perhaps these two . . .

Or was it as he surmised? That something else was happening, for surely God wouldn't allow the raising of the dead in this little parish that even the bishop of London did not care to reconsecrate.

He needed more evidence. He poked into the shelves that only contained a small sack of flour, a wedge of cheese, and a bowl of eggs. A coffer held little but ragged clothing. There was nothing of any worth, at least on the surface. But Crispin had been schooled by his own apprentice and erstwhile thief, and so he moved carefully about the room, testing the floorboards with his boot. He dropped to his knees to pull at the squeakier ones, but there were no hiding places in the floor. He ran his hands methodically over the walls, checking with particular care by the timbers, but there was no secret hiding place there either. Whatever it is they might have had in the cottage was certainly gone now.

Footsteps at the door. The stark faces of Jack and Abbot William peered inside.

'Jack—'

'I know,' he said wearily. 'Go fetch the sheriffs.'

* * *

211

It was Crispin's lot to always await the sheriffs, just as it seemed to be Jack's to retrieve them. Instead of waiting inside where the bodies were, he leaned on the wall outside the gravediggers' cottage, arms folded. The night had taken away the warmth of the day, and he found himself missing his cloak and hood.

Shadworth reined in his horse first and, for a man of his girth, sprang off the saddle and landed lightly before Crispin like a much younger man, glaring at him with a hint of scorn. 'You've found more victims, Master Guest.'

'Believe me, Lord Sheriff, I had no intentions one way or the other.'

'What? Oh, of course. But . . . dammit, Guest. You haven't solved the thing yet.'

'It is regrettable.'

'Damn well is.'

'Don't talk to him,' scowled Sheriff Vaunere, climbing down from the saddle. 'That's your problem, John. You're always talking to Guest. You'll get very little out of him.'

'Is that true, Master Guest? Will you tell us nothing?'

'Only because I have discovered nothing, my lord.'

'But . . .' He huffed a sigh and leaned into the doorway. 'By the mass.' He shuddered and crossed himself. 'I entreat you, Henry, don't look.'

'I must look. I'm the sheriff.'

He stuck his head in the doorway and just as quickly lurched away. 'God's wounds.' With a hand pressed to his chest, he breathed in tremulous gulps of air.

212

Shadworth moved into the room and looked the corpses over. 'That's nasty work, isn't it?'

Crispin, rocking on his heels, nodded. 'Indeed.'

'Do you suspect anyone?'

'Not as yet, Lord Sheriff.'

'Well?' He tore his gaze away from the ripped throat of the young Hal and glared at Crispin. 'What's taking so long?'

Crispin narrowed his eyes and turned his face away. 'These things sometimes take some time.'

'We haven't got time. I'm sure the coroner would not like us to take more time.'

'If I could hurry the process, my lord, I assure you, I would.'

Shadworth smiled and tangled his fingers with the long necklace at his chest. 'Why, of course you would. Your methods have always fascinated me. What is it you plan to do now?'

If only he knew. He configured his face to a neutral pose. 'I will . . . think on it. May I go now, Lord Sheriff?'

'Go? Now? I just got here.'

'And you can await the coroner. He knows well where to find me. It is time I get home to my bed. The abbot of Westminster is staying with me. I can't keep him up too late.' He saluted Shadworth in the doorway, and another to Vaunere leaning against his horse and trying not to vomit. Without waiting for him to speak further, he darted away to where Jack was standing with the abbot.

'Come, gentlemen. Home is calling,' he said hastily, urging them onward.

They walked into the night. Crispin wanted to

213

walk more briskly for the cold, but remembered that Abbot William wasn't up to the pace.

'I fear my presence here is no longer necessary,' said the abbot when they were in sight of the Shambles.

'Nonsense, my lord. You are a welcomed guest. And would you not stay to see the truth of it?'

'This is a game for a younger man. I think that tomorrow I shall fetch my horse and return to Westminster.'

Jack stepped up and took the abbot's arm. 'Are you certain, my lord? You wouldn't like to witness the outcome? I can tell Master Crispin is on the scent.'

'What are you talking about, boy?' Crispin hitched his belt. 'I'm nothing of the kind. I am still as perplexed as the next man.'

Jack laughed and elbowed the abbot, who turned to him with an amused expression. 'He's nothing like the "next man",' said Jack.

Crispin watched as the two talked in conspiring tones before him. They reached Crispin's lodgings and opened the door.

Isabel, who was sitting by the fire as they entered, stood to face them, a stern look on her face. 'Master Crispin,' she said in a severe tone. 'You did not tell me the truth.'

'The truth?' It was very strange to be reprimanded by a slip of a girl and to feel a disquieting sense of guilt because of her righteous anger. 'What are you talking about?'

'I *thought* you said you would take the relic away.'

He turned to his fellows with arms open. 'I did. They are my witnesses.'

Her face suddenly lost all its rosiness. She turned toward the shelves and raised a shaking finger. 'Then what is that?'

They all turned, and Jack gasped.

On the shelf, behind some candleholders and a stack of thick white candles, was the red cow of St Modwen.

Sixteen

'This can't be happening,' whispered Crispin.

Abbot William crossed himself. Jack seemed too thunderstruck to even try. 'You saw that!' said Jack. He turned a wild eye to both Crispin and the abbot. 'You saw that! It wasn't there before and now it is!'

Crispin stared. 'It appears . . . that St Modwen would not be in the Horne house any longer.'

'Blessed Virgin,' Jack murmured, crossing himself several times.

'This is most extraordinary, Master Guest.'

'Yes. I must admit. It is.' He studied it from a distance, reluctant to touch it. 'It seems the saint knows some mischief is afoot in that household and does not wish to be present for it.' He glanced at the abbot. 'What should I do with it now?'

'It is a most miraculous thing, Crispin. But it has come to you, and to you it must remain. At least for the moment.'

Crispin shook his head. 'Not I.'

'But you have been chosen. You must forget what you think you know . . . Beware of what you find . . .'

Crispin was no longer surprised that Abbot William uttered the same last words as his predecessor Abbot Nicholas. For Crispin suspected something otherworldly was behind it anyway, despite his deep-seated skepticism.

216

'But Abbot William,' pleaded Isabel, 'is it right and proper to leave it in my kitchen?'

'My dear, St Modwen was a maid, and well understood the chores of women. I think it not only proper, but a comfort to you, especially in your condition.'

She absently rubbed her belly and bit her lip. 'Oh. I didn't think of that.'

'Yes. We sometimes forget that the saints were men and women special to God by their devotion and sacrifice. But like us, nonetheless. They are our friends and helpers as well. And since the saint has chosen to reside there, I see no reason to gainsay her.' He turned to Crispin with a beatific expression. 'I think this is a very great honor to you, Master Guest.'

Crispin couldn't help but feel it was anything but. He refrained from saying so.

Isabel tried to go about her domestic duties as the others sat quietly before the fire. As the night wore on, the others began moving toward their beds. It was then that Crispin realized he would be sleeping in the same room with it.

Isabel had situated the footstool and fur for him in his chair, but he paced instead, glancing now and again at the inconspicuous red cow nestled by the candles.

'This is foolish of you,' he said to the cow once he was alone. 'To come here like this. What are you thinking? What is so wrong with Clementia Horne?'

He did not expect an answer – hoped he wouldn't get one, to be perfectly honest – but glared at the thing nonetheless.

After a long pause with clenched muscles, he suddenly relaxed and fell into his chair. He tented his fingers, pressing them against his mouth as he brooded, still staring at the shadowed object.

He studied it for a long time, before he heaved a great, trembling sigh. 'Can you help me?' he asked gruffly, breath feathering over his nails. 'My son . . . I've only just discovered him. Should I lose him now? I promise not to vex him. I promise . . . to stay away. If only he could live.'

Tears. He hadn't realized he'd shed them until he tasted their tracks. He dropped his hands to his thighs. 'I'm a pitiful man, I know. Blasphemous. Disrespectful. Dishonorable. I've made many mistakes. But I . . . I always *meant* well . . .'

The room seemed to fall into a hush. Even the fire had calmed to glowing embers. Wisping smoke curled up the chimney without a sound. No bird or mouse marred the silence. No creaking beam or settling furniture dared be heard.

The cow's painted eye seemed to watch Crispin, even as the shadows deepened around it. 'If I only knew how to help him, how to find the true murderer. Can you help me at all?'

The embers flickered, the smoke rose. The shadows wavered with the firelight. But nothing else. No thunderclap. No mysterious and comforting voices. It was as he suspected. He'd be on his own to figure it out. But with so little time left.

He thought again of those lights deep in the meadow. Were they there now? Were they only a distraction, as he had told Jack, or were they the souls of the lost, lifting from the graveyard out of unconsecrated soil?

He glanced upstairs, saw a candle still lit. Should he grab Jack to go with him? Just as he thought it, the candle snuffed out. Well, that was that. The man had a wife heavy with child. Let them have their evening together. He'd go it alone.

He crept through his own house and grabbed his hood and cloak, and eased open the front door. Gyb, his black and white cat, stood on the step, flicking his raised tail at Crispin as he sauntered over the threshold like a lord. Crispin gave him an admiring smirk. 'Why is it I feel *you* own *me*?' he pondered, allowing the cat to pass, before closing the door softly behind him.

Out into the street of the Shambles, the night lay soft and blue, without even a breeze to accompany him. He thought little of the Watch as he made his way toward St Modwen's, passing closed shutters and barred doors. The lilting song from a rebec behind the shuttered windows of an inn told of the merry-making of travelers getting acquainted, of hoist cups and camaraderie. But it did not cause a feeling of emptiness as it once had. He now had comrades, family at home . . . that he had left behind without any sort of note, he suddenly reminded himself. Should his investigations go awry, would Jack know where to find him?

He convinced himself it was so, and never slowed his pace.

It wasn't long until he saw the church, like a

stump against the sky. Its windows were all dark. The small hut where the gravediggers had lived was also silent and vacant. Poor little church. Poor St Modwen, so unloved that even a small relic gone missing again would cause nary a stir. Of course, Crispin knew where it was, and if he knew anything of relics – and God help him he did – then he knew it was in perfect contentment on his kitchen shelf. 'Foolish, St Modwen,' he chided into the night.

He opened the lychgate to the little parish and passed through the covered entrance. He could not help but sweep his gaze over the most recent of graves and was pleased to find them undisturbed. But of course they were, he admonished himself. The dead were not rising. That was merely a tale told to keep the nosey away. Even Bishop Braybrooke had said as much, that rumors of the dead rising had kept the prayerful from the church. And now it had come to its diabolical conclusion when the priest himself had been murdered.

He rounded the church and looked out toward the meadow. Faint lights bobbed out in the distance, and this time he had no fear in following them.

Stalking out into the wet meadow, his cloak sweeping beside him with each long stride, he was assured by the night that he would not be immediately seen. When he got to the middle of the meadow, he crouched low, for he could now plainly see that the lights were lanterns held by men with staffs in their hands.

'Be still, Bill,' said one to the other.

The other nodded his squared head. '*You* be still, Fred. You're the one making so much noise that I cannot hear what might be in the traps. Ah! Here is one. A fine fox it is, too.'

'A fine red one, aye. That pelt will make us a pouchful of coins.'

'Better than them coneys, to be sure.'

'Not to mention the deer. That was a surprise.'

'The king's deer for our table,' said Bill. 'Aren't we eating like lords these days?'

'But poachers always come to a bad end,' said Crispin, rising from a clump of sheltering grasses.

The poachers aimed their staffs at him. 'Who goes there?' cried Fred in a harsh bark.

'No one but the Tracker of London.'

Their eyes widened under their lantern light. 'What would you be wanting from us?' demanded Bill, adjusting his grip on his staff. His eyes darted around them, looking for possible companions.

'I should haul the both of you to the sheriffs. And you'd hang, wouldn't you, for poaching the king's game?'

Their rough faces, lit by their hanging lanterns, contorted and frowned. Bill gestured with his staff. 'You have no call to be doing that, Master Guest. We haven't done you or yours no harm. We're just making a living as best we can.'

'True that,' said Fred. 'It isn't as if we were cutting purses, or bludgeoning the innocent over the head, is it? It's just a little game. The king will scarce miss a rabbit or two. Or even this fox. It's dead anyway.'

221

'You well know that's not the point.' Crispin had not bothered to draw his dagger. He wondered how long it would take these two rustics to figure out that there were two of them, and one of him. He crossed his arms over his chest. 'I did find the remnants of your snare earlier. It wasn't too hard to find you and evidence of your presence. However, I have a mind to overlook this completely . . . if you can give me some honest answers to my query.'

Fred cocked his head. 'Eh? What is it you want, then? One of our rabbits?'

'I don't take ill-gotten gains. And I don't take bribes. No, all I need is information.'

They exchanged questioning looks with one another.

Before they could form a thought, he rushed in with, 'Your lanterns. Do you go out often among these fields? Last night, for instance.'

Bill licked his thick lips. His face was covered in uneven stubble. 'Aye. We done that. A few nights running. Looking at our traps.'

'Did you, by any chance, see any queer doings at St Modwen's yonder?'

They stretched to look over his shoulder toward the little church. Fred shook his head. 'Queer doings? What would that be?'

'Figures walking through the graveyard . . . and beyond.'

'"Figures"? I don't know your meaning, Master Crispin. What "figures" would that be?'

He took a deep breath and plunged on. 'It is rumored that the dead walk at night from St Modwen's churchyard.'

222

They both took a staggering step back. 'What?' cried Bill. 'I never seen the like. Is it true?'

Fred wiped at his face, looked back at the church, and then squared with Crispin again. A weak smile stole over his face. 'Ah now. Master Guest is having us on, isn't he, Bill? There isn't no such thing, is there, Master Guest?'

Crispin shrugged. 'It is only a rumor. I would know if it is true.'

Seeming to feel more at ease, Fred commiserated with Bill, thumbing back at Crispin. 'The Tracker is jesting with us. He's testing us.'

Bill gave a quaking laugh. 'That's all it is. I don't suppose you'd come back to our camp and have an ale with us? We have a skin or two with some fine stock. Paid for it with coin and all,' he hurried to add. 'I'll wager you have many a tale to tell, eh?'

'You don't live in yon cottage?' He gestured toward the dark house at the outskirts of the meadow.

They both looked, though they probably well knew what he referred to. 'Naw. That cottage isn't ours. I hear tell it belongs to some foreigner. He don't bother us and we don't bother him.'

'Foreigner?'

'Name of Oliver.'

'Surname?'

'Didn't catch no surname.' He shuffled, still keeping a tight grip on his staff in such a way that he'd have the best advantage if he decided to cosh Crispin on the head with it. 'Now, er, are we free to go about our business? Like you said.'

'One thing more. Has anyone by chance hired you to kill local livestock – say a goose or goat or two – and leave them for dead in their yards?'

'Us?' Bill's face molded into incredulity. 'Why would we do such a thing?'

'For money.' Crispin reached into his coin pouch and flipped a silver penny into the air and caught it again. 'Like this one. And a few more besides. They might have discovered you as I have, and asked you to do such a deed for a few coins.'

Fred rubbed his oversized jaw, watching the coin rise and fall as Crispin tossed it. 'Let us say, for the sake of argument, mind,' said Fred, 'that such a thing transpired.'

'Fred!' hissed Bill.

Fred waved him off. 'Just supposin'.'

Crispin continued to toss the coin and catch it. 'Just supposing. That they saw you out in this field and, in fact, paid you to continue your rounds with your lanterns at twilight and to extinguish them if you caught sight of anyone stumbling toward you. And I further suppose that you were paid to do as I said, to slit the throats of those animals and leave them for dead. What would that cost me to know?'

'We got sixpence for it,' said Fred.

'Shut your gob, Fred!' said Bill.

'But I'll give you a shilling.'

Both men froze. 'Master Guest,' said Bill in a hushed tone. 'Would you truly?'

Crispin replaced the penny with a shilling coin, tossing it and catching it. It was part of the money the sheriff had paid him, but it would be worth

224

it to know. 'I do not lie, gentlemen. Surely you have heard that about me.'

They both stepped back and whispered furiously to one another behind their hands. Crispin waited, tossing the coin up, and smoothly catching it again.

Fred moved forward again, eyes shining, lips parted, staring at the coin. 'And for the shilling, what would we do, sir?'

'Tell me who hired you.'

They commiserated with looks again and seemed to silently agree. It was Bill who raised an arm and pointed back toward the cottage. 'Master Oliver.'

Seventeen

Crispin handed over the coin and told them to go home. 'In future, I would suggest another line of work. I might let slip to the king's guards that there was poaching going on in this meadow. And you wouldn't want to be caught, now would you?'

They saluted and bowed to him, extinguished their lamps, and tramped off through the meadow along a narrow track, hunched together over their coin.

He watched them go and was secure in the fact that he would see the strange lights here no more. And then he turned toward the cottage.

It was dark and no smoke emerged from the tilted chimney just as before. Its thatch was worn off on some spots on the roof, revealing the timbers beneath. It had looked far better from a distance than up close. He stood observing it for some time, listening carefully for any sounds from the cottage, but could detect none. There was very little to be gained from waiting about, so he marched up to the door and pounded with the fleshy part of his fist. 'Open up, Master Oliver. Show yourself.' He was little surprised when no reply came.

He tried the door but it was locked. The white rag he had seen before was absent. He walked over to the shuttered window but it, too, was barred. Should he break in? The sheriffs would not deal kindly with that, even the fawning Shadworth. He pressed his face to the shutter, scanning the room within through the crack where the shutters met. Nothing. It looked barely habitable. Though there was a table with a beaker and a wooden plate upon it. Tilting the angle of his head, he saw a pallet with a straw mattress and bed covers. Clearly someone was there but not at the moment. Could the poachers have lied to him? The sparkle in their eyes when they saw the coin seemed to say otherwise. Though Nesta was known to cavort with her sweetheart, one by the name of Oliver.

Crispin sighed. Looking up into the night sky with its sprinkling of stars, he decided he'd worked out enough mysteries for tonight, and headed home.

The quiet streets of London were a comfort. No one to trouble him. Not even a dog or cat. He could ruminate on the problem of Horne's murder and the foolish notion of revenants without interruption.

When he arrived on his doorstep, he was careful to make as little noise as possible. What an odd sensation to realize the number of people he sheltered under his roof. It was so trivial a thing in his day as Baron of Sheen, for many were housed in his manor: servants, guests. But a houseful under his current circumstances was, he supposed, more . . . noticeable. And soon another, a babe to be born. Jack and Isabel had wasted no time, and why should they? They were young and hale and had their life ahead of them. What did Crispin have?

227

He let himself in and closed the door carefully. The fire was still lit, but low, and he slipped off his boots, laid his stocking feet on the footstool, threw the fur over his legs, and settled down in the chair to try to sleep.

It was hours and hours into the night. Gyb showed himself again and jumped onto Crispin's lap, curled into a bun, and slept. Absently, Crispin stroked the velvet head, the animal's purr gently vibrating over his legs. The cat soothed his racing thoughts enough for sleep at last, where he dreamed of Philippa.

When he awoke in the morning, the cat was gone, and Isabel was poking the fire with an iron rod, keeping an eye, it seemed, on the little red cow that cowered in the shadows.

'Does it speak to you?' he asked.

She wasn't startled that he had awakened. 'No. I wish it would. I always thought that relics . . . well. That they'd make you feel things. Comfort you. For me, it makes me afraid.'

'Why?'

'I don't know. What's it doing here, Master Crispin?'

'I wish I knew.'

She turned. Her hair was tucked up into her kerchief. But her eyes, usually so gentle and kind, were suddenly dark and penetrating. 'Should we be on our knees to it? Keep vigil?'

He shrugged. 'Abbot William did not instruct us thus. And so I see no reason to do so.'

She clutched the wooden spoon in her hand, pressed it to her breast. 'It came to you.'

'Perhaps.'

228

'Doesn't that . . .' She brushed her hand over her cheek, swatting at a stray lock of hair. 'Doesn't that bother you?'

He looked her in the eye. 'I . . . don't know.'

'You're a strange man.' She shook herself, coming back from her dreaminess. 'I'm sorry, Master Crispin. I shouldn't have said that.'

'I suppose it's true. Surely Jack has spoken of the many relics and strange occurrences we have encountered.'

'He has. And I only half-believed them. I don't doubt his stories now.'

'I know he sees them as some sort of sign. Some sort of message from God to me.'

'Is that what *you* think?'

He rubbed at his knuckles, warming them. 'I haven't decided. For I am not the better for them.'

'Maybe you don't see it that way. But there could be a higher purpose, one you aren't willing to admit.'

He blinked slowly and looked her over. 'Forgive me, Isabel, if *I* say, that you are a strange girl.'

She huffed a laugh, clutching the spoon in her hand but now holding it down at her side. 'I have time to think, you see. When I am at my work, I think about things.'

'A young philosopher.'

'You can't be in this house and not absorb a bit of Aristotle.'

It was his turn to chuckle. 'No, I suppose not.'

'Master Crispin,' she said after a moment, sobering. 'What will you do with it?'

He lay back and breathed, gazing at the

229

reliquary. 'That is a very good question. I suppose I might try to return it again.'

'But what if it won't stay returned?'

He blew out a sigh. 'I don't like to think about that.'

'You and Jack. You've come across a lot of relics.' She looked upward toward the stairs and the chambers above, where Jack was likely helping the abbot in his morning ablutions. 'Why, Master Crispin? Why do they always come to *you*?'

After rubbing his lids with calloused fingers, he looked up. 'It's a mystery I have yet to solve, my dear. Maybe it's one I can't.'

'I do hope you do. Before more show up.'

He raised his brows at that, hoping she was wrong. She turned back to her work, and he watched briefly before he rose and took care of his own morning wash and shave.

Dressed with sword at his hip, he waited until she was occupied, taking out the scraps to the back courtyard, before he snatched the red cow from the shelf, stuffed it in his scrip, and rushed out the front door.

He strode quickly away toward Mercery. He had to think. He didn't want the company of Jack or Abbot William slowing him down. Oh, he valued their help and suggestions, but at this particular moment he needed to be alone.

The relic bounced against his hip as he walked, reminding him all too starkly of his mission. Was this relic going to help him, or hinder him? There was no way to know. God seemed to move in mysterious ways, and his

230

saints in even more mysterious and sometimes mischievous ways. They were more like pixies than God's own.

When he reached the Walcote and Horne estates, he stopped and watched them both from across the street, under the overhang of a jettied storey. Leaning against the shop wall behind him, he crossed his arms, crooked a leg and rested a boot on the stone foundation.

According to Christopher, he had only been alone with John Horne when the man was on his last breaths. As much as the boy disliked him, Crispin couldn't see him stabbing him, and without arms practice – or even an understanding of the body – he couldn't have given him the fatal wounds. Though . . . they were at his height, just at the right place for stabbing.

'No,' he murmured. He dismissed that argument, though a juryman might well make it. The boy had merely found John Horne during his last moments.

What of Martin Chigwell?

Chigwell had said that he'd argued and then left his master, but he could have done the deed without letting on to Christopher and, because of his fear, let his friend be accused. He was of an age to well understand the circumstances and the inevitable consequences. He might very well leave Christopher to his fate. He had the means and the motive. And he knew the house like the palm of his hand.

He mentally counted him as number one.

Absently he reached into the scrip to make sure the cow was still there. He barely noticed when he took it out and turned it without thinking in his hands.

What of Robert Hull? Crispin knew of no particular grievance the man might have with his master. And it seemed unlikely. As unlikely as the maids Nesta and Clarice. But he'd still like to ask each of them once more.

That left Madam Horne.

She had argued with the deceased. Often, according to Hull. But her husband was her livelihood, and would one destroy one's livelihood so blithely? Well, the same could be said of Chigwell and Hull. Though Hull still had a house to run, even if the master was dead. Chigwell's fate was more uncertain. And Clementia Horne might very well be able to run the business for her husband. Many a wife did so. He'd even known blacksmiths' wives who carried on after their husbands were dead, swinging a hammer at the forge. It was rare, but it happened.

And where was she when Horne had died? She had argued with him earlier and disappeared, presumably to the solar or wherever it was women retreated to in that household. He'd have to talk with her as well. That would not be as easy.

He rolled the cow in his hands, and suddenly looked down at it with some surprise. He stopped and held it tightly, staring at the little, smudged window of crystal and to the small bone fragment within.

'What is it you are up to, Saint Modwen? You are trying to tell me something, are you not?' The cow did not reply, as expected. The only

232

result was his feeling foolish for talking out loud to the thing at all. But when he looked up, he noticed Nesta making her way hurriedly down the lane, away from the Horne household.

He pushed away from the wall and made haste after her.

'Nesta!' he called, and she wrenched her head around, halting.

When he neared her, she stared down at the cow in his hands with widening eyes. 'Why do you have that?' Her eyes grew wild and fearful. She took one look at his face and ran.

He stuffed the relic in his scrip and took off after her.

She was fast and nimble, skirting through the traffic of people, riders, and carts. But Crispin was just as agile, and ran up a cart and jumped off on the other side before the man on the cart could swear at him.

It wasn't long until he caught up to her, grasping her arm and yanking her back off the road.

She tried to scream and slap at his hand but he dragged her to an alley and took both her arms in a fierce grip. 'You will be silent,' he hissed.

She took a harsh, gulping breath and made no other sound.

When he was relatively certain she wouldn't bolt, he slowly released her. 'Now. Why did you run from me?'

Her eyes darted toward his hands, and slipped back up toward his gaze again. 'You had the relic.'

'You seemed surprised. Was that not part of my mission to find it?'

'But . . . I heard it was returned yesterday.'

'Yes . . . well . . . Circumstances . . .'

'H-how did you get it?' She waited, breathing hard.

'Never mind that. I have more questions for you.'

She pressed her lips together, seemed frightened. Crispin studied her. 'When you saw young Christopher Walcote in the chamber with Master Horne, did he have his knife?'

She shook herself, puzzled. 'What?'

'I said, when you saw young Walcote in your master's chamber, did he have his dagger?'

'I don't know.'

'Well *think!*'

'He had his sheath . . . but I don't recall seeing his dagger. Master Horne shook him and his dagger fell to the floor.'

Crispin's heart gave a flutter. The boy was telling the truth. Perhaps there had been just that much doubt in him, but not now. 'You saw that?'

'Yes. I reckon he never picked it up, because he ran out of the room . . . after he kicked Master Horne in the leg.'

'Where did he go from there?'

'He ran to the solar.'

'Where was Martin Chigwell?'

'He was nigh. Outside the chamber somewhere. He went in soon after Walcote left.'

'Did you see their argument?'

'Not so much. I was outside the chamber myself, but the door was open. I could see some.'

234

'You lingered to watch?'

'Well . . . I . . .'

'Never mind. Where was Madam Horne?'

She pressed a finger to her lip. She seemed to have forgotten her fear or apprehension. 'I don't rightly know, sir.'

'Surely you saw her upstairs? Didn't she have an argument earlier with Master Horne?'

She took a few steps back to lean against the wall. Restless fingers harried her apron. 'Yes, but . . . I had my own work to do. During the day, I am not much called upon to serve her. Only when she asks me to.'

'So she argued with Master Horne and left his chamber. And then where did she go?'

She shook her head. 'I don't know. I never noticed when she left. Maybe to her own chamber.' She toyed with her apron again, looking up shyly to Crispin. 'Why are you trying to prove that Christopher Walcote didn't kill him?'

'Because I am tasked with it. Do you believe he did it?'

She seemed to ponder for only a moment. 'I don't know. I just believed what the sheriffs said about it. But . . . I suppose if I did think on it, he doesn't seem like the sort of child to do such a thing.'

Pleased, Crispin tried not to show it.

She glanced hastily at his scrip, bulging with the reliquary. 'Can I go?'

'Where are you off to? The Horne household is that way.' He thumbed over his shoulder.

'I have . . . something to attend to.'

235

'Where?'

'It's none of your business.'

He said nothing. She took that as leave to go. He watched her for a time. She looked back at him to see if he was following. When she didn't look back again, he dove into the lane and quietly followed.

He almost lost her when he had to wait for a flock of geese to be coaxed out of the way by their child drover, but he saw her just leaving Tower Street and heading up to All Hallows. Clarice had mentioned that she had a sweetheart named Oliver and it would be the height of coincidence if there were two of that name. He waited for her to make any kind of turn near All Hallows Barking, but she kept going . . . toward St Modwen's.

Eighteen

She traversed through the churchyard between the stone markers and crosses. And then toward the cottage that belonged to the gravediggers. Crispin noted two new graves – probably for those two – that she passed by.

Poor devils. Buried in unconsecrated earth. Fie on Bishop Braybrooke!

She turned the corner at the church and disappeared behind it, between the church and rectory.

He slipped over the graveyard wall near the lychgate and kept low along the church, trying to avoid the windows. Carefully, he peeked around the corner. No one. He came around and then to the other side. She wasn't there. He pondered it for a moment and then saw movement in the meadow. She was heading, as he suspected, toward the small cottage at the meadow's edge.

Crispin waited in the shadow of the church and watched the small figure make its way across the grassy plain. He couldn't quite tell, but it looked to him as if she had gained entrance. Waiting a while, he came to the conclusion that she was not to emerge for some time. Should he interrupt them at their communion?

He wondered if he should wait and ultimately decided that he had lingered too long. She had spoken her piece to him. But she had seemed

237

unduly disturbed that he was in possession of the relic. Did she think he stole it? No, it was subtler than that. She seemed concerned about *where* he had got it. A strange thing to worry over for, surely, he would have got it from the Horne solar. Or did she know of another place?

Perhaps he *did* wish to interrupt her, for he also wanted to talk to this Oliver.

He set out toward the cottage, this time in the light of day. He was wary of animal traps along the way, but didn't encounter any. Why should this Oliver wish to scare people off from the churchyard with tales of revenants and glowing lights in the meadow? Was it he who had dug up the graves – no. He had hired those gravediggers to dig them up and they had lied to Crispin and paid with their lives. Yes, he had hired them to dig up the graves and perpetuate this story, even to deceiving poor Father Bulthius. Had they murdered him, too? Or had that deed fallen to this mysterious Oliver? Was Nesta an innocent dupe or an active accomplice?

With thoughts of her in Oliver's clutches, he moved faster, but when he got to the cottage, it was as shut up as it had been last night. There was no sign that Nesta had even entered the front door. It had the same growth of nasturtiums blocking the entrance.

Though again, there was a white rag tied to the front door latch.

He crept around the back to look for other entrances, but there didn't appear to be any. He looked through the haphazard shutters of another window but saw no life within.

There was certainly no choice. He'd have to break in and do his best to explain it to the sheriffs . . . should the occasion arise.

He gripped the shutters through the space between them and pulled. The wood was old and battered, and a plank came away easily. He pulled at the next one beside it and made equally short work of that too. Casting the boards aside, he climbed onto the sill and dropped inside. The place smelled musty of disuse, and there was dust on the surfaces. The beaker and plate he had seen last night were still there, and looked as if they had been in that same position for some time.

He looked about the sad room. Nothing there. No one there. Nothing to indicate that they had in fact been there for a very long while.

He kicked at the shredding rush mat along the floor. He knelt at it and lifted it away. No trapdoor.

Where had Nesta gone? He was certain – almost certain – she had entered here. As far as he knew, nothing lay beyond the cottage but Tower Hill.

He left as he had entered and checked behind the cottage just to make sure. Only a wooded area with a trail that led up to the tower. A fruitless enterprise if ever there was one. He felt slightly embarrassed with himself that he had allowed her to escape. He trudged across the meadow along a narrow path and passed by the church again, seeing nothing changed, and made his way home.

When he finally returned to the Shambles and

to his lodgings, he faced the solemn stares of Isabel, Jack, and Abbot William.

Jack jerked toward him. 'The relic is gone!'

'I know. I have it.'

'Oh, blessed mercy, Master Crispin,' he said, hand clutching his heart. 'You should have told us. Madam Tucker here was in a state.'

'Oh, Isabel. I do apologize. I am a man used to living alone.'

Jack made an indignant sound. 'Here now! What've *I* been doing these last eight years, then?'

'*Men* alone, then. And I certainly don't have to answer to you.'

Of course, the implication was that he had to answer to *her*. What a strange world his life had become!

'Crispin,' said Abbot William, shaking his head. 'All of us have been in a state. Do you have it still? The relic.'

'Yes.' He pressed his hand to the scrip and felt its presence there, felt that unpleasant tingle in his hand. 'I'd like to keep it close. For now. Jack, there is something I need to do. But this is what I'd like *you* to do.'

It was decided that Abbot William would remain at his lodgings, while Jack went to his task, and Crispin left for his own. The abbot had argued that the relic should remain with him, but Crispin had an unexplainable feeling that he couldn't trust where it might end up next, and so elected to keep it in his own scrip. He headed back toward the Horne household.

When Hull opened the door to him, he quickly

began to shut it again, but Crispin caught the door and held it. 'Why Master Hull, one would think I was not welcomed here.'

'You aren't. My mistress wishes to never see you again.'

'That's not very hospitable. Must I remind you that the sheriffs—'

'The sheriffs don't know you as I am beginning to.'

He smirked. Very likely. 'Nevertheless, I am here to investigate, and investigate I shall. Tell me. Which servant is it that used to serve Master Horne?'

Hull narrowed his eyes. 'I don't know your meaning?'

'There is a servant's alcove in his chamber. Who served there?'

'Oh. Well, alcove there is, but no one has ever served there. Master Horne was a private man.'

'No one stayed in that alcove?'

'No.'

'I desire that you take me up to his chamber, then.'

He quickly glanced toward the top of the stairs. 'Madam Horne would forbid it. She doesn't like you, Master Guest.'

'It is not required that she – or you, for that matter – like me. It is required that you obey me.'

He looked fit to burst, but he merely took a deep breath, shut his lips tight, and marched toward the stairs. Crispin followed, keeping a sharp eye out for Madam Horne.

They reached the room and Hull had to unlock

it. He pushed opened the door and stepped aside for Crispin to enter. Crispin moved into the room and scanned it from wall to wall. 'Master Hull, did you witness the body of Master Horne?'

He shuddered slightly and nodded. 'It was there.' He pointed to the same place that Clementia Horne had.

'And the boy, Christopher Walcote. Where was he?'

He moved to stand in the place that Christopher was discovered. He was before the bed but facing the door.

'Are you certain he didn't move?'

'Fairly certain. I came running first after Madam Horne began screaming. The Walcote boy seemed frozen to the spot.'

'And was he positioned as you are now? Facing the door?'

'Yes.'

Scanning the room again, Crispin noted that the alcove would have been to Christopher's back. 'That alcove. You say no servant beds there.'

'As far as I know, no one ever has. Master Horne was a private man.'

'So you said.' He strode toward the alcove, grasped the door latch, and tried to open it, but it was locked. 'Who has the key to this?'

'Only me.'

'Open it, if you will.'

He bit his lip and cleared his throat. 'Forgive me, Master Guest, but I cannot.'

Crispin fastened his most accusing glare on him. 'And why not?'

'Because . . . the key has been missing for a fortnight at least.'

'You are the keeper of the keys.'

'Yes. I . . . please don't tell my mistress.'

A household kept in fear. He relaxed his posture and nodded toward the steward. 'Have no fear of that, Master Hull. But I need to open that door.'

'But I don't have the key.'

'We won't need one. I have certain . . . skills.' He walked to the shadowed alcove, and knelt in front of the door. A locksmith had owed him a favor, and designed the tools he had long desired, no longer needing the sharpened blade of his dagger or the aiglet of his shirt's laces anymore. He took them from his money pouch and, fitting the curved, twig-like metal sticks into the lock, he used the two to manipulate the pins inside. They easily clicked into place, and he pulled the latch open.

Crispin looked back at the astonished Hull. 'I won't tell your mistress, if you won't either.'

He rose and stepped into the passage. Looking back, he saw a dark substance on the inside latch and door. 'Would you be so good as to fetch a candle for me, Master Hull?'

The man hurried to comply, grabbing one from a wall sconce in the corridor, and ran back inside the chamber with it, shielding the flame with his palm. He handed it to Crispin, who hovered the candle near the latch, swiped some of it with his finger, and sniffed. There was definitely dried blood on the latch and door. The murderer had entered from here, he was certain of it, and most

243

likely fled by the same route. He raised the candle to examine the passage.

'Do you know where this passage leads, Hull?'

He shook his head. 'I can't say I ever remember opening this door.'

'Then will you accompany me?'

The man paused for only a moment before he made a curt nod. His expression seemed to say that he had a new respect for Crispin. Crispin hoped that would remain once they got to where he believed that passage ended.

First, they traveled in a long arc, going downward, their footsteps echoing back to them in the tight quarters. But soon enough it rose again, and in the dark shadows ahead, they saw its end. They reached a similar door which was also locked. But Crispin did not immediately kneel to unlock this door. Instead, he leaned over to listen at the wood to make certain the next chamber was uninhabited.

He turned to his companion. 'And you have no idea what room this might be.'

Hull shrugged. 'The kitchens, I assumed, but . . .' He was thoughtful. 'We traveled upward again.' After a pause, he slowly shook his head. 'No, I don't know where we are.'

Crispin knelt and performed the same work on this lock as he had the other, and when the door latch clicked, he hesitated opening the door. He kept close to it and peered through the jamb as he opened it only a slice.

'What is it?' whispered Hull. 'Where are we?'

'I can't be certain,' Crispin whispered back, 'but I surmise . . .' He opened the door wider.

A chamber nearly as large and as well-appointed as John Horne's.

The steward stood at his back and peered in with widened eyes. 'It is Madam Horne's room,' he said faintly.

Nineteen

Hull was silent as they entered carefully. Once Crispin established that no one was there, he stood in the archway of an identical alcove to the first, and surveyed the room. Looking back, he did not see blood on the door or latch.

'As I suspected. She came through the passage to his room from this one. I surmise that she stole the key from you some weeks ago, with this very intent.'

'To kill my master?'

'Oh yes. For you said they argued at length and for some years.'

'Yes, but it doesn't follow that—'

'Do you think a wife cannot stew and plot, Hull?'

'Well . . . I never much thought about it, but—'

'Christopher Walcote was a convenience. A very handy one. It could just as easily have been put upon Martin Chigwell . . . or you.'

'No. I . . . I refuse to believe it.'

'She made her way through this passage, after having secured the key. How she must have plotted. And when she found young Walcote's dagger upon the floor, she saw her way through to it. She picked it up, caught Master Horne unawares, I imagine, and stabbed him fatally in the back. He must have turned and she gave him one final blow. She left the knife and escaped through the door by which she had come. She likely planned to lock it again, but she heard someone come in. Young Walcote. She heard their brief exchange, heard her husband fall to the floor for the last time, and burst through this door. She left blood upon the inside of the latch. Perhaps later she thought to clean the front of the latch, but not the inside. When she came in, the blood on her hands could be easily explained as she held her dead husband.'

'But I don't understand. Why didn't Young Master Walcote say he saw her there?'

'He told me she "suddenly appeared". But he was facing the door to the chamber. And she didn't enter from there. He would have plainly seen her if she had. She entered from behind him, and indeed, she would seem to have "suddenly" appeared.'

'My God.'

'Do you see the truth of it, Hull? Will you help me or hinder me?'

'She is my mistress . . . but . . . the boy. He is innocent. Should he hang for her?'

'That is the question you must ask yourself, Hull. Are you loyal to your murdering mistress . . . or to God?'

He crossed himself. It seemed that he had decided.

'Where is your mistress now?'

'I . . . I . . .'

He grabbed the man by his forearms. 'Have courage, Hull! Where is she?'

'Likely in the solar. Praying to that damned relic.'

Crispin left him. Surely, she would have noticed by now that it was missing again.

He strode down the corridor to the solar and cast open the door.

She was at a prie-dieu before the empty niche where the reliquary had been. But instead of ranting and raving as he might have expected, she was shaking her head. 'I don't understand it,' she was saying, oblivious as to who had entered. Crispin guessed that she assumed it was a maid or other servant.

'What, madam?' said Hull, coming up behind Crispin.

'It's gone again, Robert. The relic. St Modwen. I think . . . I think she is angry with us.'

'When there is sin in the household, then I suppose that is true.'

She angled her body away from her prayer book atop the prie-dieu and looked behind her. 'Oh. There is that very troublesome Crispin Guest.'

'Yes, madam. With your permission, I will have Master Hull send a servant for the sheriffs.'

She huffed and pushed herself to her feet. 'And why is that?'

'Because they will come to arrest you for the murder of your husband.'

A pause, before her face reddened. 'Get out of my house.'

'I'm afraid I can't do that.'

'You . . . you have the gall to accuse me . . .'

'I think you have plotted a long time for this, for your opportunity.'

She turned her glare on Hull. 'And you! You're helping him? Why? Why would you do such a foolish, foolish thing? Risking your position and your oaths to serve this family.'

Hull's face was awash with tears and he shook his head. 'I would see justice done.'

'Justice? What would you know of justice? What would you know what was in my heart? Or my soul?'

He shook his head again and remained silent.

She raised her chin and looked down her nose at Crispin. 'Where is your proof?'

'You obtained the key to the passage door that connects your husband's room to yours, and there you—'

'Key? Passage? What on earth are you talking about?'

The merest of shivers passed up between his shoulder blades. Perhaps it was her tone. Oh, some had lied to him. Convincingly, but not many. He suspected she was lying now. Only . . . there was something in her tone.

'The passage between your rooms, in the servant's alcove.'

She frowned. 'That door doesn't open. It hasn't opened for over twenty years.'

'We did go through it, madam,' said Crispin, 'just now, and found blood on the door *inside* the passage.'

Her indignation turned to shock, and she felt behind her for the prie-dieu to steady herself. 'Robert, is this true?'

He wiped his nose and gulped back a sob. 'Yes, madam.'

249

'And you think *I* did it?'

Crispin stepped forward in front of Hull. 'Yes.'

'Blessed *Jesu*,' she said quietly, crossing herself. 'While it is true my husband was an adulterer and a scold, he was still . . . my husband. I could not have killed him.'

'Christopher Walcote was facing the door to the chamber when he said you "suddenly appeared", but he did not see you enter, could not have seen you enter. And so I surmised you came from the alcove—'

'And that is your proof?' Her shock fell away, replaced by anger again. 'The boy was obviously confused. He had just murdered my husband! Perhaps he was not in his right mind. I came in from the chamber door. Nothing else is possible.' She clasped her hands before her. 'Bring your sheriffs. I will tell them what an incompetent fool they have trusted in you, Crispin Guest.'

'I will prove it, madam.'

'How? I swear by Almighty God, by the bones of the blessed Saint Modwen herself, that I did not kill my husband. I have been a good and faithful Christian woman. A loyal wife to my husband, a gentle mistress to my household. Tell me, Robert,' she said, facing him, 'do you truly think me capable? After all the years you have known me?'

He looked down at the floor and considered. His puzzled expression was concerning. If Crispin was to convince the sheriffs, he needed the corroboration of this servant. 'Well, Hull?' he urged.

Slowly, he shook his head. 'Master Guest, what

250

seemed a miserable certainty before, does not seem so now.'

Damn the man. And damn himself, for he was beginning to feel the same way. He closed his hands into fists. 'You could have obtained the key from Hull's key ring and gone through the passage. You found the boy's dagger on the floor, you picked it up—'

'How could I have obtained the key from Robert's ring of keys? He wears it at all times.'

A sinking feeling overtook Crispin. 'I take it, Master Hull, that you are never without your keys.'

'Never, sir. Even when I go to my rest, the keys are at my bedside. And they make a terrific noise when moved. Madam would never enter my quarters. Indeed, I doubt she has ever been there . . . or knows where they are.'

Crispin glared from one to the other. His carefully cultivated plot was unraveling before his eyes. She *could* be lying. And so could Hull. But the more he listened, and felt their confident tones, the more he doubted it himself. He walked in a circle and slammed his fist to the wall. '*Someone* has come through that alcove passage.'

'Are you still accusing me?' she asked, unafraid, it seemed.

He looked her over, and could not say with certainty now that she was guilty. 'No, madam,' he muttered.

'Very well. You may leave. And Robert, I have much to say to you.'

He hung his head. It was Crispin's fault that the man might lose his situation. And yet, was

251

it possible that the man was lying to Crispin? That he hadn't lost the keys, but deliberately got rid of them only after using them for the murder?

Grasping at straws, he told himself. 'Do not take out your anger on Master Hull,' said Crispin aloud. 'He was reluctant and I convinced him. A loyal servant he is, and loyal to God.'

Her stern face was unmoved, and Crispin backed slowly out of the room. He stood in the gallery and looked below to the entry floor, its chequy tiles, the tapestries on the walls and finery. And none of it could spare the household its sorrows and its sorrows to come.

What of Nesta? He had only briefly spoken to her. What reason would *she* have had to kill the master? If he had been toying with her, promised her things he had no intention of fulfilling, that could make a woman angry enough. But such a thing would be a crime of the blood, of passion, and done at the moment. The passage was part of this crime – the blood proved that much. And it meant planning. It meant stealing the keys from Hull, and that would require access that would not be suspicious. Certainly the maids could go everywhere, just as Hull could go every-where. Who else could go to as many places in the household?

Someone was walking across the floor below. Crispin noticed it out of the corner of his eye, and he glanced down. Martin Chigwell was carrying on his duties, a roll of cloth under his arm going on to God knew where.

It fell into place like a pin in a lock. Martin had a key.

'Chigwell!' he called.

Martin stopped and looked upward, eyes finding Crispin. Maybe there was a look on Crispin's face, betraying his intentions. Whatever it was, Martin's face lost all color; he dropped the cloth, and ran.

'Dammit!' Crispin scrambled to get down the stairs, leaping down the steps. He grabbed the railing when he reached the bottom and spun toward the door out of which Martin had exited. He cast open the door and found himself in a courtyard. He scanned through the hedges, the trees, the flowering shrubs, the walkways, but didn't see him. Then he heard a scrapping and grunting near the wall. He hurried through and found the boy making his way over the top. He grabbed his leg and yanked. Martin tumbled to the ground and struggled to rise. Crispin pulled his sword and aimed the point at the boy's chest. Martin froze, staring at the blade.

Tears veiled his reddened eyes and he breathed hard through his mouth. 'I'm sorry. I'm sorry.'

Crispin trembled with rage. 'You swore to me.'

'I'm sorry.'

'You *swore* to me. Then you lied to me. You would have let your friend *die* for what *you* did!'

'Have mercy, Master Guest.' He wiped carelessly at his face with his sleeve. 'I'm not brave like Christopher. And . . . not as honorable, I guess.'

Crispin crouched low, the sword still aimed at the boy's chest. 'You stole the key to the passage.'

His eyes widened. 'How did you . . .?' He licked his lips and hung his head. 'You know all, then, if you know that. I planned it for some time. He was such a miserable man. He said the most awful things about Christopher's mother. And about me.' He snuffled, choking on his own snot.

'And?'

He wiped his face again. 'I stole Master Hull's key. I was often in his rooms. We spoke of this and that. As an apprentice, it was part of my job to know what the steward did and what were the doings of the house. That's what Master Horne told me. I found out about the passage. I got the key off Master Hull's key ring. So easily. He never noticed. He was even in the room with me. I kept it for a long time. Then, on that day, Master Horne was a beast to me as usual. I decided it would be that day. I went in from the mistress's room and through the passage. But before I opened the door, I heard him berating Christopher. He made me so angry. And once I heard that Christopher had left, I carefully opened the door. He was alone. And I saw the dagger on the floor. And I . . . I . . . took it up and stabbed him. He was so surprised. But he deserved it.' Martin had begun to cry again. 'God have mercy, but he deserved it. And I dropped the knife. I thought Master Hull would find him, or even the mistress. I didn't know it would be Christopher or that he would be blamed. I didn't know what to do!'

'Confess. That would have helped.'

'I didn't want to die.'

'Then what happened?'

'I . . . I went through the door and escaped

254

through to the mistress's room. But I saw the blood I'd left on the door latch. I wiped it off with my apron. And it was then I realized that I must have done the same in my master's room. I dared not go back, and by then I heard the mistress screaming. It was when everyone was rushing through that I was able to get in and wipe it clean. I burned the apron.' He stared at the blade and then up at Crispin. 'Do you have to tell, Master Guest?'

'And leave Christopher Walcote to die for you? What do *you* think?'

He pressed his hand to his mouth and sobbed.

A maid screamed. Crispin glanced over his shoulder. 'Shut your mouth, girl,' he growled. 'Get Master Hull at once.'

He had liked Martin Chigwell. And Christopher liked and trusted him. And under any other circumstances, he might have found a way for the boy to escape. But someone had to stand on the gallows and it wasn't going to be his son.

Justice was justice. It wasn't a pretty thing. It was often messy and unpleasant. But it had to be so.

And yet, even as he sorrowed for Martin and a young life soon to be cut short by the hangman's noose, he couldn't help but cheer that his son would live. But even that satisfaction was brief for, in telling the Walcote family, it would be the last time he talked to Philippa. He vowed, for the boy's sake, that he would never see him or her again. There was no other way forward.

When the sheriffs arrived, Crispin explained it all, even as Martin continued to weep, but in the end, he nodded when asked if he were guilty. All through his explanation, Shadworth kept a sharp eye on Crispin. When the bailiffs took Chigwell away amid the weeping servants, the sheriff accosted Crispin by laying a hand on his arm.

'By the saints, Master Guest. You found the killer. Such a shame. I'm sure the boy had great promise.'

'But no loyalty,' said Crispin bitterly, 'to his master or his friend.'

Shadworth shook his head. 'You are a marvel. A marvel!'

'John,' said Sheriff Vaunere disgustedly, 'if you are done fawning over Guest here, are you ready to depart?'

He sighed. 'Yes, I suppose I am. Well done, Master Guest.'

Crispin bowed. Vaunere made a sound of revulsion and led the way out the door. Shadworth paused, holding the jamb as he looked back at Crispin. 'Were I a maid I would fair swoon away at your gifts, Master Crispin. You've earned your wage. Oh! Have I paid you enough?' He reached for his pouch, but Crispin, in a hurry to get away, waved him off.

'I'm certain you did, my lord.'

'Well then. I hope we can work together again, Master Crispin, before my time as sheriff is done.' He puffed up like a grouse and stomped out of the entry.

Crispin turned to go himself, stepping out over

256

the threshold and standing in the courtyard . . . when he was stopped by Clarice the maid.

She hurried to his side, clutching her apron in her fumbling hands. 'Master Guest, did this have to be so? Martin was such a good lad.'

'He's a murderer. He plotted and planned it, and when his friend was accused he stayed silent. Your definition of "good" seems lacking.'

Her fingers touched her lips. 'Oh, I suppose. It's just that . . .'

'You liked him.' Crispin scowled. He'd liked the lad, too. Sometimes he hated his vocation.

Clarice began again. 'I was afraid to tell anyone. Afraid to tell Master Hull.'

'About the murder? Did you know—'

'No, no. None of that. It's just that Nesta has gone. She said she was leaving London for good with that Noll.'

Noll? Oh yes. Noll was short for Oliver. Was Nesta his accomplice after all? 'How much do you know of this man?'

'Nothing. She'd speak so little about him. Only that his brother was a cleric nearby, but nothing of his worth, his prospects, or even his vocation. I'm worried. Such secretive behavior from her is not right. I can only think the worst, that he asked her to be silent on his matters.'

He mulled over her words, but his mind was too concerned with getting to the Walcotes. 'It happens that I am investigating . . . er, somewhat around that area. I will make further enquiries.' He pivoted, but then turned back. 'Do you believe she might be in danger?'

She balled up the hem of her apron tightly. 'I

257

don't know, Master Guest. But I fear it. It doesn't feel right. I've known Nesta since we were children. We look after each other. I would never forgive myself if something happened to her and I could have done something to help her. If I'd only known what Martin was planning, I could have stopped him. We haven't been good at being our brother's keeper, have we, Master Guest?'

He squeezed her hand and hastily gave her further reassurance before he quickly left her behind. When he passed through the gate, he glanced back, and Clarice was still watching him.

He hurried to the Walcotes' gate. He had both good news and unpleasant. Perhaps he only had to face the good news, and Christopher could be told later of the bad. For he was a coward, too, when it came to his son. He hadn't the heart to tell him about Martin Chigwell.

The steward fetched him into the parlor, but Crispin paused in the doorway, surprised. There, the whole family awaited him.

He girded himself and stepped in, eyes sweeping carefully over Philippa, who was leaning toward him with her lips parted and her eyes wide. Clarence stood beside her, his hand clutching his belt nervously. And Christopher, sullen, brooding, didn't look at him at all but was instead tossing small sticks into the fire.

'Master Guest,' said Clarence breathlessly. 'What news? We saw the sheriffs' men on the lane . . .'

'The news is good, Master Walcote. The true murderer was found and confessed. Christopher is free of all suspicion.'

Philippa cried out, and looked as if she would run to him, but he took a step back. It seemed to snap her out of it, and instead she turned toward Christopher, and much to his chagrin, she grabbed him into an embrace.

He batted at her, even as he acknowledged her kisses as the dutiful son he was. 'Mother, please. Not in front of Master Guest.'

Crispin hid his grin by bending his head toward his chest. He was unnaturally elated. At the same time, he held himself in check. He watched the boy carefully, surreptitiously. He would not see him again. Not in this life. And he cherished the moment, memorizing his features, still amazed at how much they were a mirror of his own.

And then there was Philippa. Flushed and pink with pleasure, cheeks bright and wet from tears, she was never more beautiful. How he longed to take her in his arms. With an ache in his heart so deep that it wiped the smile from his face, he took another step back, intending to quit the room and leave them to their celebrations.

He was brought out of his musings as Clarence gathered him in an awkward embrace before setting him loose and pumping his hand. There were tears in the man's eyes.

'We can't thank you enough, Guest. I owe you my life for my son's, at the very least.'

Crispin lowered his gaze from the man. Here was Clarence gushing at him, and all Crispin could think about was cuckolding the man. He muttered a prayer of strength.

'And to think how I hated you at one time,' said Clarence. 'Oh, it was only a matter of

259

moments and so long ago. For it was you who discovered that my brother Lionel murdered that man who had taken Nicholas's place. Though Lionel was never a very kind man. You might even call him cruel.' He turned to Philippa. 'My dear wife said that this Nicholas imposter had been kind to her, for all his deceit.' He chucked her chin. She gave him a cautious smile. 'Still, that whole business was very queer, and certainly convoluted, yet you managed to reckon it out, didn't you, Guest?'

'Yes. It was a puzzle.'

'By Jehovah, you are good at puzzles. And a good thing, too. You saved my son.' He wiped a tear from his eye and Crispin choked back his own. For he was pleased to save the life of his son, and content that Clarence thought the boy was his own. His future was secure.

Yet. Something in the back of his mind concerned him. Something Clarence had said that seemed to mesh with something Clarice had mentioned. 'Master Walcote, in those long-ago days, when you came for the false Nicholas's funeral, you recognized at once that this was not your brother.'

'Why, yes. Oh, he had the look of Nicholas, right enough, and many years had passed since we had seen him in the flesh. He could have certainly passed for Nicholas from a distance. But, face to face, I knew instantly it wasn't my brother. Would that we could know the circumstances of our true brother's death.'

But Crispin was staring at him. 'He could have the look of him, but if he were beaten about the

260

face, that could hide any discrepancies, and no one would be the wiser. Especially if they were . . . brothers.'

'Eh? What's that you said?'

'God's blood! I must go. Forgive me my hasty departure.' He bowed to Clarence, and turned to Philippa. It barely registered now that this would be the last time he saw her. 'Madam Walcote,' he said with deep sincerity. He almost took her hand to kiss, but kept his arm at his side, knowing how dangerous a thing it would be to touch her.

Christopher stepped forward. Crispin held his breath. 'You saved my life, just like any proper knight. You said you would, and you did.'

'It was my greatest pleasure, Master Christopher.'

'Will I see you again? I would like to show you my horse. You could teach me to joust.'

Philippa pulled at his shoulder, dragging him back against her, where she threw a protective arm over his chest. 'Master Guest is very busy with grown-up matters. He don't have time to play with you.'

'But he promised to be my knight.'

'Hush, child. He *has* been your knight. He has been a chivalrous knight to us all.' Her eyes were full of meaning, full of want, but also harbored a plea.

Do not fear me, he hoped to convey with his eyes. *We shall part as chaste as we met.*

Crispin bowed deeply to her. 'God keep you,' he said softly, his eyes on her alone. 'God keep you all.'

'And you, Guest,' said Clarence, stepping forward, blocking her from view.

It effectively broke the spell. Crispin had places to go and another murderer to find.

Twenty

He wished he had a horse to get to his destination all the quicker, though it would have been difficult rushing on horseback through the crowded streets of London. Crispin arrived at the meadow in the shadow of the tower and hurried across it to the cottage, but it was as dark as when he had inspected it last time. Yet there was a white cloth tied to the door as he had seen twice before.

It was obviously a signal, but what did it mean? And where was Jack, for he had sent him here to talk with Master Oliver. He didn't like the feeling of his neck hairs bristling.

He circled the cottage again, looking for clues. In the mud, he saw footprints. And they looked large, like Jack's long-soled boots. He *was* here, then. But where did he go?

Glancing back over his shoulder toward the church, Crispin nodded. 'Of course.' He took off running, pelting hard over the uneven meadow, splashing through the mud and running through the taller grasses. Breathing hard, he stopped at the church and raised his head, listening. Nothing . . . wait. Yes, he did hear something faint. Two people arguing, perhaps? One voice, deep and resonant, the other higher-pitched. He walked the length of the back of the church, cocking his head toward the church wall. It was fainter when he walked closer toward the church, louder when he was near the rectory. He peered into the window of the rectory but it was just as empty as the last time he had searched it. But . . .

He climbed onto the sill and stood at the glass window. It was locked, but he used his dagger to press between the windows to lift the bar. He pulled it open and leapt to the floor. No cupboards or other rooms, save for the one open space, with hearth and bed. But, noticing the floors, he paused. It looked like the church, with its chequy tiled floor. But this floor wasn't tiled. It was wood, only painted to imitate what was in the church. He walked along carefully, bent at the waist and scouring the planks with his eyes . . . there! Seams. A trapdoor. And now he could hear the argument that was plainly between a man and a woman, though it was too muffled to hear their words. He stuck his finger in the hole he found in the door and lifted.

A ladder downward, and a light.

He laid back the door as quietly as he could, and, drawing his sword, made his way down.

Of what he could see of the room, it was no larger than the one above, and was crammed with shelves full of goods. Some of the goods were in the process of being packed into coffers and sacks. Two candles burned on a high shelf, throwing light into the center of the space, while the edges remained in gloom. Two figures, a man and a woman, stood in the center, while another man lolled in a chair. Crispin could see that the man was bound.

'It's not for you to decide,' said the man in a

raised voice, clearly trying to put the woman in her place.

'But you've hurt him,' said the woman, gesturing toward the shadowed man in the chair. 'No one was to be hurt. You said so.'

'It can't be helped. It's obviously Guest's man. That was a poor choice indeed to—' He stopped and turned.

Crispin had made it halfway down the ladder and leapt down the rest of the way. 'This is a surprise,' said Crispin.

'I could say the same about you, except for your man, here.'

Crispin gave Jack a quick perusal. There was blood on the side of his face, and he appeared to just be coming out of a stupor.

'You shouldn't have hit him,' said Crispin. 'Now you've made me angry. Noll, is it? Short for Oliver. Or should I rather say . . . Father Bulthius?'

The man smiled. It was the priest in a layman's tunic and hose. His tonsure was hidden under a hat with a liripipe. 'I knew I dallied here too long. I'm afraid my weakness was this creature,' and he gestured toward Nesta, wearing a heavy traveling cloak and hood.

'What do you mean "Father Bulthius"?' demanded Nesta, staring at Crispin before she turned again to her paramour. 'What does he mean?'

'Your lover is a priest,' said Crispin, mind working on escape, arrest, saving Jack all at once.

Nesta whipped her head toward the man. 'No. You never said . . .'

265

Crispin huffed. 'He's a murderer who lies. How unique. This is Father Bulthius Braydon, brother to Oliver Braydon. You told me as much when we first met.'

Bulthius shook his head. 'By the mass, you are as clever as they say. What gave it away?'

'Oh, I had a similar case a few years ago of a mistaken identity, of brothers who were not brothers in that instance. You beat your own brother about the face to bruise and swell it, so he would be just unrecognizable enough as Oliver and instead mistaken for you. And then you switched your clothes with his, *after* you beheaded him, which explains why you felt the need to smear the clothing with blood, for surely it would otherwise have been covered in it. But to slay your own brother . . .'

'Well, you see . . .' He shook his head and knocked his thigh with his closed fist. 'He was always getting the better of me. He was the eldest. He got the money, the lands. Yet *I* was the more deserving son, more studious, smarter by far. But instead, I was relegated to the Church. And I served well for years and years. And what came of it? I knew that bastard Braybrooke planned to close my parish. And what was to become of me? Cast out. Sharing another small parish with some bumbling, inane priest.'

'But Oliver!'

'Oh, you dear, naive girl. I must confess at last, that I am *not* Oliver. That was my brother, who lies dead in my grave. I killed him and exchanged places. Though I was playing Oliver long before that. That's when I met this dear

266

thing.' He touched her chin but she shied away, as if his fingers were hot coals.

'And what did Nesta have to do with your scheme? This rising of revenants? It was she I saw trailing a white gown, wasn't it?'

She lowered her head. 'Oliver . . . I mean, *he* told me to do it. It was to frighten everyone away. So . . . so we could steal away with these goods.' She swallowed, looking about the cellar.

Crispin frowned. 'You hired those poachers to wave about those lanterns at night for effect. And what of the gravediggers? They must have been in on your scheme. It was they who went about dragging coffins. But of course. Someone had to dig them out in the first place. Did you tell them they would get their cut of your stolen goods? Was that all it was? To steal from the church?'

'Well . . . yes. I discovered this room, you see.' He chuckled as he spread his hands and looked about. 'It was filled with gold and silver goods; plate, candelabras, furs, bolts of cloth . . . all conveniently left out of the inventory. I don't think anyone knew it was here for a generation. The last priest who knew about it must have died before he told anyone. What a trove to discover! So, I saw my escape. And it was better cover for me if all believed I was dead.'

'But to kill?'

'My brother was useless. Came to me with some sad tale of his profits all lost, and what was he to do? And so I found – then and there – a use for him. He wanted me to help him. Me! Of all people. The impoverished priest. I laughed

267

in his face. But then I thought about it and plotted. And then it all became clear. A new life in France for me, with a beautiful girl at my side, all of these goods, and a new name.'

Crispin clenched his jaw. 'And you murdered those gravediggers to keep the secret.'

'I needed their help, but when it was done, they needed to be silenced. I couldn't trust that they wouldn't talk.'

'So why hire me?'

'To give the story credence. And to discover "my" body. But I am afraid I got too confident, too cocksure. You see, I've had years to work this out. And you were to be the gold-plating on the masterwork. I never thought you'd be able to work it all out before I got away.'

'Perhaps, if it weren't for Nesta's involvement, for she was part of another task for me to solve.'

'You don't say. Well. The Lord does move in mysterious ways.'

'Yes, He does. And now what?'

Bulthius looked from Crispin to the horrified Nesta; in one smooth gesture, he pulled his dagger, yanked Nesta in close to him, and held the blade to her throat. She screamed but she soon silenced when he shushed in her ear. 'Now, my love, you must be silent. For if I am to make my escape, you are to be my surety.'

'And you will escape with nothing. For you cannot hold Nesta hostage, climb a ladder, and carry away any of your coffers at the same time.'

'I have already secured some in secret places in London. I will do well enough. Not as well as if *you* were dead.'

'Why have you deceived me?' she wailed, tears streaming down her cheeks.

'Oh, my dear, I never meant to. For you were truly dear to me. What a cold drink of water you were to my parched and celibate life. It was only when I abandoned all my principles that I began to feel a breath of freedom and contentment. Killing my brother was just an added pleasure.'

'No, *no*!' She squirmed in his arms as he edged toward the ladder. 'You're a fiend! A murderer! The Devil take you!'

'I'm sure he will,' he said mildly, 'but not quite yet. You will forgive me, Master Guest, for locking you in the cellar. I'm afraid you won't be allowed to pursue me.'

'I will get out.'

'Not if you are burned to death.' He smiled. 'This old church needs burning. No one will miss it. It's to be abandoned anyway. No one will find you for many a day. And of course, by then, it will be much too late.'

Crispin frowned. 'You are a particularly vile man, Bulthius. I have rarely met the like.'

'Then I hold a special place for you. How gratifying.' He reached the ladder and shoved Nesta toward it. 'It will be awkward, my dear, but we must climb together. Master Guest is much too chivalrous to risk my slitting your throat.'

She sobbed and shook, but he pressed her hard and, with a trembling hand, she reached for the ladder.

A loud war cry behind him, and suddenly

269

Bulthius was bowled over and tumbling to the ground, leaving Nesta grasping the ladder.

Jack, still tied to the chair, stood over him, panting. 'Burn *us* alive, would you?'

Crispin leapt. He kicked the knife from his hand, but Bulthius rolled away and snapped to his feet. More agile than Crispin had credited him, he bent into a crouch. Crispin still held his sword in a tight grip. He didn't fancy it getting out of his hands and being used on him.

Bulthius looked determined. He charged, grabbing Crispin's sword hand at the wrist and pushing it away. He was strong, and Crispin struggled to keep hold of it, but with an agonizing twist to the joint, he had no choice but to drop it.

'Don't let him get the better of you, master!' cried Jack, struggling to free himself from his bonds.

'I'm trying!' he croaked, as Bulthius got his hands round Crispin's throat.

Gritting his teeth and struggling to breathe, Crispin reached up and grabbed the man's head. With lessening air reaching his lungs and his sight dimming, he dug his thumbs into the priest's eyes and pressed hard.

Bulthius cried out and released Crispin as he stumbled back.

There wasn't time to catch his breath. Crispin saw the glint of a dagger on the floor and dove for it at the same time Bulthius did. Crispin was faster. He clutched it tight and rolled over and over with it against his chest. He staggered to his feet, coughing. Bulthius crouched against a shelf, squeezing shut his eyes.

'You're a whoreson, Guest,' he gritted out.

'And you are a demon. I'm particularly suited to fighting those.'

Bulthius snapped open his bloodshot eyes. 'Then demon it is.' He yanked on the shelf. It teetered and started to fall. He lunged out of the way as it careened toward Crispin.

Jack was in its path, just freeing himself. Crispin grabbed him by the collar and yanked with all his might.

The shelf crashed down, splintering its wood and dashing all its goods in a scatter across the floor, missing Jack by inches.

When Crispin looked beyond it, Bulthius was halfway up the ladder.

'Jack!' he yelled, pointing.

Jack leapt for the ladder, grabbing hold of the man's ankle. Bulthius kicked out, landing a blow to Jack's temple. It opened the wound on his head again, trickling blood into his eyes but, with furrowed mouth, Jack held on. With a cry, Jack pulled hard and Bulthius clattered down, falling in a heap at Crispin's feet.

Crispin quickly placed his boot at Bulthius's throat.

Sobbing, Nesta flung herself into Crispin's arms. He fought to juggle her and his prisoner.

Jack wiped the blood from his forehead and blinked. 'Oi! What about me?'

The sheriffs collected a bound and soured Bulthius. Their bailiffs conveyed him to Newgate.

Nesta watched him go, hugging herself. 'I

should have known. I should have known,' she muttered.

'How could you have?' said Crispin.

'Because . . . he asked me to secure funds for travel, too. Even if I had to steal them. *His* words. And, may God forgive me, but I did. The mistress was always saying how valuable that relic was. So it was I who stole it. When I saw it in your hands, I was sure you knew. For how else could you have secured it?'

'It . . . is a long and curious story.'

She sniffed and shook her head. 'It doesn't matter. I've got no man. And I might have lost my situation.' She burst into tears and buried her face in her hands.

Crispin felt little need to comfort her.

'Master Guest,' sighed Sheriff Shadworth as the bailiffs marched away with their prisoner, 'two murderers in one day! I am astounded. You see, Henry. The man *is* a marvel.'

'Yes, yes,' said his recalcitrant companion. 'But how did you know where to find him? You said you saw the white cloth as a signal. But how did you know what it meant?'

'The cottage was untouched without a cellar or secret room. And I had seen when the cloth was there and when it was not. I assumed it meant a signal. And once I had reckoned that Oliver was in fact Bulthius, I realized it must mean that he was present in the rectory, so that Nesta would know to go there.'

'Seems unnecessarily elaborate. Why would she simply not go directly to the rectory?'

'Because he had intimated that what they were

272

doing was secret. Even so, she couldn't help mentioning to her friend Clarice that she was seeing a man named Oliver, but she would divulge nothing else. The Walcote affair sparked an old memory about brothers and murder, and I was able to ferret it out.'

Sheriff Vaunere folded his lips and rubbed his beard. 'That was impossible to unbind, Guest.'

'It is my bread and butter, my lord.'

He lifted his face and scowled. 'Oh *is* it?'

'Henry,' said Shadworth, 'you know very well that it is.'

The sheriff grunted and made a dismissive gesture. 'Priests as murderers? What is this town coming to?' He stalked away toward his waiting horse.

Shadworth beamed. 'I am quite amazed, Master Crispin. And at you, too, Master Tucker.'

Jack snapped up his head, surprised. He bowed, saying nothing.

'What's to be done with this treasure?' enquired Shadworth, tapping his lip with a finger. His eye had a gleam to it.

'I suppose it rightfully belongs to the Church,' Crispin answered.

The gleam faded. 'Yes, I suppose it does. I shall have to call upon Bishop Braybrooke. How that man annoys me.'

Crispin merely cocked a brow.

'Frankly, I'm amazed, Master Crispin, that you aren't wealthier. This talent of yours is indescribable.'

'Clients are always scarce, my lord.'

'I can't imagine it. You are better than any jury.'

'It would content me if you could convey that to the citizens of the city, my lord.' He bowed.

Shadworth smiled. 'Of course! Glad to do it. Well! God keep you. And you, Master Tucker. You take good care of your master. London needs him.'

'I do me best, m'lord.'

He waved and headed toward his horse.

'Blind me,' muttered Jack as he came up beside Crispin. 'Did we ever have a sheriff who outright liked you, sir?'

'I can't remember one who was as enchanted.'

'He is that.' He winked at Crispin, and Crispin cuffed him for his trouble.

'We should get back home, master. I'm sure the abbot will be anxious to know what has transpired.'

'I think you should tell him.'

Jack smiled. 'Me, sir?'

'You have a colorful way of description.'

Jack puffed up like a dandelion head. 'I do at that. I try to make the telling as exciting as the doing. That's the trick.'

'You go on. I'll catch up. There is something I must do.'

Jack's smile faltered. 'As you will, sir.' He paused for an explanation, but when none was forthcoming, he trotted along the churchyard path and out the lychgate.

Crispin touched the bulge in his scrip, satisfied it was still there, and turned toward the church.

There had been many comings and goings

today, but the church was as empty as he'd seen any. Stripped of its altar goods, including its cross, the structure was bare nave, empty font, and plain altar. The day was drawing on apace, and the sun slanted long upon the darkened floor. He stepped into the nave, his boot scraping on the tiles, and gazed up to where the rood screen was. Not what one would consider accomplished carvings, the screen nevertheless did the job of delineating laymen from cleric. Though there was none of either save Crispin.

He strode up the nave, his own steps echoing back to him. He passed the rood screen and climbed the one step up to the altar. Simple carvings in stone, as ancient as the building's arches and vaults. He gazed at the sad state of it before reaching into the scrip and pulling forth the cow. Placing it on the altar, he stepped back to look at it. 'I think this is where you'd like to be, is it not, St Modwen?'

He felt suddenly lighter. It had been a full day, to be sure. And much had weighed him down, not the least of which was saving his son. But that was now done.

He bowed to the little cow. Its bright red paint a startling contrast to the gray of the stone and the dark shadows.

Movement out of the corner of his eye caught his attention, and he turned toward the window overlooking the meadow. As the late afternoon light warmed the plain, tingeing the edges of the grass heads with golden light, a woman with a staff went striding on. She seemed to be urging a cow ahead of her. A red cow.

275

Pressing his face to the window, Crispin stared hard. And just before she disappeared behind a hedgerow, she turned and looked directly at Crispin.

He started back, a chill shaking him, but before he girded himself and regained his place at the window, she had vanished.

Twenty-One

A feeling of satisfaction like no other came over Crispin as he strolled back toward the Shambles. He had accomplished much and, for once, he felt he had risen above all the pettiness of his tasks. For though he would not see Philippa or his son again, he had served them well . . . as would any knight errant.

He inhaled deeply of the end of the day. Shops were still open, citizens were still at their shopping and crowding the streets. A stray dog followed behind a beggar and Crispin even stopped the man to offer him a farthing.

He turned at the Shambles and was in sight of the old poulterer's when Jack burst out of the door and merely stood in the street, dazed. Crispin trotted toward him and grabbed hold of the wild-eyed apprentice. 'Jack, what's the matter?'

'Isabel. The baby! It's coming!'

Crispin looked up to the second-floor window. Hadn't they both anticipated this moment? But now that the moment was here, they both froze. Jack moved first. 'I must go fetch Eleanor.'

He jerked from Crispin's grasp but Crispin lunged for him and grasped his arm. 'Don't be a fool, man. You stay. I'll go.'

'Oh master! Bless you, sir!'

He raced back into the house and now it was

277

Crispin's turn to stand immobile in the street. Her cries rang out over the lane through the open window and soon he heard Jack's soft reassurances.

Crispin blinked. *Wake up, man!* Off he ran toward Gutter Lane. He turned at the corner and nearly skidded into a wall. He threaded his way quickly through the carts and horses, stepped on a chicken before it squawked and flew up at him. He waved it away before he reached the door of the Boar's Tusk. Casting it open, he stood in the doorway. Panic as he had never known consumed him, and he rushed in, searching for the plump alewife. There! Scolding their servant Ned, who was tending to the fire.

'Eleanor!' he shouted above the throng of people occupying tables with their beakers and clay bowls in hand. They barely looked up. 'Eleanor, for God's sake!'

She turned her wimpled and kerchiefed head. Her smile was wide on seeing Crispin, but soon turned wary when she saw his expression. He shoved his way through the men at their tables and wobbly stools, not even hearing their threats and oaths.

She reached out to him. 'Crispin, whatever is the matter?'

He was out of breath and light-headed. He leaned over on his thighs and breathed. 'You must come, Eleanor,' he panted. 'Isabel is at her childbed.'

'Oh gracious! I'll get Gilbert.'

He grabbed her arm. 'There's no time!'

She had the audacity to laugh in his face. 'Oh, you silly man. Of course there is time.'

In disbelief, Crispin watched her unhurried pace as she retreated to the back of the alehouse in search of her husband. What was the woman doing? Didn't she realize that her niece was about to give birth . . . in *his* house?

Scowling, Crispin waited, tapping his foot. At last, Gilbert appeared. They were both wearing cloaks and Eleanor had a bundle in her hands. 'Let's off, Crispin. Oi, Crispin. You look white as a sheet.'

'Will you please make *haste*?'

Eleanor chuckled as she followed Crispin at a trot.

Never had the Shambles seemed so far away, though, intellectually, he knew it was a scant half-mile. He urged her into his lodgings when they arrived, but they stalled in the doorway.

'God's blood! What are you waiting for?' When he peered over their shoulders he saw what had stopped them: Abbot William kneeling in prayer before the hearth.

'Jesus mercy!' cried Eleanor. 'What's happened?'

The abbot looked up. 'Oh, Crispin. And friends.' He rose and wiped at his knees. 'These must be Gilbert and Eleanor Langton, dear Isabel's uncle and aunt.'

'And this,' said Crispin curtly, 'is Abbot William of Westminster Abbey. He's been our guest for some days.'

Eleanor looked back at Crispin with widened eyes. 'You might have warned me.' She curtseyed to the abbot, even as Gilbert bowed and swept his hood off his head.

There was a wail from upstairs and everyone stared at the rafters.

'Well,' said Eleanor, recovering, 'I must get to it. Gilbert, make yourself useful by collecting linens.'

He saluted. 'Aye, m'love.'

Eleanor hastened up the stairs with her bundles, and everyone heard Jack exclaim, 'Oh, thank Christ!'

He was shooed out of the room and was soon hurrying downstairs. 'I'm to get Anne Lymon, the butcher's wife,' he said. Before Crispin could say another word, Jack was gone.

The men stood in silence, preferring, it seemed, to look at their feet rather than at one another.

Finally, Gilbert heaved a sigh. 'Well, I'd best get the linens or the wife will give me what for.' He ambled toward the ambry and gathered what linens he could find; towels, tablecloths and other small pieces within the cupboard.

The abbot moved to a chair and sat, running his hand over his head. 'I was going to return to my abbey today. God knows what they are thinking at my continued absence. But I certainly can't leave now that there is to be another soul brought into the world.'

'Crispin,' said Gilbert, his face suddenly in front of him. 'You look pale. Here. Sit down.' He pushed Crispin into one of his chairs.

Crispin sat, perplexed at his inability to do anything, to think. When Gilbert shoved a goblet of wine into his hands, he didn't hesitate to drink nearly all of it.

The tavern keeper laid a large hand on his

shoulder. 'I take it you've never been nigh a child bed?'

'Don't be absurd. There was plenty of that at court, and at Lancaster's household.'

'Ah, but not like this. This is Jack Tucker's babe. Almost like your own. No one's ever been this close to you before.'

He drank another dose and pondered. 'Gilbert, you might be right.' He dropped his head into his hands. 'Never have I felt more helpless.'

'That is your love for them,' said the abbot with a warm smile.

He said nothing more. The door burst open and Jack stumbled in. He pointed up the stairs. 'She's up there.'

Roger Lymon's diminutive wife grabbed her skirts, lifted them, and scurried forward. Crispin somehow noted that she had red stockings.

'Day to you, Master Crispin,' she said as she rushed past. 'God keep you all,' she added over her shoulder after sweeping the group of men with her eyes. Up the stairs she went, closing the door after her.

Jack stood at the foot of the stairs, staring upward. 'Do you suppose she'll be all right? My Isabel?' He turned to Abbot William. 'My lord, should we pray?'

'I have been doing so, Master Tucker. And you should as well.'

But Jack was pacing instead, rubbing his hands through his curly hair. 'I can't. I can't think. Master Crispin, what have I done?'

Gilbert chuckled and slapped Jack on the back. 'You've done as every father before you has,

281

lad. You've loved your wife and done as God intended. Now it's up to Him to watch over her.'

Jack spun toward Crispin. 'The relic! St Modwen! Have you still got it, master?'

'I . . . no. I returned it to her church.'

'You what? But we needed that!'

'Peace, Master Tucker,' said the abbot. 'She has already blessed this house. Do you think it matters so much whether her relic is here or not?'

Jack blinked, fluttering his lids, and slowly commenced pacing again. 'I . . . I suppose not.'

He stopped when wailing came from the upstairs room again.

Suddenly, the chamber door above slammed open and Eleanor leaned over the railing. 'This babe wishes to come as fast as he can. Where are those linens, Gilbert? They'll be a great deal of cleaning needed anon.'

'Coming up!' He gathered all the linens in his arms and waddled up the stairs. Eleanor relieved it from him, and hurried back into the room, shutting the door.

Jack locked desperate eyes with Crispin's.

Crispin slammed to his feet. 'This is absurd. Babes are born every day in every corner of the world.' He pointed sharply up the stairs. 'That child will be hale, and strong, and . . .' He faltered, but instead of sitting again, he stood beside Jack, putting his hands on his shoulders. 'It will be all right.'

'I just pray that they will both be well.'

'Our hope is in God,' said Abbot William.

Sounds of crying, grunting, shouting came

from above, and Jack cringed. Crispin hadn't known when the boy had leaned into him, but he swung his arm around Jack and held him tight.

He suddenly realized he had missed this part of fatherhood. When Philippa had been in *her* labor pains, it had been Clarence who had paced, for Crispin hadn't known about it. He hadn't been there when the boy smiled for the first time, or walked, or said his first words. He had missed it all. Some would say he was there for the most important part – to save his life. And while that was true, he couldn't help thinking he had missed so much more.

Well, not this time. He'd be there for Jack's child. And a foolish notion it was. Why should he be so concerned with a servant's babe? But he pushed those arguments away. He was long past caring about those differences. He wasn't a lord, would never be again, but this he *could* do, and dammit, he was going to do it.

A baby's cry.

The men froze.

The abbot was the first to move as he rose from his seat. 'God be praised,' he murmured.

Crispin held on to Jack, for the boy's knees seemed to have given out.

Eleanor came to the edge of the upper stairs, a grin wide on her face and toweling her hands. 'Master Tucker, you have a baby boy, and he's a loud one. And your dear wife is just as fine as can be. Come on up.'

Jack gasped and burst into a sob. Crispin turned to him and suddenly gathered him into an

283

embrace. 'A boy, Tucker,' he said into his ear. 'That's a marvel, isn't it?'

'I'm a father,' he said, dazed.

Gilbert slapped him on the back, sending him stumbling forward. 'Did you think you wouldn't be? Get up there, Tucker.'

Jack grinned. 'Aye. I'm a father!' He bounded up the stairs and Eleanor ushered him into the bedchamber.

'Well!' said Crispin. He could feel the smile on his face stretching the muscles. 'We must have wine!' He grabbed the jug already on the table, and poured wine into what goblets he had. He handed one each to the abbot and to Gilbert.

'You pour just as much as you like,' said Gilbert, 'for I will fetch as much as we need from the Tusk.'

Crispin held up his goblet. 'Here's to Jack Tucker and his son!'

'God bless them both,' said the abbot. They clinked cups and drank.

It wasn't long after that Jack leaned over the railing. 'Master Crispin,' he said in a hissed whisper, 'will you come up, sir?'

'Me? But . . .'

'Please, sir. Isabel wishes to speak with you.'

Crispin exchanged a worried expression with Gilbert, put down his goblet, and slowly made his way up the stairs. He had never been in that room, save for the one time when he'd first rented the house. There was little need, after all. It was to belong to Jack and, very shortly afterward, it had belonged to Jack and his new bride.

But this time, at the top of the landing, he

made the turn right, instead of left. Jack took his arm and dragged him in. 'There's no need for that, Tucker,' he grumbled.

Isabel was sitting up in bed, with a tiny, red-faced babe swaddled in her arms. Her face was shiny with sweat, and her hair was plastered to her forehead, but she was beaming. Anne Lymon and Eleanor were bundling wet and bloody linens into a bucket.

'We'll just leave you for now,' said Eleanor, elbowing Madam Lymon, then out the door they went, bundles and bucket in hand.

For some reason, Crispin feared to go closer, even as Jack urged him to. But when Isabel looked up at him and even reached out her hand, he could not stand back any longer. He took her hand and squeezed it, before letting it go. 'You are well?' he asked softly.

She brushed a wet lock from her cheek. 'Yes. Thank the Almighty. He has delivered me and my son.'

'Master Crispin,' said Jack, an anxious look to his eye. 'Isabel and me . . . well. We want to thank you, sir.'

'Thank me? For what? I had little to do with this.'

Isabel chuckled and looked down adoringly at the red face of her child. Crispin knew that babies were supposed to be beautiful. But he rather thought the babe looked more like a wizened crab apple than a beloved child. Was it supposed to look like that? It hadn't troubled Eleanor, so he supposed it was true. Surely the boy would become more handsome as the days drew on.

285

'We want to thank you, sir, for being such a kind and generous master,' said Jack. 'Thinking of Master Horne and his apprentice, well. I've realized I could have had it much worse. I'm speaking out of turn, I know, but you're more like a . . . father than any man I've ever known.' Tears glistened in his eyes.

'Tucker . . .'

'It's true, sir. You've made me the man I am today. And I hope I do you proud.'

Crispin cursed the boy for making him blink back tears. 'Jack . . .'

'And so, Isabel and me, we . . . we wish to christen the boy "Crispin" . . . but only if you think it right and proper.' Quickly, he added, 'I'd not insult you, sir, if you thought that a servant had no right to your name. It's just that we would give you something, sir, for all that you have given me. And . . . with your own son out of reach, as it were . . .'

Crispin ran his hand over his face and wiped his runny nose. 'Dammit, Tucker.' He had to swallow that warmth away from his throat a few times before he could speak. 'You honor me, Jack. Of course I will consent.'

'I'm so pleased,' said Isabel. And then she looked down at the tiny babe who didn't seem to look as bad as Crispin had first thought, and whispered, 'Welcome to the world, little Crispin.'

Afterword

Perhaps you were looking to refresh your memory about Philippa Walcote. You can find her story in the first Crispin book, *Veil of Lies*.

And if you were looking for the church mentioned in this story, be at peace. There is no St Modwen's Church in All Hallows Barking (and isn't that a great name?). There never was one in London. I added it. There is only one parish in England devoted to St Modwen, and that is in Burton upon Trent in Staffordshire, part of the Diocese of Lichfield, where she founded her monastery. It was the only liberty I took . . . besides walking corpses and murdering people who didn't exist, of course.

St Modwen or Modwenna was an Irish noble-woman who made a pilgrimage to Rome and became an abbess of some repute, performing miracles of various kinds. You won't find any images of her, or much of a surviving cult. Henry VIII's men, led by Thomas Cromwell, who went about the country dissolving monasteries and setting the monks and nuns adrift, made sure the relics, statues, and portraits of saints were destroyed so *'that there should no more idolatry and superstition be there used'*. So said Sir William Bassett in 1538, when he was instructed to remove the image of St Modwen. *'I did not only deface the tabernacles and places where*

287

they stand,' said Sir William, '*but also did take away the crutches, shirts and sheets with wax offered, being things that did allure and intice the ignorant people to the said offerings, also giving the keepers of both places admonition and charge that no more offerings should be made in those places till the King's pleasure and your lordships be further known in that behalf.*'
The statue of the saint was said to stand with a red cow and was equipped with a staff that could be removed, which was supposedly helpful to women suffering labor pains when they leaned on it. I suppose Isabel could have used that.

Also, a word about walking corpses and blood on their faces. There were reported incidents in the Middle Ages and in slightly more recent times of such fears, when freshly interred corpses' graves appeared to be disturbed. Animals, certainly, dug into turned earth, but more likely the culprits were grave robbers, looking for easy pickings. People would bury loved ones with their prized possessions, such as daggers and swords as well as jewelry, to take with them to the afterlife. After all, they've been doing that since ancient Egypt and before. But when grave robbers opened coffins they'd find that face cloths around the mouth were bloodied, and instantly ascribed it to the late-night wandering of the corpse. Of course, we know now that once any kind of animal dies, it can no longer rely on living enzymes and circulating blood to prevent the bacteria from breaking down the body, and some of that putrefaction of decay creates liquid waste, some of it being blood and plasma, which excretes where it can. Some of that results in gases that expand the body and split it open. But, not to put too fine a point on it, there are other openings of the body. One is the mouth. It's naturally occurring, this appearance of what seems to be blood on the mouth. But they didn't know that then, and all sorts of fanciful tales emerged, like those of vampires.

You might have noticed that I skipped a year from the last book, *Season of Blood*, to this. I was interested in moving Crispin's story along. We might be skipping another year in the next book, *Traitor's Codex*, to 1394, involving Crispin with a mysterious manuscript that the Church is willing to kill to get their hands on. See all about Crispin's books, including discussion guides and the series listed in order, at JeriWesterson.com.